AND SOMETIMES I WONDER ABOUT YOU

WALTER MOSLEY

AND SOMETIMES I WONDER ABOUT YOU

W&N

WEIDENFELD & NICOLSON

First published in Great Britain in 2015
by Weidenfeld & Nicolson
an imprint of the Orion Publishing Group Ltd

Carmelite House, 50 Victoria Embankment
London EC4Y 0DZ
An Hachette UK Company

1 3 5 7 9 10 8 6 4 2

This edition published by arrangement with Doubleday,
an imprint of The Knopf Doubleday Publishing Group,
a division of Random House LLC.

The right of Walter Mosley to be identified as the author of
this work has been asserted in accordance with the
Copyright, Designs and Patents Act 1988.

All the characters in this book are fictitious,
and any resemblance to actual persons
living or dead is purely coincidental.

A CIP catalogue record for this book is
available from the British Library.

978 1 474 60042 2 (cased)

Printed and bound by Clays Ltd, St Ives plc

The Orion Publishing Group's policy is to use papers
that are natural, renewable and recyclable products and
made from wood grown in sustainable forests. The logging
and manufacturing processes are expected to conform to
the environmental regulations of the country of origin.

www.orionbooks.co.uk

For Carine Desir, who shares my cracked view of the world

1

Taking the local train from Philly to New York's Penn Station may not be as smooth as the Acela's ride but it gets the job done for a few dollars less and sometimes, like that Monday afternoon, the car is nearly empty and a man has time to think.

My nearest neighbor across the aisle was a slim and dapper gentleman, well past retirement and dressed in an out-of-season white seersucker suit with light blue pin-striping. It was cool that fall and he would have done well with a heavier fabric, but maybe that was just the octogenarian's style—or maybe his only suit. He was napping, talking in his sleep. The unintelligible words came from his lips like a sporadic spoken-word song in another language. Maybe it was a foreign tongue.

Six rows back, I knew, sat a behemoth of a man wearing black-jean overalls and a heavy, long-sleeved blue-and-white-checkered work shirt. From a thick steel chain around the big man's neck depended a real horseshoe that had never been attached to any hoof. The man was in his forties, over four hundred pounds, with red hair and the raspberry and cream–colored skin of a Norseman. His regular breathing, when you got within two rows, was loud enough to hear over the clacking of metal wheels on metal tracks.

At the front of the car, in a seat facing backward, there perched a small black woman who was somewhere around my age, clutching a red, yellow, and green calico carpetbag by its worn brown leather handle. The fifty-something lady looked worried but this seemed like a regular state of affairs—not any specific problem that plagued her at that point in time.

2

Specific problems have always been my stock-in-trade. As a young man I delivered this unwanted commodity; nowadays I remove it—for a price.

A woman came through the semiautomatic door behind the worried grandmother. This potential new resident of our low-occupancy car was harder to define.

She was beautiful. Her bright skin was the russet brown I associated with the Caribbean, her hair was untreated and a little wild, and her eyes a color somewhere between brown and bronze. I noticed her eyes because this was the third time she'd gone past gazing at me, considering, and then rejecting whatever thought it was that those eyes harbored. Past thirty but nowhere near the next decade, she'd still be lovely when she reached the age of the sleeping man who muttered across the aisle.

I wondered what she might have asked if I had met her expectations. This thought caused me to look around just in time to see her stop at the behemoth's row. She asked a question and he grumbled something. She asked something else and he shook his head vehemently, gestured with his left hand, and then turned away—which was no mean feat for a man his size.

She nodded at him, almost a bow, and made her way to the end of the car. There she punched the chrome plate that engaged the sliding door.

The passing thought that it might have been nice to hear her question firsthand was soon displaced by the certainty that whatever she said would not have improved my life. In my experience beautiful strangers rarely give as much as they take and they almost always ask for more.

After she was gone I pulled out my cell phone and entered the characters M-A-R, then touched a button that had the image of an upright receiver emblazed upon it. The phone rang once and she answered.

"McGill and Son detective agency."

I had never asked her to answer the phone like that but Mardi had her own aesthetic and she had become, in just a few years, an indispensable part of my office.

"Hey, Mardi."

"Mr. McGill. How are you?" Her voice was soft like a satin finish on polished steel.

"Just fine. I get anything on my *New York Literary Review* ad?"

"No, sir. I checked just this noon."

I didn't expect an answer. William Williams was in the wind. It was no great loss; like the dollar bet on a hundred-million-dollar Lotto—you were bound to lose but you had to play.

"A man named Hiram Stent called asking for an appointment any-time today," Mardi murmured.

"What's his problem?"

"He didn't say but it sounded pretty, I don't know . . . urgent."

"I'm not coming in today," I said. "I'm going straight to the sanatorium from the station. Give him a morning slot, first thing."

"Yes, sir. Are you finished with the Martinez case?"

"Yeah."

"Did it turn out okay?"

"He ran once," I said. "Who's to say he won't do it again? Twill in?"

"No," she said but her tone said more.

"Where is he?"

"He didn't call in today. I think he's probably at home studying the tapes you had me give him."

There was something off in Mardi's voice, something that had to do with my favorite son. I would have asked about it but just at that moment I felt a presence at my side. Looking up, I saw the brilliant vision of the beautiful woman who flitted around our car like a hesitant butterfly over a sticky flower.

Her dress was a shade deeper than coral, and though it wasn't tight it expressed her figure just fine.

"I'll have to call you back, M, something just came up here."

"On the train?"

"No problem," I said, "just somebody wanting a section of my paper."

"See you tomorrow," she said, and I broke the connection.

"Hello," I greeted while putting the phone in the breast pocket of my all-purpose blue suit.

"I didn't mean to interrupt you," she said. Her voice was somewhere in the lower register of gold. Her black satin purse was cinched at the top like a miniature burlap potato sack.

"No problem. I was just calling in to the office."

"Oh." She glanced at the door behind her. "Um . . . can I sit next to you?"

I was on the aisle so she was asking for a window seat—with a buffer.

"Is that what you asked Haystack Calhoun back there?"

She didn't get the cultural reference but still understood the joke. Smiling and frowning at the same time, she said, "I think he's afraid of girls."

"Good for him. Some men never learn that lesson."

"Have you?" the nameless beauty asked.

If I believed in angels they wouldn't be the sweet beneficent kind with fluffy wings and halos but rather haughty, removed Valkyries that tore the soul from your dying breast. That kind of angel would have asked the question she put to me. And, I knew, I should have answered like the colossus with the horseshoe necklace.

"My name's Leonid," I said, "Leonid McGill."

"May I sit on the other side of you, Mr. McGill?" she asked.

If I wanted her name I was going to have to work for it.

I grabbed my brown rucksack from the empty seat next to me and then stood making a gesture with *my* left hand, the same and yet the opposite of the behemoth. She smiled and brushed past me. At that proximity I got a whiff of something both acrid and sweet, like some ancient forests I'd been in. It was a mild scent that caused a strong reaction in a section of my heart that had almost been forgotten.

When she was installed there next to me I knew that the next week or so would be trouble. I smiled and laughed a little. She nodded and then grinned.

2

"What kind of work do you do?" she asked, turning in her leather seat and lifting her right ankle up under the left thigh. That way she could look at me while watching both ends of the nearly empty car.

"There's a guy named Eddie and a woman named Camille," I said.

My new neighbor leaned back against the window and smiled. She didn't mind hearing a roundabout answer.

"Eddie is, or at least he was, a what you call undocumented laborer from Central Mexico, a farmer that could read and write. Camille is an investment banker, more Madison Avenue than Wall Street."

"What's the difference?" my temporary companion asked.

"What's your name?" I replied.

That turn got her to grin. She looked both ways down the aisle like a cautious pedestrian and said, "Marella. Marella Herzog."

"Interesting name," I mused. "Where's it from?"

"I think the origin for Herzog is German." Her smile was as opaque as the answer. "Marella is Italian."

"Wall Streeters are solitary sharks, Marella," I said, relishing the name. "Madison Avenue is populated by social animals—mostly wolves."

"What about Eddie and Camille?" she asked.

"At the same time and in very different spheres Camille and Eddie got tired of their roles in life. She began doing charity work, not giving money but rolling up her sleeves and going down to shelters. She also represented dozens of undocumented laborers in court—gratis.

"Around then, Eddie was honing his English, becoming a florist's assistant, and studying for his citizenship exam."

"Don't tell me," Marella said. "He was arrested by the INS and she got his case."

Before I could answer, Marella looked up suddenly, seeing something at the front of the car. I turned my gaze and saw a tall, olive-skinned man with a scar along the right side of his nose like an editor's diacritical marking. He was wearing a long-sleeved black shirt and gray slacks. Slender and likely strong, he reminded me of an unsheathed hunting knife—both haft and blade.

I say "tall" because he was a shade or two over six feet, but really most American men are tall compared to me. I'm half an inch under five and a half feet. What I lack in height I like to think I make up for in muscle. I weigh one eighty-three most mornings and not too much of that is fat.

The taller man's body didn't slow down as he passed our aisle but his eyes did. Those dark slits took her in—glanced at, and then dismissed, me. He didn't look crazy and so I remained calm.

When he passed through the back door of the car I said, "No. Eddie brought a woman from his Bronx apartment building to Camille's after-hours, downtown office on Bowery."

The woman calling herself Marella Herzog took in a deep breath through her nostrils and looked back at me with what I can only call a bit of pride.

"And he spoke such perfect English that she fell in love with him," she said.

"Something like that. Eddie knew a world that offered her something, and she was like the Statue of Liberty as far as he was concerned. They shared intelligence, he passed his citizenship test, and she stopped worrying about where banking could take her. It was like a multicultural fairy tale until about a month ago."

"So you're a marriage counselor?" Marella guessed.

"One morning Camille woke up in her Park Avenue South condo and found Eddie gone. He'd taken with him his four pairs of cotton pants, six shirts, shoes, and toothbrush."

"You're a PI."

"She called me after the police told her that it was just a man leaving a woman. I found a trail of calls and a few bills that led me down to Philly. I spent the week in the City of Brotherly Love buying roses. It took longer than I expected because Eddie had opened his own kiosk in Reading Terminal Market. I talked to him about Mexico in my best Cuban Spanish and he said that he loved it in America. After fifteen minutes of yacking I told him that I worked for Camille and that she wondered why he ran away."

"What did he say?" I think at that moment she had almost forgotten the olive-skinned hunter that had marked her with his slow eyes.

"People were always looking at him," I said. "White people, other Mexicans, policemen. He had started to feel that he didn't belong with Camille or in her world. He felt that he brought nothing to the table and the table belonged to her."

"Wow," she said, pursing her well-formed dark lips. "That's some kinda man, huh?"

"I told him that my father told me that the first thing a farmer learns is that the man doesn't own the soil but the earth owns him. The same thing, I said, was true of tables and monies and fancy streets."

"Your father sounds like a wise man."

"Yeah. Maybe too wise."

"What did Eddie say?"

"He hugged me. Threw his arms around my neck and pressed his cheek to mine. I think he must have been hoping for a sign to go back home."

"To Park Avenue," Marella said.

"To Camille."

"So did he?"

"She came down this morning, paid my fee, and took her man to the Belmont Arms."

"That's a wonderful story," Marella Herzog said. She placed a hand on mine.

"Why don't you tell me one," I suggested, turning my palm upward to press against hers.

"What would you like to hear?"

"Why a stunningly beautiful woman like you would ask to sit next to an old, off-the-rack straphanger like me."

"You looked like a strong man and so I wanted to sit down next to you."

"Not before you asked Haystack back there," I said.

"He looked a little stronger," she admitted with a smile.

"And what use do you have for strong men?"

"You saw the guy who walked by?"

I nodded.

"He works for a man that I was engaged to down in DC. I saw him on the Acela to New York and got off in Philly. I guess he saw that and followed me."

"And what does this man want?" I asked.

"To take me back."

"Why?" I said, thinking about Camille. She was a plain woman with naturally blond hair and a figure made for a '40s film. She asked me to find Eddie, and when I did she came to him.

"He broke off the engagement. I'm pretty sure he wants the ring back."

"Why not give it to him?"

"Because it became my property when he gave it and I accepted," Marella said with all the commitment of an outer-borough storefront lawyer.

"But if he's so adamant why not let him have it anyway?"

"Because I will not be intimidated by thuggery." Something about her choice of words seemed . . . unnatural.

"If that was true you wouldn't be using me as a buffer."

She turned to look out the window. We were entering the outskirts of Newark, New Jersey.

After a moment or two she said, "I sold it, got quite a bit of money." Then she turned to face me again. "Are you a strong man, Mr. McGill?"

"I think so."

"Can I trust you?"

"In what circumstance do you mean?"

"I need protection."

I pretended to think about her request, but the answer was a fore-gone conclusion. After a beat, maybe two, I nodded. "Sure."

"Sure I can trust you or sure you will help me?"

"Both."

"And, if you don't mind me asking, why should I trust you?"

"Because I work for money."

Marella's smile seemed to enhance her forest scent.

3

"My bag is two cars up," she told me a few minutes before we pulled into Penn Station.

"Let's go," I said, in a tone that I hoped exuded simple certainty.

We jostled through the cars as the few other passengers were standing up, gathering their jackets and bags.

The train's swaying made our walking like a conga line on a drunken beach somewhere.

"That's it," she said, pointing at an overhead rack. It was a substantial black bag festooned with large pink polka dots. The decorations were frivolous so I was a little surprised at the weight of the suitcase.

"You put this up there yourself?" I asked and then grunted, lowering the bag to the floor.

"Two young men helped me," she said.

It has always amazed me how a woman's eyes and her words can find a direct line to my animal heart.

I wrangled the festive bag out onto the platform, then rolled it with Marella at my side. We rode up a half-stage escalator into the middle aisles of Penn Station. She was looking around nervously but I stared straight ahead. I had already seen the man-knife in the reflection of a window on our train. He was close behind us but nearly hidden behind a redcap's overfull cart.

Even when I lost sight of him I knew he was near us somewhere.

I made a turn down a fairly empty corridor and Marella asked, "Where are we going?" There was fear in her voice, but whether it was due to her pursuer or maybe to some danger I represented, I could not tell.

"Baggage elevator," I said. "This sucker is too heavy to lug up the stairs. What you got in here anyway?"

"My whole life."

"That's either way too little or far too much," I said as we reached the dull and pitted chrome doors of the elevator car.

I pressed the Up button but the light was out. I couldn't remember a time when it worked.

"You're different than you were on the train," she said as we stood there.

"Then I was on the train," I said, "now I'm on the job."

"That reminds me, what are you charging to carry my bag?"

"That depends."

"On what?"

"Well . . . if all I have to do is walk you to a taxi I'll accept a handshake and a kiss on the cheek. But if I have to play bodyguard and make sure that you're unharmed then the going rate is fifteen hundred dollars."

"Fifteen hundred!" she exclaimed with a broad smile on her lovely mouth.

"I couldn't be trusted for less."

Her nostrils flared and I wondered if I had paid my latest life insurance premium.

"Are you really as tough as you act, Mr. McGill?"

"I truly hope that neither one of us has to find that out today."

The elevator doors opened and people began to disgorge; five travelers and a bright-eyed redcap whom I'd run into over the years ferrying first-class and infirm passengers along the uncharted routes of the station. His name was Freddy Mason, and his wife I thought might have been Yee.

Marella and I stood aside as the crowd moved past. Then Freddy came out pushing his cart. When he saw me he nodded and frowned. Then, seeing my pickup client, he smiled.

There was no one else waiting for the elevator, which I regretted, and there seemed to be no one else around. So I ushered Marella Herzog into the empty chamber and girded myself for what I knew was coming.

When she was against the corrugated back wall of the metal car I set the suitcase up in front of her—to create an extra buffer. I looked up at the polished metal reflector in the left corner and saw him coming even before Marella yelled, "Watch out!"

He timed it almost perfectly. The doors were already closing when he lunged through. There was something in his left hand. It could have been a pistol but I suspected a more intimate weapon. Either way I'd have to turn before he could expect me to cower in fear.

All those years working out in Gordo's boxing gym had honed my reflexes until they almost had minds of their own. I couldn't go ten rounds anymore but in a profession like mine survival was rarely about endurance.

Already low to the ground, I crouched down and spun on my left heel. I grabbed his left wrist and broke it with one fast torquing motion but I had no intention of stopping there. I raised up and delivered a left uppercut to the tall man's jaw before seeing the hunting knife he had dropped when his wristbone broke. I grabbed his head with my right hand and slammed it against the wall. It bounced very nicely and my client's stalker, whoever he was, fell unconscious to the floor.

I glanced up at Marella. If she had any response it was not in her face.

Moving quickly, I set the olive-skinned man in the back corner to the right so that it looked as if he was sitting there, grabbing some sleep where he could. That way the first thing an unsuspecting passenger might have thought was that he was a drunk using a public conveyance as his bedroom.

I noticed that he was still breathing.

That was fortunate.

Our luck held, because there was no one waiting for the baggage elevator. We had taken nineteen steps before someone yelled for help.

Twenty-eight steps later we were taking the escalator up to the Eighth Avenue exit. It was there we saw four uniformed cops come barreling down the stairs.

"Should we try to run?" Marella whispered in my ear. Those were the first words she'd spoken since the encounter.

"Only if we want to get caught."

There was a long line waiting for cabs at that time in the afternoon. The sirens of two police cars and one ambulance wailed to a stop not half a block away from us. While policemen and paramedics hurried into the station, Marella and I attached ourselves to the end of the taxi line.

"I guess I owe you some money," she said after a few minutes' wait.

"Fifteen hundred."

"Will you take a check?"

"No."

She put a hand on my shoulder. She wasn't more than half an inch taller than I but her caramel heels added an inch to that.

"I like strong men," she said.

"Why? So they can protect you?"

"I like to watch them come."

A woman standing in front of us turned slightly, cocking her ear in our direction.

"How's that?" I asked.

"Underneath, on top, or looking over his belly button," she said. "Strong men who know their strength give it up because they don't have to pretend."

The woman in front of us on line touched the shoulder of the guy she was with. They were both white and in their twenties. She leaned over to whisper something and he turned to look.

"Is that offer in lieu of my fee?" I asked.

"Next!" the cab controller shouted. He might have said it more than once.

The nosy couple realized that he was calling to them and reluctantly returned to their lives.

"I'm staying at the Hotel Brown in the East Sixties," she said.

"I know the place."

"I should have the money in the next hour or so."

I took out a business card and handed it to her.

"Call me when you're ready to pay up," I said, and she smiled.

"I guess you are as tough as you think," she said.

"Next!"

4

Marella Herzog's cab pulled away leaving me a little stunned. My heart was beating like it was being played by a one-armed Japanese Ondekoza drummer pounding slowly on his seven-hundred-pound drum with a caveman's club at twilight. It was this unusually calm and yet powerful beat that allowed me to go back into Penn Station. I guess I felt somewhat invulnerable and unconcerned with consequences or danger.

The main hall of the transportation hub was a little more frenetic than usual; like an ant colony that had just perceived some kind of physical threat. I counted nine police uniforms and actually saw the wheeled gurney that carried our unconscious attacker toward the front exit.

I was taking a greater chance than most civilians because half the NYPD had at least passing familiarity with my face. In my younger days I had been the danger. I was a private investigator who only worked for underworld figures setting up other crooks for their crimes. I had relinquished my evil ways but the police never forget and rarely forgive, so cops who weren't even out of high school when I was active knew my mug shot.

I wasn't worried because the police would have assumed that our attacker's attacker had fled. Also I wasn't going to be in the area of their ad hoc investigation for more than thirty seconds.

At the bottom of the escalator I took a hard left past the public toilets, through a short hall that housed a newsstand and a doughnut shop, and then down a concrete stairway into the long hall that led to the station's commuter trains.

The lower-level arcade was a triple-wide passage with dozens of shops selling everything from orange pop to used books. If you were on your way out of the city, headed for some suburban home, you could get whatever you needed on that unnamed, underground, two-block-long street.

Strolling among the crowd, I considered the fight I'd just had along with the concept of organized sport. One day elevator fighting might become a recognized competition. The walls, floor, and ceiling would be made from transparent, steel-hard plastic and its audience mostly young and dissatisfied. The gladiators might enter the car on the first floor and travel upward, stopping at each stage to take on another challenger. The height of the ride would be the classification of the fighter, and anyone who made it to the top would be champion.

Why not?

Halfway down the arcade was an upscale coffee shop named Cheep's. There was no logo for the espresso joint so I never knew if the name came from the false promise of lower prices or the cry of a small bird. At any rate, Cheep's had two young black women and an older black man taking orders and serving overpriced coffee in paper cups. There were four small tables in the recess, three of which were most often untenanted because commuters were defined by forward motion, not sitting and sipping in a man-made hole.

One small round table had a regular occupant, however—a man known to most as the Professor. An older and diminutive white man, the Professor always wears a loose-fitting, threadbare suit, the color of dust. His cotton T-shirt is invariably navy and his back forever against the wall. The Professor is one of the many sources I go to to find out what's happening in my town.

I got on line for coffee, watching the passageway peripherally. A few cops walked down looking for someone to raise his hand and say, "I did it. I beat up the guy holding the knife and then came down here to hide."

"Can I help you, mistah?" the young woman who took orders asked.

Her straightened hair was maybe two feet long and equal parts pink, turquoise, and dark brown. She had golden pins through either side of her upper lip and eyes that had seen things.

"Large coffee," I said. "Dark roast."

For some reason my order, or its delivery, made her smile. As had been its purpose since humans became a species, the smile socialized me.

"How are you today?" I asked.

"Rather be out there with you, Mr. McGill."

My reaction to being recognized was twofold. First I lost the feeling of invulnerability. She had pierced my imagined force field with just a few words. Then I wondered who she was. Maybe twenty and a few pounds over the limit imposed by American TV, movies, and fashion magazines . . .

"Sherry, right?" I said. "Shelly's friend."

"That's good," she complimented. "I was only over at your house one time."

"Can you guys hurry it up," a man's voice said from behind. "Some people have trains to catch."

I turned around, the full 180 degrees. He was, of course, a few inches taller, what passes for white, and younger than me by two decades. But that wasn't enough. I'd lost my immunity to injury but my super strength was solidly in place. The gray-suited man gazed at me with his light brown eyes and then looked away.

When I turned back, my coffee was there in front of me, Sherry smiling over it.

"How much I owe you?"

"This one's on the house," she said.

"Thank you."

"If you come back sometime in the morning it won't be so busy."

"I will," I said and then moved to the side.

I had never been flirted with by one of my daughter's friends. At most other times I'd have probably shrugged it off, but Marella's explosive intrusion had torn up the tracks of my regular route and I was now on foot in unfamiliar territory.

———

"Professor," I said, standing at his table.

"Leonid," he answered in a soft, sophisticated tone of erudition. "How are you?"

"Pretty good," I said. "I was passing through and thought I'd drop by and say hello."

"Sit down. Drink your coffee."

I lowered into the chair at his side so that I could see out and see him at the same time.

"How are you?" the Professor asked again.

"My wife tried to commit suicide a few months back," I said. "Dealing with her, I may have gone off orbit a bit."

The Professor was one of the select few whose vision I trusted. There are all kinds of categories in the streetwise intelligence business. There was Sweet Lemon Charles, who had given up the Life for poetry but still wandered the old streets and passed rumors that most likely had roots in reality. Alphonse Rinaldo was the most powerful man in city government and yet he had no official post. You only went to Rinaldo for Category 5 difficulties. Luke Nye had specific information on criminals only.

But the Professor was another thing completely. Born Drake Imago, he was once an Ivy League philosophy professor teaching in the gulfs between Hegel and Marx, Marx and the Frankfurt School, the Frankfurt School and certain political activists in '60s European and American politics. He'd had a rivalry with another professor, a man named Hendricks, for years. Hendricks always stayed ahead of the Professor, getting the bigger grants, awards, and more prestigious accolades.

One day the Professor came home to find Hendricks in flagrante delicto with his wife. After calling the police, the Professor sat down to his manual typewriter and, with his hands still wet with the blood of his victims, typed a confession starting with the first crime committed against him by Hendricks: when he stole the Professor's idea about *Obfuscative Language and the Tyranny of Philosophy*.

Receiving a life sentence, the Professor spent twelve years in maximum security—this because he showed no remorse for the brutality of his crime. During the first eighteen months he'd been beaten, raped, slashed, nearly starved to death by criminals that stole his food, and driven temporarily insane by the sights, sounds, and smells of nonstop human distress. That, as he is happy to tell all and sundry, was his basic education.

Then he met a young man named Bronk. When the Professor was being beset by a rat-faced con with tattoos all around the edges of his face, Bronk saved him and asked if he could write down what Bronk felt. Completely illiterate, Bronk had committed a string of armed robberies and was then incarcerated without having the chance to communicate with his family. His mother lived in the hills of Kentucky and didn't have a phone. The Professor sat down with Bronk and after a series of twelve questions he crafted a letter that expressed things that Bronk had not even realized he felt.

For the next ten and a half years Bronk and the Professor were cellmates, bosom buddies, and maybe even lovers. No one bothered the Professor after that, and he became a fount of information and advice for the gen pop of the maximum security prison.

"I'm sorry," the Professor said about my wife—Katrina. "How's she doing now?"

"Okay. All right. I have her in a sanatorium because she's still a little loopy."

The old man gave a sad smile and sipped his coffee.

You go to Sweet Lemon, Rinaldo, or Luke Nye when you want more or less specific help. The Professor is a thinker and a witness to the world whose insights change the lenses of perception.

If an ex-con comes to him he might have a line on a legitimate day job or maybe a connection for something a little less savory. If you find yourself at a crossroads in life he's the traffic light. And if you just drop by . . . who knows? The Professor's eyes are always open, collecting data like a water filter catching all the impurities the seven seas have to offer.

"Got anything for me, Drake?" I asked.

"I've seen your son Twilliam walking back and forth down here a few times," he said. "He was wearing tattered blue jeans and a T-shirt with a grease stain on the back hem."

"Twill was?"

"He was indeed."

I finished my coffee, put a twenty-dollar bill down on the table, and bid the educated killer good-bye.

5

I reached Tivoli Rest Home a few minutes past 7:30 that evening. I decided to walk up to East Eighty-fourth rather than take a subway or taxi because the meals were served at 6:00 and the staff, mainly nuns, were strict about allowing their patients to eat in peace.

"Mr. McGill," Sister Alona Alfred said in greeting as I entered the admissions hall.

"Evenin', Sister."

"I haven't seen you in a few days. I was wondering where you were."

"Down in Philadelphia doing a job."

"Were you successful?" she asked. Sister Alona was youngish, in her thirties, and had a complexion that a runway model would have slashed for. Her smile was both infectious and as far from seductive as one could get.

"I reunited a married couple," I said.

"Bless you."

Katrina's private room was on the sixth floor of the nine-story building. I don't think she'd left that floor since the day I delivered her six weeks earlier.

The door was open so I didn't knock. She was lying in the bed; actually she was languishing there. Her left arm was thrown up over her eyes and her right hand hung over the side of the mattress. The blankets were on the bed but not over her because the small room was warm. There had been a cold snap and the heat had been turned on—high.

There was a chair and a window, pine flooring, gray-green walls, and a cream-colored ceiling that would not tolerate a very tall man. There was a vase of flowers, yellow pansies, on the writing desk she never used and a stack of fashion magazines that our daughter, Shelly, had brought a month before. They hadn't been touched.

I went to stand over her but said nothing.

After a few moments she let the left arm fall to the side. Her pale eyes were staring at me. All I recognized was in that steady stare. Before she tried to kill herself Katrina's beauty denied her fifty-five years. She could have been forty and, on her better days, thirty-five. She exercised and used all the right unguents to preserve the skin and eliminate wrinkles. But now her flesh seemed to sag and you could see all her years like Marley's chains.

"Leonid."

I sat. "Baby."

"I vas vorried about you." Usually her inexplicable Swedish accent didn't come out unless she was drunk. Maybe the drugs they had her on also caused it.

"Just a job," I said. "I told Twill to tell you that."

"He did. He came tvice and sent Mardi once. She seems a little vorried."

"How about Dimitri and Tatyana?"

"She comes every morning before school but D gets too upset to see me like this."

The wounds from her attempted suicide were there on her wrists; jagged lacerations that had cut deep. She looked like she was dying, and our Dimitri loved her more than anything. Of course he'd stay away.

"We should talk, Katrina."

Making a monumental effort, she pushed herself up until she could rest her back against the wall that abutted the head of her bed. In rising she seemed to shrug off a decade or so.

"What is it, Leonid?" she asked.

"I'm worried about you, baby. You don't seem to be getting any better but the doctors all say that there's nothing physically wrong."

"They ask me how I feel every Tuesday and I tell them that I have lost interest in living. Then they go away and I fall asleep again. I've been dreaming about my parents and my brother." Somehow sitting upright stripped her of the accent from a country that she had never even visited.

"So you still want to kill yourself?"

"No," she said, looking toward the small, shaded window. "No. I don't want to live but I don't have the will to try suicide again."

"Did you tell the doctors that?"

"They never ask."

She turned her gaze to me. I wondered if I should take her home; maybe in familiar circumstances she might begin to feel better.

"Do you remember when we used to watch the television in the little front room after the children were in bed?" she asked.

"Whenever I wasn't on a job."

"I'd make you another supper and you would sometimes rub my feet."

"I always liked that fourth meal. You're the best cook in the world," I said, and I meant it, too.

"Remember what you would say when we watched *Law & Order* and all those crazy crimes?"

"'Sometimes I think that everybody in the world is crazy,'" I said, quoting myself, "'except for me and you—and sometimes I wonder about you.'"

The smile that crossed her face brought back the old Katrina for a moment, surfacing in the gloom like the body of a whale breaking the surface and then disappearing beneath the waves.

"Would you like it if I brought you home, Katrina?" I asked. "Dimitri and Tatyana could move back in and I'd watch TV with you and rub your feet."

She mustered only half a smile and said, "Sometimes I'm too weak or too sad to go to the bathroom by myself. I won't be a burden."

"Do they make you walk?" I asked.

"Every day at four. I spend an entire hour preparing for Sister Marie to come and pull me out of bed. We walk from here down to the elevator. She asks me if I want to go down to the recreation area in the basement and I tell her, 'Maybe tomorrow.'"

I wanted to say something kind, to slap her and tell her to snap out of it. I would have torn out my hair if I wasn't already bald.

Katrina looked down at her hands. "I've disappointed you."

"No, baby," I assured her. "You're going through a hard time and we just have to see it through."

"You are a good man, Leonid."

"We both know that's a lie, Katrina."

"No, Leonid," she said with conviction if not strength in her voice. "I strayed. Twill and Shelly are not your children. You have always known but you raised them with love and you never ran away. You were always there for us."

"That's like complimenting a beaver for having big buckteeth," I said, "or a lion for his deep voice."

"Or a man," Katrina said, "for living by his nature."

I felt uncomfortable receiving these accolades. Katrina and I had been alternately bickering and cheating on each other for decades, and now there she was speaking truth to me. We hadn't been partners or lovers for so long that in a way we were strangers.

"You have anything you want me to do about the kids?" I asked. Maybe thinking about them would help her make it down to the recreation room.

"Twill is into something," she said. "Do you have him on some case?"

"No. He's just studying the tapes I recorded when I was following people."

"When he came to see me he was too happy. You know when things are good with him he just acts, I don't know, kind of cool. But when something is going on he gets that glitter in his eyes."

I knew the look. The problem was I hadn't seen my son in seven days.

"The Professor said he saw him wandering around the lower level of Penn Station, said he had his shirttails out."

"You saw Drake?"

I'd forgotten that the academic ex-con had come to a picnic we once gave. He and Katrina talked for hours about ancient recipes he once studied. He might have even written a monograph on the subject as a footnote to his doctoral thesis.

"What about Shelly?" I asked.

"That man followed her up to SUNY."

"Seldon Arvinil?"

"He left his wife and daughter to be with our little girl. I suppose she's happy though. Who am I to deny her that?"

"You're her mother."

"If I was a good mother she wouldn't have needed an older man to shelter her heart."

Hearing these words reminded me of Sweet Lemon Charles for the second time that day. The next time I saw the prison-made poet I'd ask him what he knew about the poetry of despair.

6

The Hotel Brown was nestled between two Middle Eastern consulates on East Sixty-seventh, not far from Fifth Avenue. It was an old hotel with an excellent security staff and high-ceilinged rooms that were well appointed and large. Not a cheap joint.

I stood across the street and called the hotel operator with the help of 411.

"Hotel Brown," a woman said. "How may I direct your call?"

"Marella Herzog," I said.

There was a hesitation and then, "Who may I say is calling?"

"Leonid McGill."

The next thing I heard was a ringing phone.

"Hello, Leonid," she said on answering the third ring. "I was wondering when you'd call."

"How'd you know it was me?"

"I told the front desk only to allow calls from you. It was getting so late that I thought maybe I'd have to wait until tomorrow."

It was 9:39 by my watch and tomorrow seemed very far away.

"Are you calling about your money?" she asked when I was silent.

"I guess that's part of it."

"What else?"

"I didn't get my kiss on the cheek."

"Where are you?"

"Across the street."

"Come on up," she said, "room eight twenty-five. I'll tell the front desk to let you by."

———

There was a time when black men were not allowed to visit fancy hotel rooms unless they wore a service uniform and were delivering flowers or dinner on a tray. There was a time when dark-skinned women would not be allowed to stay in those rooms. But those days are long over. There's still racism of course. People of color still struggle mightily against misconceptions that are half a millennium old. But these days I can take the elevator up to a femme fatale's room and no one would bar my way—or warn me off.

I knocked on her door and she answered—in the nude. The nude. She wore absolutely nothing. Her entire body was an even reddish brown, telling me that she spent a lot of time on unregulated beaches.

Walking across the threshold, I closed the door with my left hand, went to my knees, and pressed my mouth into the nexus of her legs.

"Oh," she said.

Working my head and neck to separate her thighs maybe four inches midway between the pelvis and the knee, I jabbed softly with my tongue.

"Oh," she said with a bit more feeling.

But it was when I got the left thigh on my shoulder and stood straight up that I believe she was more shocked than I was to be received by a russet-skinned beauty at a door on the eighth floor of a room which, not all that long ago, excluded our ancestors.

She grabbed onto my hairless head but she didn't have to worry. I wouldn't have let her fall. Between my shoulders, hands, and tongue she either had a powerful orgasm or did a very good job at pretending.

"Let me down," she said when the shudders subsided.

I moved my shoulder and then my chest until I was holding her in the cradle of my arms.

"You're very strong," she said and then kissed me for the first time.

I rubbed my nose against her chin.

"Lucky I don't have an engagement ring in my pocket," I replied.

She hugged my head then with even more passion than she had shown before.

"Lie down with me," she commanded.

And so there we lay: her completely naked and me fully dressed and fully erect.

She touched the urgent bulge in my trousers and said, "We'll take care of that in just a bit."

"We better," I warned, "before it takes care of itself."

Marella laughed out loud, actually guffawed and punched my arm. She was a solidly built woman; in her thirties, as I've already said, but with the pampered body of a woman ten years younger.

"Do you think you killed that guy?" she asked.

"Naw," I said dismissively.

"How can you be so sure?"

"I went back in the station after you left."

"You did? Wasn't that rather reckless?"

"Nobody saw us," I said.

I considered explaining my idea of the elevator-gladiator sport.

She unzipped my blue trousers.

"He saw us," she said while fishing around for the flesh in my pants.

"Um . . . he was still out."

"How do you know that?" She found what she was looking for. Her fingers were cold.

"Oh," I said. "He passed maybe twelve feet away from me on a wheeled gurney pushed by two women."

"Your turn," she told me and we didn't talk about anything for a while.

"I think I can safely say that I have never met a man like you," Marella Herzog said at 1:51 by the lighted digital numerals on the clock next to her side of the bed. We were both naked by then, drinking honor-bar cognac. My pants, which were neatly folded on a plush red chair that sat against the wall, had an extra fifteen hundred dollars in them.

"I can say without a doubt," I replied, "that I have met all the failed attempts that first the Hebraic and then the Christian God made trying to come up with a woman like you."

"You're good," she said. "It's a wonder that you haven't been shot down by a town full of frightened citizens."

It struck me that our conversation was like an aged wine rather than a freshly squeezed juice. If I believed in the gods I swore by, or maybe their Hindu counterparts, I would have said that we were old souls that had known each other at many other times, in other reincarnations.

"So what do you plan to do about the man that wants his ring back?" I asked.

"How old are you?"

"Almost fifty-six."

"And you laid that guy out and held me up on your shoulders like my daddy did when I was a little kid."

"I hope not just like that."

"No. The other way around."

"You needed a man who wouldn't mind the ride," I said. "I guess I needed a woman like that too."

She leaned over toward her end table and poured another miniature bottle into her near-empty glass. I realized, watching that supple and sinuous movement, that life was the only magic all humanity could agree upon.

"I don't think I have anything to worry about, Mr. McGill. You nipped that problem in the bud."

"Rich men sometimes have armies of guys like that one on the train," I advised.

"I don't think it'll be a problem," she countered. "I still have your card if something comes up in the next day or two, and after that I'll be far, far away from here."

Who was I to question the perfect Lilith, the precise Mary Magdalene?

"Can I sleep here with you tonight?" I asked.

"Only if you don't mind if I wake you up once or twice."

7

I was back down near Penn Station at 5:17 the next morning, making my way up the stairs of a nondescript brick building just a few blocks away. When I'd woken up at 4:00 Marella was still asleep. After an ice-cold shower I threw on my blue suit, kissed her, and said good-bye. She sighed, smiled, and turned the other way.

I left the Hotel Brown certain that my business with Ms. Herzog was yet to be completed. I was wondering if this was a good thing as I pushed open the door to Gordo's Gym on the fifth floor of the nameless, unremarkable building.

There were already a dozen boxers and half that many trainers hard at work. Two of four makeshift rings had opponents practicing how to dismantle their opposition. My usual heavy bag near a murky window was being used by a featherweight named Brian "Fat Fudge" Lowman. He was making that bag sway, which is no mean feat for a man that small.

"Hey, LT," a gravelly voice hailed.

It was Gordo Tallman, the red-bronze surrogate father who had taught me that my best talent was absorbing pain and then giving it back with some interest. He had thought that I'd use that equation getting a light-heavy championship belt, but instead I plied it on the streets.

"Gordo," I said. Standing face-to-face, we were the same height. He didn't weigh much more than Fat Fudge but his will was unbreakable. "How you doin'?"

"I'm gettin' married," he said.

"You and Elsa set a date?" I asked.

"Me and her broke up."

"Broke up? You just got engaged. What happened?"

"Sophie." It was a one-word treatise on Gordo Tallman's life.

Sophie Bernard was the little sister of Gordo's third wife, Helen. Helen was from Houston, Texas, and after she and Gordo got married she brought a few members of her family up to New York. Sophie came to live with Gordo and Helen. She was a small woman with big eyes and rich with the empathy that hard men want but can never ask for.

After three months of living with the sisters, Gordo found that he talked more with Sophie than Helen. The marriage foundered sometime soon after that. After a year had passed, Gordo came to Sophie and asked her to marry him. She said that she wanted to but wouldn't because it would break her sister's heart. Sophie had promised Helen that she never did anything wrong with Gordo, so if they got married Helen would think that she'd lied.

"Sophie?" I said. "I didn't even know that you still talked to her."

"She called," Gordo said, a little shy. "She called to tell me that Helen had died."

Oh.

"I said I was sorry and me and Elsa went to the funeral over in New Brunswick, New Jersey. After the ceremony we sat with Soph at a pizza restaurant the family rented out. It was just a nice time, you know? But on the train ride home Elsa says to me, 'You're in love with that woman.' I just laughed. I hadn't seen Sophie in twenty years. I liked her. I liked her fine but the past was gone.

"At least that's what I thought. But that night I couldn't go to sleep. I sat up remembering what it was like those three months I saw Soph every morning over coffee. Elsa was my nurse, she saved my life. I love her but there was something in my heart for Sophie that I couldn't shake.

"Maybe if Elsa didn't say anything . . . But no. I would have been thinking about Soph after that."

For a moment my old mentor was lost in thought.

Finally he said, "Two days later Elsa told me that she was going back to Germany."

"What did you say?"

"I couldn't say a word. I wanted to. I tried. But all I could manage was this miserable face. Elsa kissed me and a few days later she was gone."

"And then you called Sophie and asked her to marry you again?"

"I'm eighty-three years old, LT. My time is nearly up. I should'a been dead from that cancer. I cain't tell my heart what to do. Sophie asked me how was Elsa and I said she'd gone back home. Two minutes later I asked her to marry me and she said all right."

I knew Elsa. I hired her when I thought Gordo would die from cancer. She was a good woman but I could hear the love in Gordo's voice.

"Congratulations," I said. "How's Helen's family feel about this?"

"Most of 'em back down in Texas" was his answer. "I'm flyin' up twelve of 'em to come to the ceremony."

"That's a mighty big nut, G. You sure you can do it?" I knew he could. Gordo was a rich man. He was a brilliant trainer but his genius was real estate.

"I gotta couple'a things I need from you, LT," he said instead of taking the bait. I could tell from his tone that talk of love was over.

"What's that?"

"I got this Chin'ee kid from Hong Kong can fight. Middleweight, you know. Fast as Sugar Ray Leonard with the bones of Marvin Hagler. Ain't nevah lost a fight an' been in the ring nineteen times."

"What's his name?"

"Chin Wa."

"Never heard of him."

"Never fought in the States or on TV. He think he the real deal but I believe that the competition was lacking."

"And?"

"Fudge be on your bag all mornin'," Gordo said. "Got him tryin' to get some pop in them punches, so maybe you could do a couple'a rounds with Chin and see if he got the seven covered."

"Where's Iran?" I asked. Iran Shelfly, a heist man that went to prison, partly because of my hidden perfidy, now worked for Gordo.

"He down doin' a undercard in Philly. I told him if he won I'd get him a real fight. Maybe with that Irish kid ev'rybody love so much."

I went in a corner, shed my clothes, and donned trunks that Gordo kept in a drawer for me. The old man laced my gloves and I entered the center ring with no headgear.

"He gonna hit you," Gordo warned. I heard him but Marella's spell of invulnerability was on me again.

After a few minutes a young Asian Adonis came out of the locker room; only Gordo's prospects, or "health club" customers, got lockers and dressing areas. The rest of us had to rely on the modesty provided by corners, and we took our showers at home.

Chin Wa didn't have one ounce of fat on his 157-pound frame. He was lithe and smiling. When we faced each other in the middle of the ring I said, "No headgear?"

"You won't hit my head," he said. "But I sure hit you."

And he did, too. I was trying to cover up, throwing uppercuts up top but he knew how to punch and he moved his head like a king cobra on speed. Maybe fifteen seconds into the first round he'd hit me as many times. After a minute or so my uppercut fell a bit and I caught him in the rib cage on the right side. One. I got two more in before Gordo hit the bell.

When the bell to the second round started I could see Chin Wa was angry that I was able to answer. He threw a flurry at me, landing every punch, and I connected once five inches below his diaphragm. Four. For the next minute or so his volume and velocity of punches slowed though he might not have realized it. I got in two right hooks on his left side before Gordo hit the bell again.

By this time we had an audience. It was my guess that most sparring partners that got in with Chin were daunted by his speed.

When the third round started I put my hands down, he smiled, hit me four times and then I let out with a straight right hand to his lower core. He looked at me with real surprise on his face. He tried to raise his arms as if to protect himself from the blows that might be coming but instead the movement twisted his gut muscles and he spun to the canvas like a corkscrew.

"Inside'a your lip bleedin'," Gordo said as I put on my clothes in the corner.

He lifted the left side of my lip with two fingers and rubbed a crystal of pure alum against the cut. It stung for a moment and then came the tangy taste of the chemical. The intimacy of boxers and their trainers is something akin to love.

"Thanks, LT," Gordo said. "It would'a taken Chin up to the middle ranks to learn that a heavy hitter can have a brain. You could'a been the best in the world at one time."

"The way I take hits I would have most certainly been punch-drunk by now."

Gordo looked down then. He knew the ravages of the sweet science like anybody else.

"Have you seen Twill around?" I asked my oldest friend.

"Not for ovah a week now. But Dimitri come in every night, him and that Mata Hari girl he been datin'."

"Does Tatyana box?"

"Naw. She just stretches and do that yoga stuff while he in trainin'."

"But no Twill?"

Gordo shook his head and shrugged.

8

got up to the seventy-second floor of the Tesla Building at a few minutes before 7:00. Now and then I try to get into the office before Mardi. It's a kind of competition for us. Though usually quiet, and always reserved, Mardi is likely to give me a certain look when I come in and she's already there. The look says, *You see? I am the better worker here.* So now and then I like to come in early to stick out my tongue at her.

But when I turned the corner headed toward my office I forgot about the silly rivalry.

Standing there beside my office door was a medium-sized white man in an ill-fitting brown suit. He was five-seven or -eight but with bad posture and a sagging belly, though he was not overweight.

When he saw me approaching, the man forced a hopeful look into his depressed features. As I came up to him he said, "Mr. McGill?"

"Yes?"

"My name is Stent," he said. "Hiram Stent."

His features were what I could only call indistinct. There was no ridged border between his lips and the surrounding skin. His eyes were murky, neither brown nor green. And Hiram Stent's skin was tan but not from day labor or last summer's visits to the beach. His leathery rind came from long hours of overexposure and a little too much alcohol that worked to cure this finish from the inside out.

"Oh yeah." I was working the first of seven keys on the office door. "Mardi gave you an early appointment. But you know, Mr. Stent, we don't open till ten."

"I didn't know so I came early so I wouldn't miss you or anything."

I was pretty adept at the locks and so the door soon came open and I ushered my scruffy would-be client in.

I crossed past Mardi's big blond desk and went to the metal door that protected the greater part of my office suite from the outside world. I placed my electronic card next to the little screen at the right side of the door. This caused a virtual number pad to appear. On this pad I entered the seventeen-digit code and the heavy door swung open.

"After you, Mr. Stent."

As he went by I noticed two things: a scent and his shoes. The odor had a dry earthy bouquet that I remembered from when I was a happy child with a mother and a father playing in the dirt. The shoes were the real giveaway though; black at one time, they were now turning gray and wearing thin, almost shapeless from many more miles of walking than they were designed for. Those soles knew the pavement from long association and little or no respite.

"This way," I said to my visitor.

I led him down the long aisle of empty cubicles toward my office.

"You have a large staff," he said, looking from side to side at the empty desks.

"Only the receptionist and my son."

"Then why all these offices?"

"I have the ambition of being a big fish one day. I figure if I have the room to grow there's a chance it might happen."

By then I was shepherding him into my office.

I went behind my extra-large ebony desk and sat with my back to the window that looked down the isle of Manhattan to the swirly new World Trade Center.

"Sit," I told my guest, and he perched on the closest red and boxy office chair that Mardi said looked better with my black desk.

"Thanks for seeing me, Mr. McGill," Hiram Stent said.

The man's physical presence was a puzzle in itself. The hair on top of his head had turned a dirty blond. The tier under that was the brown of a pecan shell and there was a spotty ridge below that which was almost all gray. These layers showed that Mr. Stent was much in the sun, a natural brunet, and very possibly under great strain. He was no more than forty but some of those years had been long and hard.

I was silent while studying the middle-aged man.

He was getting nervous.

"I'd like to hire you, Mr. McGill," he said.

"How did you find your way to me?" I asked.

"What do you mean, um, I took the number six train."

"I'm asking you where you heard my name. I don't advertise."

"Oh," he said, nodding. "I heard your name from a man called Rooster."

"Red Rooster Collins?"

"I don't know his full name."

"Black man, red hair and tall?"

"That's him."

Rooster was a man I knew; not an important man but a well-connected one. He was a diagnosed schizophrenic and so often spent his time, when off his meds, in places that might house a man like Stent.

"How can I help you, Mr. Hiram Stent?"

There was a story behind his vague features, the burning coal of a problem that turned his stomach and kept him up at night. But when asked he was struck dumb.

"Why did you want to see me?" I said, hoping that a rearticulation of the question would loosen his tongue.

"My name is Hiram Stent," he said. "I was the CFO of Lipsky, Van der Calm, Tryman, and Wills for twelve years." He said these words and stopped, hoping to have made some kind of impact.

"Chief financial officer," I said to urge him on.

"They're an investment company," he said, "specializing in midsized corporations and family businesses."

"Okay."

"Because," he said, and then he cleared his throat. "Because most of the work is done on computers and the phone, Charles Wills decided that the firm should move to Wyoming, where real estate is cheap and so we could either lower costs or increase our assets. The downtown Manhattan landlord was raising the rent from six to sixteen thousand a month."

"That's a lot of money," I noted.

"I guess it is. That's why they decided to relocate. They offered to take me with them."

"But you didn't go," I surmised.

"My wife didn't like the idea and I . . . I thought that I could, I could get another job easily enough. I mean, I have an MBA and twelve years' experience working for LVTW."

"But that was the time of the market slump," I said.

"Exactly, the economic slump," he said, grabbing onto the phrase like it was a lifeline. "I couldn't get work anywhere, anywhere. And even when things got better no one wanted a CFO who'd been unemployed for three years. I only knew how LVTW worked and I was too old for most entry positions. My wife took the kids and left to go stay with her family while I was job hunting. She connected with an old boyfriend . . ."

I didn't need to ask anything; his story was as obvious as a pair of worn shoes.

"I kept looking," he said. "When I asked Lois to come back she said no. When I called again she'd had her number disconnected. Her mother wouldn't tell me where she went. I haven't seen my children for two years."

There were tears in his reptilian eyes.

"After a while I lost the condo on Thirty-third and now I stay in a rooming house on Flatbush in Brooklyn when I can get enough money together . . ."

"So why are you here, Mr. Stent?"

"Lois's old boyfriend is a handyman. He doesn't make much. I was being paid nearly two hundred thousand when LVTW moved out west. If I had that kind of money now I could buy a plane ticket and go down to Florida and get my family back."

His tone was plaintive, his dreams the dreams of a child. I felt for the guy.

"But why are you here?" I asked.

"I need to get back on my feet, Mr. McGill," he said. It seemed to me that he'd lost the thread of his purpose.

"And how could I help with that?"

"By finding, locating Celia Landis."

I was half convinced that Stent had lost his mind from sorrow, homelessness, and alcohol consumption. But then he uttered a real name. I wondered if there was an actual person attached to the name.

"And who is that?" I asked.

"I don't know. I mean I've never met her."

"Then why are you looking for her?"

"A guy, a man named Bernard Shonefeld, sent a letter to my old address and a neighbor who knew me sent it on to my post office box. You know I keep that box in case my children ever need me—they'll know how to find me."

"Bernard Shonefeld," I said.

"He's doing work for a law firm in San Francisco—Briscoe/Thyme. They're looking for this Celia Landis woman . . . young woman. I think she's twenty-eight or -nine. That's what Mr. Shonefeld said."

"Why is a law firm in San Francisco asking you about a woman that you don't know?" I was fascinated by the twists and turns of his hapless story.

"They said, Shonefeld told me that, that this Celia Landis is a distant cousin on my mother's side. I never heard of her but Briscoe/Thyme had been looking for her for a long time, eleven months, and all they could locate was me."

"What did they say they wanted with Celia?" I asked.

"Her grandfather, on the other side of her family, people I'm not related to, died and left her many millions of dollars. The estate tasked the lawyers to find her for a ten percent fee. Shonefeld told me that they'd give me ten percent of that if I could find her."

"Did this Shonefeld ask you for money?" I asked.

"No. No. He just said that I should find her and I'd get ten percent of ten percent of over a hundred million dollars. That's at least a million, more than enough to go down to Miami and get Lois and the kids back.

"I used the computers at the New York Public Library to try and find her through the genealogy search engines. But there wasn't anything. I tried every kind of search but there was nothing."

"Did you try asking your mother?" I asked.

"Mom died when I was seventeen and she was estranged from her family because they didn't like my dad because he was Catholic. He's dead too. Dad's family is from Canada somewhere and I'm an only child. But I did find one of Mom's sisters in Newark. I called out there and told her that I was looking for Celia because I didn't have any family and I heard she might be in New York. Mr. Shonefeld told me that he believed that she was in New York. She, my aunt Charlotte, said that she had a picture of Celia from a high school graduation photograph. She said that she'd sell it to me for seventy-five dollars. After that I did day work and collected bottles until I had enough to take a train out there and buy the picture."

From the breast pocket of his threadbare brown suit he brought out a tattered square of paper. He stood up and leaned across the desk to hand it to me. It was a snapshot of a pretty girl, somewhere in her late teens, with long brown hair and red lips. She was smiling at the camera, pushing her left shoulder forward in an inviting way.

"You paid seventy-five dollars for this? Why?"

"I thought maybe a private detective could find her. I mean that's what she looks like and she comes from around Princeton, New Jersey."

"Did you look?" I asked.

"Just on the Internet and in the phone book. She's not there and Aunt Charlotte said that most of her family is dead or in the wind. That's the words she used—'either dead or in the wind.'"

"And what do you want from me?"

"Find her, Mr. McGill. You're a detective. You can do things that I don't know about just like I can work with monies in ways that you probably don't understand."

"Speaking of money," I said. "How do you plan to pay for my services?"

"Ten percent."

"Ten percent of ten percent of ten percent?"

"I figure that to be a little more than a hundred thousand dollars," he said, his voice filled with impossible hope.

"Mr. McGill, are you in?" Mardi Bitterman said over the intercom.

"Hey, Mardi, I'm back here with Mr. Stent."

"You're in early."

"Earlier than you," I said with just a hint of satisfaction in my voice.

Then I turned my attention back to the homeless man who dreamed about millions. If I were ever to teach a class on being a PI the first thing I'd say is to never take a case like Stent's. There's no percentage in it—ten or otherwise.

"I can't help you, Mr. Stent," I said.

"I'll sign any contract you want."

"It's not that. It's not that you're unemployed or distressed or lost. I like you. I feel for your predicament but I don't believe that what this man is telling you is true."

"I have the letter."

"I'm sure you do. I'm sure there's a Celia Landis out there somewhere and that some man calling himself Shonefeld is looking for her. But wealthy people don't offer poor people a million dollars for a name and an address; not unless there's something hinky going on."

"But they said that they're looking for her. What other reason could they have?"

I stood up and walked around the desk, handed Hiram back his frayed photograph, and gestured for him to stand.

"What am I going to do?" he asked as if I was his only friend in the world.

Maybe I was.

"I don't know what to tell you, Hiram. I can't take this case because, in my professional opinion, something in this story stinks."

"But . . ."

I put my hand on his shoulder and he stopped talking. I walked him down the untenanted aisle, past Mardi's desk, and through the front door.

He never said another word.

9

I watched Hiram Stent walk down the hallway toward the elevators. He didn't look back. I almost called to him. After all, I had money from Camille Esterhouse and Marella Herzog (if indeed that was her real name). I could afford to do a good deed for some poor schlub down on his luck. But the truth was that Hiram couldn't be helped. Whatever I did, it would just turn out bad.

"How are you this morning, Mr. McGill?" Mardi asked my back as Stent turned the corner.

I closed the door and turned to my pale assistant, slight and white. Her gray-blue eyes carried all the sadness of the last days of autumn and her voice was so soft that it could have been a memory.

"Fine," I said. "And you?"

"I'm okay."

"How's your sister?"

"Just entered middle school. She loves the ocean and wants to be an oceanographer."

I sat down in one of the blue-and-chrome visitor's chairs that used to be in my office.

"You're hardly ever in this early anymore," she said.

"I used to be this early?"

"Mmmm-hm. When I first worked here."

She was right. My schedule had slowly shifted since Mardi began to shoulder some of the responsibility. She had been Twill's classmate. Barely in her twenties and she made more difference in my life than almost anyone ever had.

"Now that I'm here you can tell me about it," I said.

"About what?" she said, searching her desk for something to do with her hands.

"Twill."

She picked up a bright yellow disposable mechanical pencil and set it in a ceramic mug used to hold such things. This process took just long enough for the door buzzer to sound.

I was sure that it was Hiram Stent come back to beg me. I would have probably given him a day or two—after all, failure is a big part of being human.

"It's Ms. Ullman," Mardi said, looking down at the monitor I had installed in her desk drawer.

I could feel my Adam's apple writhe in my throat.

I got to my feet and, stumbling a little, took the two and a half steps to the entrance.

When I pulled the door open Aura said, "Oh!"—shocked that it was me.

Tall for a woman, she had a few inches on me. Aura was the color of pure gold that hadn't been polished for some years. She was nearing the midway mark in her forties with a generous figure that would never go out of style. Her hair was naturally wavy and darkly blond. Her surprised eyes were not brown but that's as far as I would go trying to define the color. Her mother, I knew, was Danish and her father black Togolese.

Aura was the plant supervisor of the Tesla Building. She was very efficient at her job. The only task she ever failed at was getting me evicted. She tried, and might have succeeded, but then we kind of fell in love.

"Didn't expect me?" I said to my sometime lover.

"Um," she said. "I wanted to ask Mardi something."

"She's right here," I said, moving backward and to the side, allowing her room to come in.

Mardi was already on her feet.

"Good morning, Ms. Ullman," she said. "How can I help you?"

"Um," she said again.

"I'll go back to my office and let you ladies talk."

"No," Aura said with more emphasis than was necessary.

"Why don't I go downstairs and get you guys some coffee and bagels?" Mardi offered.

"Thank you," Aura said to my assistant.

The next thing I knew, Aura and I were sitting in my old visitor's chairs more or less facing each other.

We had a lot to talk about and nothing to say.

When we met, my wife had left me for a banker named Zool. He turned out to be an embezzler who ran off, somewhere down in South America, leaving Katrina and my blood son, Dimitri, high and dry. And so Katrina returned just when my relationship with Aura was beginning to take form.

We, Aura and I, broke up for a while and had started to get back together a few times. The latest breakup had to do with Katrina again. Aura felt guilty making love to a man whose wife was suicidal.

"How's Katrina doing?" Aura asked.

"Kinda faded, I guess."

"Does she need new medication?"

"She needs something," I said, "but don't we all?"

Aura decided to ponder that question.

It struck me that sadness had as many striations as a rainbow—only in grays. Hiram Stent was sad because of a miscalculation. He believed that his education, his station in life, would allow him to make choices about how he might live. He lost his job, his wife, and his children; he'd lost his vanity and hope all because somebody named Wills wanted to do financial planning while living on a ranch.

Aura and I, on the other hand, loved each other fiercely but when together we turned morose and downcast.

Mardi had been molested as a child, repeatedly and over many years, and so her sadness descended when there was nothing for her to concentrate on.

"My daughter got into Mount Holyoke," Aura was saying.

"Good for her," I said.

"Are you working?" she asked then.

"I'm not sure."

"What do you mean?"

"I finished one job," I said. "That was a domestic beef. Those kinds seem to resuscitate now and then. I helped a woman who was being stalked but that only treated the symptom. And then there's Twill."

Aura smiled. Most people's moods lighten when they hear my son's name. He's just that kind of guy.

"What about him?" Aura asked.

"He's been absent and then seen wearing clothes not his style. He hasn't called in to me and that usually means that he's into something either illegal or dangerous, or both. Since he's working with me now it's more than likely that he's taken on a job I wouldn't approve of."

"He's got a lot of facets," Aura agreed.

The jeweler's term brought Marella to mind. I realized that her skin was very close to the same hue as Aura's. I wondered if that was the reason I'd taken such risk. Maybe I thought that if I put my life on the line I could receive a night of familiar love.

"What are you thinking, Leonid?"

"That we should have dinner one night next week."

"I'm free for lunch next Monday," she said.

Lunch—a single word that says, *I don't want to be alone with you in the evening when you might, and I might, get confused and break the unspoken rules that were chiseled for us on the tombstone your wife almost made.*

I didn't answer and then the door came open. Mardi entered with a small gray cardboard box holding our coffees and bagels.

"That was fast," I said.

"The coffee cart is usually on floor sixty-five this time of morning," she said.

Aura stood up and told us both, "I have a meeting down in my office in a few minutes. I'm going to have to take my coffee and run."

I stayed in my chair.

Aura gathered her coffee and bread.

"So we'll have to make a plan for Monday," she said.

"We'll see," I replied.

She looked a little lost for a moment and then left.

When the door closed I took out my smartphone and started entering a text.

"She seems a little upset," Mardi commented.

I erased what I had been typing and said, "Both of us I guess."

I started typing again.

"She's a nice lady," Mardi continued, trying to draw me in.

Instead of answering I sent the text to Aura's phone. It read: I LOVE YOU.

10

was looking at the closed door, thinking that everything was possible but little of that possibility was likely. Life was like a rat's maze tended by some insane god that tortured and shepherded us for some reason he (or maybe she) could no longer remember. Hiram Stent's fate was etched on a pauper's grave somewhere, probably before he was born. He would always make the wrong choices, always come up a dollar short. He could have been the ambassador to France and still the handyman would have taken his wife and children.

"Are you okay, Mr. McGill?"

I turned to look at my assistant. She wore a dress that was something like the flappers wore back nearly a century ago. It was sewn from flimsy fabric somewhere between cream and light pink, the hem coming down to her calves. There was faded beading here and there. It occurred to me that this ensemble had a hint of sexuality to it. This was, to say the least, unusual.

Not for the first time I thought of my assistant as a soul that didn't so much haunt as spiritually guide by a sense of the world that was more intuitive than anything else.

"Mr. McGill?"

"Have a seat, M."

Mardi made an abortive move for the walnut swivel chair behind her desk but then decided to take the visitor's chair Aura had been sitting in. I turned my head so that I was looking into her eyes. Mardi didn't like people looking directly at her—a leftover from childhood, I imagined.

She turned sideways in the padded chair and looked over at her desk; no doubt searching for another pencil to put in its place.

"Tell me about it," I said.

"What?"

"Twill."

"What about him?"

"Something's goin' on with him. When Twill disappears I get the feeling that there's a door somewhere that should be locked but isn't."

Mardi smiled because she understood and appreciated my imagistic bent.

She shook her head.

"You're his best friend, M," I said. "You can't tell me that you don't know what's happenin'."

"He had a meeting with somebody on Monday, after you left," Mardi admitted. "But then I was out Tuesday and Wednesday. He covered for me. I didn't see him almost all week."

Listening to her words, I remembered the dictum—*Truth is the best lie*.

"Who did he meet with?"

"I don't know. It was out of the office. A woman called, a young woman."

"You didn't tell me you were taking time off," I said, trying to take on the authority of a boss.

"I'm sorry." Mardi looked at her desk again, willing me to go so she could get away from the inquisition.

"Is something wrong?" I asked.

The expression on her face was equal parts surprise, anger, and *don't you know who the fuck you're talking to?*

"Talk to me, M."

"My father has been writing me from Ossining over the past year," she said. This truth dispelled her shyness. Now she was returning my stare.

Mardi's stepfather was Leslie Bitterman. Once he was an office manager by day and daughter molester by night; that was before he became a full-time resident of the maximum security prison.

"You want me to talk to some people?" I offered.

"What?" she said, almost angrily. "No. No. At first just getting the letters really upset me but not after a while."

"Does he want something?"

Mardi clasped her hands and pressed her lips against her left wrist—a kiss that was not a kiss.

"Mardi."

"He sent a letter every week for seven months before I even opened one. He said things like nothing ever happened between us, like he was a normal father trying to reach out to me and Marlene. He asked about my job and if I had a boyfriend . . ."

The motherfucker.

"I just thought it was sick," she said, "that he was trying to fuck with us even though he's locked away."

Mardi had never cursed in my memory.

"Then I answered him," she said. If any four words ever sucked the air out of a room it was these.

"What did you say?"

"I was angry. I told him that he didn't even have a right to think about us much less send letters. I told him that he destroyed my life and he was going to do the same to my sister. I told him that he made me into a murderer because I would have surely killed him if you hadn't gotten in the way. I don't know everything I said but it was eight handwritten pages long."

Mardi wrote in a tiny chicken scrawl. And she only used purple ink.

"Did he give you an answer?" I asked.

"No."

"No? Then why did you go up there?"

Mardi looked at me and I saw that she had become another person; someone related to the young woman I knew and loved, but now she was both stronger and weaker, more vulnerable.

"I kept thinking about the letter I wrote to him," she said. "The anger inside me was bigger than anything I'd ever felt. It was even more than the fear I used to have when he'd come into my room when I was a child. I realized that that anger was the largest part of my heart and if I ever wanted to be my own person, my own Mardi, I'd have to do something . . . extreme."

I wanted to ask but my breath wasn't acting right.

"I wrote another letter," she said. "It was very short and I wrote it in pencil because I erased it a dozen times until it was exactly what I wanted to say."

"And?"

"I wrote, 'I forgive you' and signed it 'M' because when you call me M I always feel that you're my father. And so I was your daughter letting go of that old corroded anchor that was pulling me down."

I don't know how long the silence was that followed those words. I don't remember reaching out but at some point I realized that we were holding hands.

"And," I said. I had to clear my throat. "And did he answer?"

"He sent another letter. It was the same old gibberish. Me growing into a fine woman and how much he'd learned and thank you about a hundred times. I didn't read it very closely. I just wrote him and said that I was coming to visit; that I was only coming one time and so he should know what he was going to say."

"Wow." For some reason I thought about my earlier sparring session with Chin Wa. If he'd had Mardi's will I'd've never won that match. "And so you went last week."

"It was horrific," Mardi said. I'd never heard her use that word before. "They took me to what they call an isolation hut and had me meet him in a room with two guards standing on either side of his chair. Before they'd even let me in I had to let a woman guard give me a body search."

The conversation stopped for a minute while all the experience and feeling coalesced in the young woman's mind.

"He had aged twenty years," she said. "His hair was gray and falling out. He had scars from a knifing and over the left side of his face where somebody had thrown acid on him. He's blind in his left eye and something's wrong with his right hand. It was curled up like a bird's claw."

"Yeah," I said, nodding. "Nobody likes a child molester in prison. Nobody."

"He was pathetic. They had him in isolation because otherwise he'd be dead. You know, I wondered why he didn't mention anything about his troubles in the letters and then I understood that he was trying to pretend that nothing ever happened.

"We had forty-five minutes and talked the whole time. I don't remember anything we said but he asked if I would kiss him good-bye and I said no."

That was the end of her story. Her posture was saying that she needed to get up and walk away from the tale. But she stayed in the chair because of me and my relationship to her self-enacted deliverance.

I still wanted to know about Twill but couldn't bring myself to question her further.

"You're a strong woman, Mardi Bitterman," I said at last.

"You think I did the right thing?"

"Every moment since the day you were born."

11

The rest of the morning was spent behind my big ebony desk going through the mail that had piled up while I was down in Philly. The bills all had checks attached to them, filled out with everything except my signature. Mardi was thorough in that department too.

I endorsed the back of the check given me by Camille Esterhouse for the return of Eddie Martinez and put it, along with the fifteen hundred-dollar bills Marella gave me, into a black envelope that I placed in the outbox on the right front corner of my desk. Mardi knew by the color that she had to make a deposit.

There were phone messages on little pink pieces of paper, phone messages on the service, and e-mails by the score. But there was nothing important, nothing I felt that had to be answered immediately.

At some point I sat back in my chair and swiveled around to look down on southern Manhattan. I had lived on the island my entire life; running wild, committing almost every crime imaginable. For the last six years I'd been trying to climb out of the dung pit and wash myself clean. I think it was just then, on that Tuesday morning, that I understood the metaphor of baptism—it's funny how some truths hide away in a pocket or a forgotten drawer and show up when they hardly matter anymore.

Considering and then giving up on the notion of salvation, I turned my restless thought-pad to the last twenty-four hours. This had been my time to encounter powerful women: Katrina, who had the will to end her own life either by knife or just waiting in that sanatorium bed to expire; Mardi, who could face the greatest terror in her life and make something good out of it; Aura, who loved me, I knew that, but whose morality was more powerful than our needs. And then there was Marella Herzog, a woman with a dog whistle that could call out the beast in me. I felt that if I could spend a week in her company I might grow back a full head of hair.

These were people who faced their fears and created the world as they moved through it. For some reason this notion made me take out my telephone. I'd call Twill myself and ask what he was up to.

"Mr. McGill?" Mardi said over the intercom.

"Yeah?"

"It's Captain Kitteridge."

"On the phone?"

"At my desk."

Had I heard the buzzer? I didn't think so.

"Send him on," I said.

I put the phone down and stared at it. I was experiencing one of those moments in life where I was not the central character but part of a small supporting cast that was there more for atmosphere than for pushing the story forward.

"LT," he said from the doorway.

Captain Carson Kitteridge was my height but weighed little more than the featherweight Fat Fudge. His skin was carved from porcelain, his eyes the faded blue of a mostly cloudy sky. He always wore cheap suits and ties that had wallpaper designs stamped on them. Carson might have been small and off the rack but when it came to his job he was a like a Jack Russell terrier, willing to go up against a foe ten times his size.

"Come on in, Kit," I said. "Have a seat."

We were usually civil. Our paths had crossed many times over the years. It was at least in part due to me that he'd been promoted to captain but it was still his mission in life to get me locked away for the rest of mine.

He stepped in, stared at my new red chairs with something like disdain, and then sat in the same seat that Hiram Stent chose.

"How can I help you?" I asked.

"A confession would be nice."

"You want a general admission of guilt for you to fill in the crime or is there something particular you had in mind?"

He reached into the side pocket of his sad brown suit jacket and came out with an electronic tablet device. He laid this flat on the table and slid it over to me.

"Just turn it on," he said, "the rest is self-explanatory."

I gave the little screen a sneer and then pressed a silver button on the lower left side. Immediately an image appeared; a familiar tableau from a different vantage point. It was the picture of a tall whitish man faced by a smaller, chubby black man with his bald head bowed so that the camera did not catch the features of his face.

I looked up and said, "So?"

Kit reached over and tapped the screen ever so lightly with his middle finger. The picture then turned into a video. The smaller black man squatted down and torqued to the left and a look of pain passed over the white man's face. I could clearly see the knife falling from the taller man's hand and then the shorter man coming up with a pretty-well-put-together uppercut.

Lucky for me the attacker's body hid my face from the camera as I stood.

Then, with my back fully to the lens, I grabbed the back of the enemy's head and slammed it against the metal wall of the chamber.

The rest of the film-short showed Marella's face but not mine as I set the man in the corner, grabbed the fanciful suitcase, and walked out of there while searching the floor for loose change that might have fallen from my pocket, or his. I knew the camera was there.

The video stopped for a moment with the attacker and his knife lying quite still, and then the image jumped back to the first frame.

Looking up again I said, "So?"

"That's you," Carson said.

"You can't even see his face."

"I know your moves."

"But I am sure the jury does not."

There came a subtle hum; my phone was set on vibration. I looked down and saw that the call was coming from the Hotel Brown. I tapped the Ignore icon and asked, "Did the man with the knife expire?"

"No."

"Is he in a coma or unconscious? Do they expect him to die?"

"No."

"Has he made a complaint or identified me from photos you must have right here on this tablet?"

Kit got tired of repeating his one word in our short play and so he shrugged.

"How about the woman?" I asked. "Have you identified her?"

"Not yet but we expect to. Maybe you could tell me who she is."

"I don't even know who the men are." I tried to keep the smug out of my voice. After all, Kit represented the NYPD and they really didn't need a reason to break my head—I knew this from firsthand experience.

"The victim," Captain Kitteridge said, "is Alexander Lett, recently from Virginia. He woke up in a hospital bed with a broken wrist and a knot the size of a tangerine on his forehead. When we asked him about the knife he said that he just found it and was bringing it to the lost and found. He said that the attacker must have thought he was threatening him with said knife and acted out of reflex."

"If he told you all that then why are you here?"

"What's goin' on, LT?"

"I don't know."

Kit stared at me. It's a wonder that he could make such dreamy eyes into a threatening glower. I felt the danger but I'd been surrounded by danger my entire life—that was my stock-in-trade.

I guess this truth was apparent; Kit stood up.

"You know, LT," he said. "I believe you when you say that you're trying to clean up your act and get it right. But this is not the way. Lett seems like serious business. This bug is going to sting you—if you're lucky."

He turned and walked out.

My smartphone buzzed at me again like the hornet Kit was warning me about. I waited for the vibrations to subside and then I picked up the little transmitter to make my own warning call.

"Hello?" he said on the fourth ring, just when I was sure I'd get his service.

"Twill?"

"Hey, Pop."

There was music playing somewhere—loud music. The heavy beat was accompanied by the hubbub of many people talking, laughing, shouting, and jostling around.

It was 10:56 in the morning.

"What's goin' on, Twill?"

Before he could answer, someone spoke to him calling him something with the word "itch" in it. Twill answered whoever it was with a word or two and then said to me, "Hold up a second, Pop. I'll go someplace a little more quieter."

The party sounds slowly subsided until they were just background noise, like traffic heard through a storm window.

"What can I do for you, Pop?"

"Where are you?"

"At a warehouse party in the Bronx."

"At this time of mornin'?"

"It only started at three," he said pleasantly, as if talking about a favorite TV show. "I'm workin'."

"On what?"

"Missin' person."

"Missin' person for who?"

"Kathy Ringgold."

"Don't make me ask you for every detail here, Twill. You're supposed to be in the office."

"Okay, Pop, okay. You don't have to get mad. There was this girl I went to high school with named Kathy Ringgold. She broke up with this guy Roger and then, after a week or two, wanted him back. But he was gone from his room and his phone had been disconnected. Nobody knew where he went and Mardi had told her that I was a detective now, so she asked me to find him. I ain't chargin' her or nuthin' but I figure

I can work on my detective chops doing a simple girl-wants-boy-back kind of job. Like you on the Martinez gig. Did you find him?"

Ignoring the question, I asked, "That's why you're at this party?"

"He think he's a DJ and so he always around places like this askin' for work. I'm just doin' the do."

"Have you been to see your mother?"

"I'm goin' there this evenin'," he said. "Right after I take a little nap."

"I want you in the office tomorrow."

"I'll be there."

We said our good-byes and I put the phone down.

The only thing I got out of our discourse was that Twill was lying and his trouble was deep.

12

The rest of the day I concentrated on the e-mails that didn't need answering. Seventeen of these were replies to my ad in the *New York Literary Review*. Some Bills and Williams, lonely johns, and a few vanity presses thought that I might really be looking for them. But none of these people or places were the self-named Tolstoy McGill, my missing father. For half my childhood and all of my adult life I had thought the anarchist-revolutionary had perished in South America fighting some dictatorship or another. But Tolstoy wasn't dead. I'd made an appointment to meet him for dinner one night but Katrina decided that afternoon to kill herself and my father once again faded into speculation.

By 7:14 I was through for the day. Mardi was still at her desk. I sometimes got the feeling that she would work twenty-four hours a day if she could.

"Who's looking after your sister?" I asked.

"Marlene's staying at our downstairs neighbors' apartment tonight. Their daughter Peg is her best friend. They move back and forth between the apartments."

Mardi looked up at me and I turned away before our eyes could focus on each other.

"Am I going crazy or did Kit just knock on the door?" I said to the door.

"I had Bug give me a button to turn off your buzzer when I'm in," she said. "I figure we both don't have to be bothered."

"What if you forget to turn it back on?"

"It's on a two-hour timer. After that it goes back to both."

I would have liked to find something wrong with her logic but Mardi was a bright kid with an old soul; just the kind of employee you wanted in a world filled with a starstruck workforce and electronic memories.

Even her smile was knowing.

"In the old days," I said, "when I was younger than you are now, people would say 'you're a good egg' to people who did right most of the time."

"Really?"

"You're a good egg, Mardi."

"Am I?" she said, looking me straight in the eye.

A microsecond of fear clutched at my heart, not quite long enough to get a good grip.

"I'll see you tomorrow," I said, thinking for the second time that this week was going to be a challenge.

I ran up all ten flights to the eleventh floor of our family apartment, a block east of Riverside Drive on the Upper West Side. There was a new locking system since a pair of East European assassins had broken in and tried to end my career. I used two keys and a remote control so small that it was hardly larger than the button that worked it. The kids didn't argue about the new process because I left the bullet holes in the wall where the killers missed.

Another reason the kids didn't mind was because two of them had moved out and the youngest, Twill, rarely spent the night.

I'm not what most people would think of as a family man. I don't come home for dinner every evening—many nights I don't come home at all. But over the decades I got used to a wife that cooked and kids that complained. The muted sounds through the large prewar apartment had made a place in what some might call my heart. And so the emptiness in the apartment felt . . . wrong.

I went to the dining room, poured forty-year-old cognac into a crystal snifter, and sat at the big hickory dining table. It wasn't lost on me that I'd sat behind a desk all day long only to come home and pull up a chair at another table. Maybe I could invite Mardi and her sister to live with me.

When I was pouring the third drink I decided to call Marella.

Somewhere in the afternoon I had picked up the phone and stared at her number. I realized that talking to her would just call for more passion—and I didn't think I had any more to give. But saying good-bye to Mardi, thinking I should invite her to live with me, made Marella a necessity, not an option.

When I informed the hotel operator of my name she put the call through.

"Hello, Leonid."

"Hey."

"Are you downstairs again?"

"No. I'm home."

"Do you want some company?"

"Who is Alexander Lett?"

"Who?"

"Alexander Lett. That's the name of the guy I slammed into the wall yesterday."

"I didn't know his name. I couldn't prove that he was sent by my ex. But he did follow me from DC."

"And this all over an engagement ring?"

"Yes."

"Why does it seem like more than that?"

"It's a very, very expensive ring."

"You called me this morning," I said.

"As soon as I woke up."

"What did you want?"

"You."

"For protection?"

"I never had a man put me on his shoulders backward before."

"That was my first time too." I was feeling that beast thing again. I liked the heavy beat it brought to my heart.

"You want me to come over?" she asked. "Maybe I could ride you on my back this time."

I once knew a man named Robin. He was a handsome man with beautiful eyes. For a while in the '90s Robin was a source of information I used quite a lot. He always denied that he was what he was, a heroin addict.

I asked him one day after watching him shoot up, "How can you say you aren't addicted when you shoot that shit in your arm every damn day?"

"Not every day," he murmured, his eyes like twin planets bathed in the radiance of the sun. "Every once in a while when the hunger gets too strong I make myself wait for two days before takin' it. As long as I can do that I keep my options open."

"How about dinner tomorrow night?" I suggested to Marella, thinking of how Robin died of an overdose before the new millennium. "There's a French place not far from your hotel. It's called the Chambre du Roi."

"Why not now?"

"I have to talk to a man I know," I said. "His name is Robin and he always has good information for me."

"Well, I guess if I have to . . . I'll wait."

There was a short spate of silence then, the kind of quiet that occurs when two strangers feel a passion in full bloom—what else is there to say? They have no history, only a future.

Marella was the wrong woman at the wrong time, but how long could I hope to survive anyway?

The buzzer from downstairs interrupted our communion.

"Somebody's at the door," I said.

"That Robin guy?"

"Maybe."

"What's the name of that restaurant again?"

"Chambre du Roi. I'll make the reservation for eight."

"Don't stand me up," she said.

"Not even if I could."

We ended the call and I just sat there a little stunned by the teen-aged hormones flooding my good sense.

The buzzer sounded again.

I walked down the hall to the foyer and pressed the onyx button on the brass-plated intercom.

"Yes?"

"It's your father, Trot."

13

I pressed the button to release the lock eleven floors below, then opened the front door and went out into the hall. Standing there, I watched the digital number plate that the landlord had installed over the elevator doors on every floor. I preferred it when there was a pewter arrow that swung in an arc, pointing to copper numbers beaten into a black iron half-circle that had flames coming from it like it was a sun and the elevator car was some kind of spaceship.

The display was counting backward, 8, 7, 6, 5 . . .

Trot. That's what he called me when I was a boy; Leonid Trotter McGill. He had given both Nikita, my brother, and me Russian names in honor of the Revolution he harbored in his heart.

"I'm leavin' your slave name McGill," he often said, "because it's slaves that riot and revolt. When you boys come to the end and the slave master has been overthrown, then you can choose names that will usher in the new world."

The display had an emerald *1* glistening in its blackness.

"It's only men with blood on their hands can claim the end of history," Tolstoy, my father, would say. "That's because the capitalists and their lackeys have blood from the soles of their feet all the way up to their ankles. They walk on the workers' blood, stride through it like hyenas after slaughterin' a whole flock'a sheep."

Whenever my father talked about the workers I got a little confused. Of the four of us only my mother had a job. Was it my mother's blood that the hyenas strode through?

The display made it to *3* and then stopped. I felt like I did when I was a boy waiting for the clock to tell me when my father was coming home.

"You're a good boy, Trot," my father said one afternoon shortly before he went away forever. "But you're a little soft. You don't understand that the police and the army and the government are your enemies. The school and the corner store, the tax collector and even the traffic lights are dead set against you. You will have to fight every day of your life against these enemies. They'll probably kill you but your brothers in arms will walk over your body to take the world. That's how tough you gotta be."

I remember wondering what the difference was between the capitalists walking in my blood and the revolutionaries walking on my body.

The elevator doors came open and a slender black man in a long black trench coat came out. He was an old man balding on top, and then some, like me. When he saw me he smiled and tilted his shoulders forward to get his feet moving in my direction.

I honestly wondered who this man was. The father I remembered was a giant with fists the size of cantaloupes and teeth that could bite through iron nails. Tolstoy had wild hair and eyes that often seemed to be electric with their intensity.

"Trot?" the old man said when he was just a few steps away.

"Yes?"

"Don't you recognize me, son?"

Even his voice was nothing like the man I had known. When Tolstoy spoke it was almost always in the tone and timbre of a rabble-rousing political speech. This man's tones were soft and palliative, like a doctor with bad news.

"Dad?"

He walked right up and put his arms around me, murmuring, "Trot, Trot."

"Dad, is that you?"

He took a step back and looked into my eyes. His smile was sad but resolved, knowing and somehow wishing he didn't know.

I still did not recognize him. He was a good-looking man, pretty far up in his seventies. But he was not the father I remembered—not at all.

I tried to think of why someone would want to impersonate my long-dead father. What possible profit could anyone make from such a scam?

"Leonid," he said in a solid tone that was somewhat reminiscent of the father I knew.

He reached in a pocket and came out with a small square piece of stiff paper; this he handed to me. It was a worn Kodak snapshot, from the early days of color. It was a picture of Nikita and me, my mother, and my father posing at a studio on the Lower East Side. The man in the picture was my father and he was also the man standing at my door.

"Can I come in, son?"

Ushering the stranger in, I took his coat and hung it on a cherrywood rack in my office. I brought him down to the dining room and poured him a cognac. He wore black slacks and a gray shirt. Taller than I but not nearly the height of the father I remembered, he was thin, his movements fluid for a man his age. There had only been the slightest limp to his gait. His dark skin and slender grace would have marked him as Twill's grandfather if I didn't know for a fact that Twill was the son of an African man that Katrina had a dalliance with.

"How are you, Trot?" the man calling himself my father asked after his second sip of brandy.

"I can only tell it's you by lookin' at this picture," I said.

"Memory is more like art than fact," he said.

"Are you Tolstoy McGill or William Williams?" I asked.

The question seemed to hurt him. He put down the glass and looked at his upturned hands. They were very large hands; the kind of paws you would expect on a man who was a sharecropper in his youth. The muscle had softened but it was still there.

"Tell me what happened," I said. The hands had convinced me. This was my father. With this certainty returned all the antipathy I felt.

"When?" he asked.

"When you left me and Nicky to fend for ourselves and our mother to die."

"I thought that maybe you could tell me a little about yourself first," he said softly. "That other stuff is so painful."

"That's all I'm interested in, man. I watched my mother die praying for you."

The sadness in his face almost dissuaded me. Almost.

When he realized that I would not back down he said, "I was wrong, Trot. Wrong about everything I thought to be true. I believed in the Revolution but I didn't know then that it was just a means to an end for people who couldn't even imagine the great socialist state. I was wrong about your mother being the good party member's wife who could survive the pain of loss and raise his children to be soldiers. Everything and everyone I believed in either betrayed me or was destroyed."

"If you knew all that, then why didn't you come back?"

"I fought for three years throughout Central and South America," he said, his eyes pointed up toward the ceiling. "I was wounded in Chile. Then I was captured and imprisoned for eight years; sometimes by dictators and then by the U.S. government men. I was under a death sentence most'a that time. Then finally one day me and some other prisoners were bein' moved in a caravan and there was a mortar attack. I was wounded but got away. Your mother had already been dead for years, and you and Nikita was grown men.

"A man named Cavalas found me and hid me in a cave in Uruguay. When I was better I moved back to Chile. I spoke the language and pretended that I came from Cuba by boat. I was a wanted man, a terrorist. At night I read and reread Marx and Lenin and Mao. And one day it hit me—the perfection imagined by socialist theory was impossible for human beings to attain. The philosophy was right but we were poor vessels for it."

"My mother is dead and you're blaming the misinterpretation of philosophy?"

"I was wrong."

"You're a motherfuckin' bastard."

"I'm still your father," he said with an inkling of the old rebel.

"Not since the day you left Mom to die and me and Nikita to make our way in the streets. Now I'm trying to make up for all the hurt I've caused bein' mad at you, and Nicky is in prison."

I was ashamed of my self-pity. Here I was holding my father responsible for his crimes and mine, too.

"Nikita's not in prison."

"I talked to him there last year," I said.

"A lot can happen in a year."

For some reason I didn't want to hear any more about my brother right then. I had reached my limit since coming back on the train from Philly. Between Marella, Twill, Mardi, Aura, and now my father, I didn't want to take in another thing.

And so, of course, the phones rang; the house number and my cell phone, too. This wasn't a regular ring, the kind with another person on the other end of the line. This bell, from both devices, was a fast triple-ring; a mechanical call set off by a specific set of circumstances.

I picked up the receiver of the house phone and a prerecorded pastiche of voices said, "Mr. Leonid McGill . . . the security system in your office in . . . the Tesla Building . . . has been breached. The proper authorities have been notified. Do not attempt to go there yourself."

"I'm sorry, Bill," I said, suddenly as calm as Buddha. "Somebody's breaking into my office."

"In the Tesla Building?"

"Right."

"I'll come with you, son."

Just those five words almost brought me to tears.

14

We caught a taxi on Broadway and cruised down to the Thirties and the Tesla Building. A middle-aged doorman I didn't recognize was sitting behind the high Art Deco reception desk. He was a bronze-colored man with light caramel eyes.

"Can I help you?" he asked in the slightest of Spanish accents.

His question was not an offer. This made me wonder how serious the break-in was.

"Leonid McGill," I said.

"Oh," he said, derailed by a name. "Um, uh . . . There's been a, a break-in . . . Somebody was hurt."

"You stay here, Pop," I said to my father. Even then it wasn't lost on me that I called him what Twill called me.

I headed for the elevators.

"You can't go up there," the doorman commanded.

I pressed the elevator button with my left hand and felt for the pistol in my pocket with the right.

My father came up beside me and when I looked at him he nodded. He'd seen me retrieve the .45 from my office drawer.

"I'm with ya, Trot."

"You can't go up there," the guard said again. His voice was filled with threat.

I took the gun out of my coat pocket and let it hang at my side; he calmed right down.

———

When we got to my office the door was gone and Rich Berenson, what stood for a third of the nighttime security force for the building, was standing in the gap.

It was no mean feat breaking down my office door. It was reinforced with titanium bars. There was a burned scent in the air and so I suspected an explosive of some type.

What kind of trouble could I have been in, to be invaded by professionals with bombs?

"LT," Rich said.

When I approached the door the guard's posture stiffened, telling me that it was probably worse than I imagined.

Rich is a tall white guy, bald on top with a graying ponytail down past his shoulders in back. He'd once been a policeman in Ohio somewhere, then retired at fifty and came to New York to be a security guard. There was a divorce and a married woman in the mix of his decision but all of that was over and done by the time we'd met.

I'd put the pistol back in my pocket in the elevator but the downstairs guard had probably warned Rich, his boss.

"Step aside, Mr. Berenson," I said.

"The police are in there," he replied as an explanation of his refusal.

"My office," I said. "My cops."

"Let him in," a voice I knew declared.

Rich stepped aside and I entered Mardi's reception area trying to make sense of the quiescent detritus left by the carnage that had hit the room.

The first thing I saw was the man-sized hole in the wall next to my impregnable inner-office door. I had always known that it would be possible to break down the plaster and wood wall, but I thought that I'd be on the other side with weapons ready if that were ever to happen.

The man who allowed me into my own space was the uniformed Sergeant Jess Dalton of the NYPD. He was glaring at me and my father. Behind him another policeman came out through the wounded wall. Just seeing that enraged me. I might have said something but I kept my peace in deference to the dead man stretched out in front of Mardi's desk. He'd been shot and then bled quite a bit before his heart gave out.

"McGill," Sergeant Dalton said—it was not a greeting. "What do you know about this?"

"You kiddin' me, right, Sergeant? I mean I hope you don't think I broke down my own damn door and killed Hector Laritas because I wanted to get rich on the insurance claim."

I knew the dead man. He was another third of nighttime security at the Tesla. Young when I'd last seen him and always with a smile, he was Twill's age and my anger was growing.

"You got it all worked out, huh?" Dalton said with a grin that clawed at the single shred of civility I had left.

Dalton was tall, his first mistake with me, and bulky from the wrong kind of exercise. He was forty years old, no more, and the color of a white napkin stained with olive oil.

"You better back up, man," I said to the cop. "Back up or back it up."

Buddha had departed the building, and all that he left was rage. My office, my door, my wall, my guard, my father . . . Dalton's hand moved toward his firearm. His younger partner looked a little confused. I was absolutely sure of what I'd do. I didn't have to draw out my gun—just reach in the pocket and shoot them both through my coat.

"What's happening in here?" my archenemy/guardian angel said.

Carson Kitteridge came in behind me. It wasn't the first time that his mere presence saved someone's life.

"Break-in, Captain," Sergeant Dalton said, suddenly compliant. "We got a call from Seko Security System about this office. By the time we got here it's like you see it."

"Seko called you too, LT?" Kit asked. He was standing on my fallen front door and so had a couple of inches on me.

"Yeah."

"Don't they tell you to wait for the police to call?"

"Would you?"

A glimmer of a smile crossed the veteran cop's lips and then he looked down on the dead stare of Hector. The humor dissipated and Kit's dreamy eyes were suddenly awake.

"What were they after?" he asked me.

"I can't tell you," I said. "Everybody so far's been body-blockin' me."

"Let him in the office," the captain said to the sergeant.

The uniforms moved to the side and I took a step toward the hole in the wall.

"Who are you?" Kit asked.

I turned and saw that the question was addressed to Tolstoy. He had almost successfully become a shadow in the corner of the office, but when I moved he made to follow.

"Bill Williams," he said, not extending a hand. "I'm an old friend of Trot's father. We were having a drink when the call came through."

Carson Kitteridge is a human lie detector and all his antennae were up. But since most of what my father said was mostly true, the captain did not pounce.

"This is an active crime scene, Mr. Williams," Carson did say. "You'll have to leave."

My father looked like the man I once knew for a moment there. He was an outlaw at heart, like every true revolutionary. The rules did not apply as far as he was concerned. But he could see that Carson was a man to be reckoned with.

"Yes sir," he said to my own personal cop. "See you later, Trot."

He turned and walked out through the broken doorway.

I watched him go, wondering how many decades it would be before I saw him again.

15

From the hole end of the long aisle I could see that my office door was closed, the way I'd left it earlier that evening; there was no way to tell if it was still locked. I walked down there, checking the cubicles as I went. Twill's space wasn't visibly desecrated. Only the cubicle that held the office computer system seemed to be out of the normal. There were papers on the floor and one of our heavy-duty USB memory devices connected to its side.

Before checking out the mainframe specially built for me by Bug Bateman, I went to test my office door. It was still locked but somebody had used some kind of lever, probably a crowbar, trying to pop the mechanism there. My personal door was almost as tough as the one they circumnavigated getting into the inner sanctum, and they'd most likely used all the explosives—or maybe they were trying to make a space for more fireworks.

Looking back down the aisle at the captain and his pickup army of cops, I imagined the chain of events. Men, most likely three or four of them, came and blew out the front door to the suite then went right to work on the wall. Two or three of them came through, leaving one standing guard, probably just inside the hole they made. One of the men went to the computer and the others went to work on my office door. But Hector was on his rounds. Maybe he heard the explosion or the pounding; maybe Seko did their job right and called Rich Berenson after alerting me. When Hector walked in, the guardian shot him, yelled for his accomplices, and then they all ran.

Maybe they went down the stairs or hijacked the freight elevator.

"Let's see what happened," Kit said to me.

For a moment I thought he wanted to look inside my head but then I remembered.

It took me and Sergeant Dalton to pull the warped office door open. We all got behind my desk and I turned on the monitor system in the bottom drawer of my desk. Whenever someone enters the front door of the reception area three cameras come on for ninety seconds. The first few frames were smoke-filled but then the three intruders appeared through the haze. They wore face masks, of course, and gloves. Before the minute and a half was up they'd started beating on the wall with two oversized sledgehammers.

"They knew what they were doing," Kit said. "They knew you pretty good, LT."

I didn't reply because whatever I said would have only been redundant.

"What did they want?" Dalton asked.

"Information," Kit and I said together.

"They tried to download the computer files." I was gesturing at the big memory stick they'd attached to my Bug-special computer.

"Is that your device?" Kit asked.

"Yeah. Yeah. Hector probably came in and the sentry shot him. The office door was givin' 'em problems and the system wouldn't cooperate. They knew a lot but they didn't know that my files are downloaded every night, erasing whatever was held in the temporary files. They realized it was useless and just ran, just ran."

"Who was it?" Kit asked me.

"You saw 'em, man. They had masks and shit. How'm I gonna know who it was?" I was that taciturn teenager living on the street again.

"What are you working on?"

"I don't have a job right now."

"You still say that wasn't you smashing Alexander Lett's head into that wall?" Kit suggested.

"It ain't him."

"He checked himself out of the hospital."

I looked Kit in the eye so that his wetware lie detector had full access.

I said very clearly, "It ain't him."

"What about Twill?" Kit asked.

"He's out workin' with some girl he knew in high school. Her boyfriend changed his phone number and he's lookin' for the new one," I said but I was wondering about Twill too.

"It's a murder," Kit told me. "We've got to do this by the numbers."

"I know."

My father and I got to the Tesla just after midnight. It was 4:00 in the morning before the police finished their questions. They didn't take me down to some precinct because I hadn't witnessed the crime firsthand. I answered their battery of questions four or five times, all the while Kit staring at me, searching for the lie. But I passed and the coroner's men came. Hector was taken to the morgue and Rich Berenson was saddled with the unenviable task of calling the young man's wife. Better him than the cops.

While all of this was happening the forensics team came through dusting and vacuuming, photographing, crawling through, and in other ways examining the crime scene.

They left admonishing me not to touch anything before forensics came in later.

After that I lifted the front door and wedged it into the hole, went down to my office, and sat.

When the phone rang I knew it was Aura.

"Are you all right?" she asked me.

"Fine."

"Do you need me to come down?"

"No."

"Are you okay, Leonid?"

"Not quite right yet but I intend to be."

———

It wasn't until about 6:00 that I signed on to my personal computer. The first thing I looked up was the inmate list for the supermax Indiana prison where my brother was slated to spend the greater portion of the rest of his life. Most systems couldn't get that kind of information but Bug had hacked every important database in the United States and then some. He let me use his access because I was the man, with Iran Shelfly's help, who had turned him from a blob into an Adonis.

My father said that Nikita was no longer in prison. My computer couldn't tell me who decided to break down my doors but at least I could see where my brother had gone.

But there I failed too.

There was no record of Nikita McGill ever being incarcerated there or anywhere else in the federal system of prisons. When I looked deeply enough I found a death certificate that was issued a year *before* the last time my brother and I had talked. He died in Columbus, Ohio, the obituary said.

A homeless man identified as Nikita Angus McGill died of coronary complications at Sutter Street Homeless Center leaving no family.

"Coincidence" is a word that had been removed from the detective's lexicon. Maybe Marella was just a lucky happenstance. Maybe my father ringing the doorbell when I was on the phone with her was a mere fluke. But when a convicted criminal disappears from prison records and a dead man decorates my front hall—that had to mean something, but for the life of me I couldn't think what that something was.

It wasn't until after 7:00, after Mardi called on my cell phone and I went out to reception to let her in, it wasn't until then that I remembered Hiram Stent.

16

started by using another of Bug's programs. The unproclaimed genius had created an entire virtual world for himself. He even had programs set with updatable key words that *read* the papers and websites for him in the morning, delivering edited versions of the news before he dove in for himself.

All I had to do was type in the name "Hiram Stent" and I got six hits on his death.

He was found at around midnight, not long after someone had used a bomb to break down my office door, in an alley off a side street half a block from Flatbush Avenue in Brooklyn. Hiram had been stabbed multiple times in the torso, neck, and face; his pockets had been torn out. His wallet had probably been taken but the canny indigent had hidden his identification (and probably a few bucks) in his shoe. The authorities suspected a mugging. There were no witnesses and the investigation was ongoing. Anyone with information was to call Crimestoppers.

While reading the articles about Hiram I decided to take his case. I had failed the sad man in life but maybe I could make up for some of that.

While dedicating myself to a dead man's quest, a name popped into my head—Twitcher. That was what the voice I'd overheard on the phone had called my son: Twitcher.

That's how my brain works: a question, maybe not even articulated, goes down through my mind and I stew on it until an answer comes, or not. Sometimes I simmer over a question for years and suddenly one day the answer just appears like Athena from her father's brow.

"Mr. McGill?" Mardi said. She was carrying a cardboard box from the upscale coffee shop on the first floor. Therein were a large black coffee, two apple-fritter doughnuts, and a real apple—this last item because she felt that I should eat at least one healthy thing each day.

After laying the box on my desk she said, "I called Mr. Domini about the door. He said that he'll come fix it by end of day. Seko Security said that a temporary security system will be installed before the end of the day and that they'll have a permanent solution by the middle of next week."

I had good insurance on my office and my systems. It's not if something will go wrong, it's when.

I spent the rest of the morning searching the Net, and elsewhere, for two women: Celia Landis and Lois Stent.

Hiram's wife was easy. She was born Lois Miriam Bowman to Lawrence Frank and Melissa Marie Bowman in Tampa, Florida, in 1983. She married Hiram in 2003, had Lisa in '04 and William in '06. The separation came in '11. In that same year divorce papers were served but that hadn't gone very far. Hiram's lawyer was a man named Tracey Tremont.

I called Melissa Marie Bowman because her husband, Larry, had died of a heart attack three years earlier.

"Hello?" she said on the first ring.

"Ms. Melissa Bowman?" I asked.

"Yes?"

"My name is McGill. I'm calling in place of Mr. Tremont, Hiram Stent's lawyer."

"What?"

"I have information about Mr. Stent that I believe your daughter would be interested in."

"Information," she said. "What kind of information?"

"I'm sorry, ma'am, but I can only share that with your daughter."

"Lois doesn't want to talk to Hiram."

"I can assure you, ma'am, that I will not put them in touch."

"I can't give you her number." The woman sounded hesitant. Maybe she liked Hiram or disliked the handyman.

"Let me give you my number," I said. "If she decides to call then she can. If not there's nothing lost."

"Okay. Can I tell her what this is about?"

"Sorry."

While waiting for Lois to call back, or not, I started looking for Celia Landis. There was too much information there. There were dozens of women with that name across the nation. It was impossible for me to find out if any of these women were the right age, related to Hiram, or the subject of a search by a law firm in San Francisco called Briscoe/Thyme.

I called information in SF asking for the number for the lawyers but was told that there was no such law firm with those names under any possible spelling.

I decided to call all of the women within fifty miles of the city with that name. That tree wasn't likely to bear fruit but I had to do it—for my client.

Before I could make the first call, Mardi interrupted.

"A Terry Colter on three, sir."

"Who?"

"He said his name like he thought you should know it."

"Leonid McGill," I said into the line.

"Who are you?" an angry male voice asked.

"Can I do something for you?"

"Why are you calling my wife?"

"That depends, who's your wife?"

"Don't get smart with me," the angry man replied.

"I can't help my IQ, brother. Maybe you should put somebody smarter on the phone."

"Maybe I should come up there and kick your ass."

"I'll be here from nine to five most days. You're welcome to come up and try." I was serious as a hangover.

My caller understood this and took a minute to reorganize his approach.

"I'm Lois Bowman's husband," the man calling himself Terry Colter said.

"For how long?"

"What business is that of yours?"

"Well," I reasoned, "if it was before yesterday your wife is going to prison for bigamy."

Another few moments and a woman's voice said, "Hello? Who is this?"

"Leonid McGill."

"And you represent Hiram's lawyer?"

"Not exactly," I said. "I'm calling you with information that his lawyer would have given you if he knew what I knew and he knew how to call you."

"What are you saying?"

"Hiram Stent was murdered last night."

Lois Stent gasped. There was a knock against her receiver and another sound that was very human and probably sincere.

"What?" she cried after making other wordless laments.

"He was stabbed in the face, neck, and torso," I said. "You can get the full details on the Internet editions of any New York paper."

"Who are you?"

"Hiram came to me yesterday wanting to find a woman named Celia Landis. He said that if he found her he'd make enough money to fly down Florida way and reclaim his wife and children."

"He said that?"

"Almost word for word."

"And so, so you're calling to blame me for his death?"

"Through sickness and health," I said, "poverty and wealth."

"I . . ."

"He was living in a rooming house, Mrs. Stent. He was trying to leverage a million dollars out of a case over a missing woman named Celia Landis. Have you ever heard of her?"

"No." She was crying.

"Had he told you anything about what he was doing?"

"We haven't talked for a long time."

"You should call the Brooklyn police and ask about him," I said. "Somebody needs to come up here and put him in the ground."

"I didn't know," she said miserably.

"No," I agreed. "You didn't."

I wasn't being fair. I had no insight into what went on between husband and wife. She had a right to live any life she wanted. But Hiram Stent was my client. *I* had let him down. He died on my watch and I wanted somebody, anybody, to pay.

"What else did he say?" Lois asked.

"He came in here with holes in his shoes," I said, wishing I could stop. "He asked me to find this mystery woman and I kicked him out because he was poor and he smelled like the earth turned on a fresh grave. He said he kept a PO box so that Lisa and William could send him a letter if they needed to."

The sob that came from Lois Stent's throat a thousand miles away stopped my tirade.

"I'm sorry, ma'am," I said. "I'll make a deal with you. You come up to bury him and I'll bury the people that did this."

A red light started blinking on my phone. That meant someone else had called.

"I never meant for him to die," she moaned.

"It's not your fault," I said. "It's whoever it is stabbed him."

With a blunt index finger I pressed the button to break the connection. I had no help for her. Maybe Terry Colter could soothe her guilt.

I didn't even put down the receiver, just hit the intercom button and said, "Who was it?"

"Is it," Mardi corrected, "he's still on the line. A guy named Josh Farth. He says he wants to hire you."

I wanted to do a search on Bernard Shonefeld but something made me stop my blundering and say, "Put him on."

"Hello," a strong male voice said.

"Mr. Farth? This is Leonid McGill. How can I help you?"

"I hear that you do missing persons cases," he said.

"Hear from whom?"

"Around."

"Around where?"

"I have a friend in the NYPD that says you do a good job because you dig deep."

"What's this friend's name?" I asked.

"Well"—Josh hesitated—"he's more like an acquaintance. His name is Peter Morton. He's a sergeant in Queens."

I jotted down the name and asked, "Who's missing?"

"A young woman."

"When can you come in, Mr. Farth?"

"I could be there in less than an hour."

"I'll be waiting for you."

17

"Mardi?" I said over the intercom.

"Yes sir?"

"Find a number for Sergeant Peter Morton of the NYPD in Queens, then call him for me."

"Through regular channels?"

"Fast."

"Okay," she said. "Mr. Domini was here. He looked at the door and the wall. I told him about your door, too. He said he'd be back with a crew this afternoon."

After getting off the phone with my brave assistant I stood up and walked most of the length of my deserted hallway. I made it all the way up to the hole gauged through the wall and stuck my head through to peek out at Mardi. She was just putting the phone down.

"It's so strange to see you come through the wall like that," she said.

I didn't respond, just pulled back in and walked almost to my door. I did an about-face and went all the way to my utility closet. I had a bottle of Cuban rum in there but I didn't reach for it.

"Peter Morton on line seven," a disembodied voice called out over the office PA system.

I picked up a phone at a vacant cubicle and said, "Sergeant?"

"Are you really Leonid McGill?"

"Yes I am."

"Wow."

"Glad to see you know who I am."

"Know who you are? I've had papers calling for your arrest on my desk half a dozen times."

"I hope that's not the case right now."

"Not from this morning anyway."

I liked the banter. Had I my druthers we'd have gone on like that for a minute or two and then I'd have downed a glass of rum, gone to Gordo's, and watched the boxers whale on each other.

"What can I do for you, Leonid?" Sergeant Morton asked.

I didn't like the familiarity. It meant that he was treating me like a suspect or a snitch.

"Josh Farth," I said.

"He's an um . . . friend of mine from Boston . . . he, uh, called me a couple of days ago asking for a PI who didn't mind looking under slimy rocks. Like I said—you're famous."

Morton wasn't a very good liar. Josh Farth, I was pretty sure, had called his cop friend to cover his story, whatever that was.

"You don't know me, Sergeant. Why throw him my name?"

"He asked a question and your name was the answer."

"What's his business?"

"Security and research for some big company."

"Which one?"

"I forget."

"You forget."

"Yeah. One day I'll get so old that I won't even be able to recognize my own shoes unless I'm wearing them."

The buzzer to the front door still worked. It sounded and I said, "I have to go, Sergeant. Thanks for the referral."

"Anytime."

I was wondering if the NYPD had a file on me that included the layout and the general security systems of my office. They'd be sure to have my address.

I went through the wall into the reception area and gave Mardi a questioning look.

"It's a man in a suit," she said, looking up from the monitor in her desk drawer. "I've never seen him before."

Grabbing the front door by the handle and bracing it up high with the palm of my left hand, I dragged the portal open and leaned it against the wall.

"Mr. Farth?"

"Mr. McGill?" He wore a light-colored pearl-gray suit with a dark green dress shirt—no tie.

"That wasn't even ten minutes."

"Less than an hour."

I couldn't argue with his math so I said, "Come on in."

He walked through looking at the loose door and the tarp that mostly covered the dark stain on the floor. His face was that odd combination of unsightly and yet well manicured. The nose was too big but he'd had a facial, the hair was too thin but his barber was a hairdresser too. His knuckles were like mismatched stones though the nails and cuticles had been trimmed and varnished.

He turned his gaze on me with eyes that were the color green you expected a frog to leap from.

"Redecorating?" he asked.

"Something like that."

"So what can I do for you, Mr. Farth?" I asked when we were ensconced in my almost unmolested office.

"I wanted to hire you but you look busy enough already."

"Just a break-in. The cops have already made their report. What do you need?"

"Was that blood on the floor?"

"No. There was a gallon jug of molasses on my receptionist's desk. The burglars must have knocked it over."

Farth paused for maybe ten seconds or so. He was trying to look as if maybe there was too much happening in my office and he should take his business elsewhere. If he did that I'd forget him.

"I'm looking for a young woman," he said at second eleven.

"Aren't we all?"

"Her name is Coco Lombardi," he said, ignoring my lame joke. He reached into his jacket pocket, taking out a three-by-five glossy. "She's dropped out of sight and her family is quite worried."

I took the picture and studied it. Sitting on a barstool she was lovely the way strippers are lovely, all decked out in glitter and little else. Her eyelashes were over two inches long and her makeup was thick enough it might have stopped a bullet. Maybe someone with no experience would have been fooled, but I could see that the twenty-something burlesque dancer and the teenager in the photo Hiram had showed me were either closely related or one and the same.

"Girls like this go missing every other day," I said. "They usually turn up—one way or the other."

"It's the other that her family is trying to avoid."

"Boston family?"

Feigning surprise, the well-put-together and ugly man said, "I didn't know I had an accent."

"Peter Morton," I said.

"You're thorough."

"Rich family?"

"My client is."

"Who's that?"

The ugly man tried to put on a sympathetic-but-sorry expression and failed.

"That's one thing I can't tell you," he said. "My client likes privacy. That is my first concern."

"So how do I know that you aren't using me to wipe out a state's witness or to get revenge for a jilted john?"

"You watch too much television, Mr. McGill," Farth admonished. "People do things like that in old books. In the new world criminals stick among themselves. Anyway, I just need you to find Ms. Lombardi and tell her that I'd like to have a conversation with her. You can set that up any way that makes you comfortable."

He was very good. If I hadn't met Hiram Stent, seen the photo of Celia Landis, had my office invaded by professionals, and been the cause of two innocent men's deaths, I might have believed about 2 percent of what he was saying.

"The reason I'm here," Josh said, now affecting honesty, "is because Coco is in trouble with some bad people. She knows some things that she shouldn't know and maybe has taken things that don't belong to her."

"From your client?"

"No, no. My client is close to the family. I'm here on a mission of mercy, not vengeance."

"And how do I fit into this mission?"

"Peter told me that you are often a person of interest to the police."

"And yet you want to hire me anyway."

"I believe that I will need a man like you to find Coco."

"A man like me." I was liking our back-and-forth. It was a way to hone my skills.

"A professional who isn't afraid of the law," Farth explained.

"Do you have an ID, Mr. Farth?"

"Why?"

"Just so that I can say, if asked by the constabulary, that I at least checked that you were who you said you were."

He smiled and took a wallet from his back pocket. From this he produced a Massachusetts driver's license. Joshua Farth, DOB December 1971.

"Ten thousand dollars," I said.

"What?"

"Ten thousand down payment for the search and another ten when I find the girl and facilitate your talk."

"Twenty thousand dollars for a simple missing person case?"

"That's the going price for a man not afraid of the law."

"That's outrageous," he said in a tone that carried no outrage whatsoever.

Farth or Shonefeld, or whatever his name was, gave me a frown that ever so slowly turned into a smile. I doubted if this man ever had an honest expression in his life. Everything he said, every response he gave, was planned. Too bad for him his plans were scrawled in crayon.

He reached into the same pocket that held the stripper's photograph. From this he brought out a stack of hundred-dollar bills bound together in thousand-dollar packets. He counted out ten of these and put them on the desk, returning the rest of the treasure to the all-purpose pocket.

Gathering up the cash I asked, "What else can you give me about Coco?"

"Since she's come to New York she's been an artist's model, a topless dancer, a personal assistant to a painter named Fontu Belair, and once she was arrested for kiting checks. She got out on bail and disappeared."

"So the police are looking for her," I said.

"Maybe in their sleep. She's been in New York nearly a year."

"What about before then?"

"I really don't know."

"Did she live in Boston?"

"Possibly. The only information I have about her is since she moved to New York."

"What about her family?"

"My client is protecting them from the complete truth about the girl. I haven't even met them."

"Is Coco her real name?"

"I doubt it," Josh said. "Like I said, I don't even know if she's originally from Boston. One guy said that she told him she came from out west somewhere."

"What guy?"

"A man called Buster who worked at the Private Gentleman's Club on Thirty-ninth Street."

It's funny how a word can trigger a deeply felt response. Josh said "Buster" and I suddenly had the strong desire to jump across my big black desk and bust his head. Killing him would have given me great pleasure but that's not what Hiram had posthumously hired me for. He hired me to get his 10 percent and use that to bring Lois and the kids back into his life, such as it was.

18

The meeting with Farth lasted a quarter hour more. He gave me a couple of addresses and informed me that the money I'd been given didn't have to be reported. He gave me an address or two for witnesses and a phone number where he could be reached.

"There's a sense of urgency on behalf of the girl's parents," he said after rising to leave. "My client would like to limit their friends' pain and so the sooner you find Coco the better."

I walked Josh Farth down the hall, through the hole, and out the front door. I didn't like him and he, I believed, could have easily ended my life without remembering my name in the morning.

After he was gone I levered the heavy door back into place.

"What did you think of Mr. Farth?" I asked Mardi. I'd learned over time that her insight on human nature was at least as keen as my own.

"I don't know," she said, considering. "He's kinda like a ghoul—there in his body but not in his eyes."

"Are you going to tell me what's going on with Twill?"

"You know Twill," she said, once again staring me in the eye. "He's always doing something he shouldn't. When I was in the tenth grade I stayed away from him because everybody said he was one of the bad kids."

"And what is my bad child doing today?"

"You'll have to ask him, sir. He's my best friend and I won't tell his stories."

She was right of course. I looked away because her eyes had gained the power of a woman since she admitted putting her stepfather in his place.

"You should go home," I told her.

"You're firing me?"

"No. No, I'm trying to protect you. I won't have you sitting behind a door that might fall in at any moment when there's a good chance that the real bad guys might return." I handed her the black envelope from my outbox and the ten thousand Farth had given me. "Put this in the safe and stay home until I call for you to come back."

"Are you going to be okay?" she asked.

Before I could think up some wise-assed retort the buzzer sounded.

Bells and buzzers had begun to bother me. They seemed like evil portents insinuating themselves between me and my loved ones.

"It's Mr. Domini and some other men," she said.

I did my exercise with the front door, revealing a crew of six.

Westley Domini was a short Italian man, though not as short as I. He had white hair and skin as close to white as it could get. He was my Mr. Fixit and a former member of one of the more powerful New Jersey mobs. He'd done some bad things in his life but then met a woman named, of all things, Ginger and decided to leave the mob business to do the thing he loved most, which was, like his immigrant grandfather, working with his hands.

This decision brought him to my office. He'd heard that I'd gone straight and wanted, for lack of a better term, a blueprint for success. We talked and drank and drank and talked for fifty hours. At the end of the session Westley had promised to work for me whenever I needed it.

For my part, I rarely called on him.

"Looks like they took your fancy door off with a firecracker" was the first thing Westley said.

"Yeah. Can you fix me?"

"Quintez, Li," he said to two of his crew. "Let's start diggin' this wall out."

Domini had a multiracial crew culled from New York. I had convinced him that he had to break daily ties to his old friends in Jersey.

"How long?" I asked the reformed pimp and murderer.

"By nine tonight," he said. "We'll get to your back-office door too."

"Some guys from Seko Security will be here along the way," I said. "Let 'em do what they need to do."

Back at my desk I called Zephyra Ximenez, my Telephonic and Computer Personal Assistant (TCPA). I rarely saw this pillar of my information jungle; if we met face-to-face two times in a year that was a lot. Most of our work was over the phone or via the Internet. It's not that I didn't want to see the Dominican/Moroccan beauty from Queens. She had skin the color of polished onyx and poise that would have put Princess Grace to shame. But Zephyra plied her trade for her many clients by wire, satellite, and microwave beams. She eschewed office work. I couldn't blame her.

"Hello, Mr. McGill," she said, answering on the eighth ring. She had my number and therefore my name.

"Hey, Z, how's it goin'?" I could hear the Domini crew banging from down the hall.

"All right I guess," she said.

"Problems?"

"A little bit."

"We'll get back to that in a minute," I promised. "First I need you to do some research for me."

"That's what I'm here for."

"There's supposed to be a law firm in Frisco called Briscoe/Thyme. I think the last name is spelled like the Simon and Garfunkel song but it could be temporal." I liked talking to Zephyra because she knew all the words in five or six dictionaries. "I can't find 'em so I thought you could look."

"Sure thing."

"Also I'm looking for a young woman named Coco Lombardi. She's a stripper here in New York but she might be from Boston originally. Celia Landis might be her alias or vice versa. And there's some other names I'd like you to look up," I added. "Josh Farth, forty-four, private investigator or security specialist; Alexander Lett, around forty, from down in DC. He's a strong-arm so probably listed as security too. Then there's a Marella Herzog. That name is almost definitely a.k.a. but it's probably used down in DC for a wedding registration at high-end stores. I'd like to know who she's marrying and what her backstory is."

"Got it, got it, and got it," Zephyra said; her voice sounded cheerier when she was working. "Anything else?"

"Yeah, yeah. Check out the social media sites for somebody named Twitcher."

"Male or female?"

"Man."

"Age?"

"It's Twill."

Silence, then: "Okay."

"What's wrong, Z?"

"I don't think I want to talk about it."

"Then let me do the talking," I said in my most avuncular tone. "There was once a fat man named Bug Bateman who lived in a hole clutching a stick of dynamite in one hand and his dick in the other. A Spanish princess named Ximenez dragged him out of there, made him do push-ups and shop at Armani, and then, just when he was exactly what she wanted, she told him that she needed the freedom to see other guys. He found out that there are many women who want a guy like him."

"He rubs my nose in it."

"Any guy you know that you wouldn't mind spending a few weeks with?"

"There's this man that calls himself Petipor the Younger. A Turkish technology importer. I think his father is a Thracian prince."

"After you finish with my searches go away with him."

"And you'll tell Bug?"

"I won't need to."

"Where do you want me to start with your work?"

"Do a cursory on Coco first and get that to me as soon as possible."

"You got it, boss."

19

"I'm leaving now, Mr. McGill," Mardi said via intercom maybe five minutes after my talk with Zephyra. "Do you need anything else?"

"Tell Twill I'm askin' about him if you see him and take your sister to some musical on the office account."

"Thanks."

"And one more thing," I said.

"What's that."

"Try to find yourself a boyfriend."

"Bye."

I called the Chambre du Roi about midafternoon to make a reservation.

"*Âllo?*" a young woman who was not French answered.

"Leonid McGill," I said. "I want a table for two at eight tonight."

"I'm sorry, sir," the woman replied, dropping all pretense at a French heritage. "We're booked solid until the beginning of next week. If you want to make a reservation you have to call at least a week in—"

"Let me speak to Henry," I said, cutting off her misplaced sense of hierarchy.

"Who?"

"In that French class you failed they called him Henri. But this is America and I want to talk to your boss."

"Um," she said and then she put me on hold.

"*Âllo?*" a man who was French said after maybe fifteen seconds.

"Hello, Henri, Leonid here."

"Tonight?"

"Two at eight."

"See you then," he said.

I disconnected the call feeling the little triumph of defeating the snobby young woman. I had many ins in New York. Most of these I'd earned by doing people favors saving their lives, getting them out of legal jams, or shedding a little blood here and there—but in Henri's case it was simply that I tipped him a hundred dollars every fourth time I ate at the Chambre du Roi.

I stayed at my desk trying to see if I could find out anything about Coco Lombardi. It would have given me a great deal of pleasure if I beat Zephyra to the finish line on that search. I guess, looking back on that afternoon, I was trying to feel superior after my office had been violated like that.

Gordo sent me a text saying that Chin Wa wanted a rematch. I spent a good while wondering what I could do to the fast, hard-hitting middleweight now that he knew that I knew how to count to seven. Not coming up with a satisfactory answer, I failed to respond to the text.

At 6:30 I was prepared to walk up to Marella's neighborhood. My head was telling me that maybe I should cancel but my pulse had a whole other set of expectations. As a compromise I called for a limo to pick me up at 7:30 and then called a number that was answered by a switch-board operator uptown.

"Tivoli Rest Home," a woman answered.

"Katrina McGill."

"Hello, Mr. McGill," the operator said. "This is Sister Monica."

"Hi, Monica, how are you?"

"I'm taking a group to the Metropolitan Museum of Art tomorrow. I asked your wife to come. She said that she'd think about it but she hadn't signed up by dinner."

"I'll talk to her," I promised and Sister Monica put my call through.

"Hello?" she answered on the fifth ring. Katrina never picked up the receiver before the fourth ring. At least she retained something of her premenopause sense of self.

"Hey, babe."

"Leonid. Is everything all right?"

"You're up there and not home with us. That's not okay."

"You know I'm too weak to maintain a home. Maybe I should give you a divorce and you could go get a younger wife."

Maybe, I thought.

"Sister Monica says that you haven't signed up for the museum trip," I said. "You love the Met."

"Too much walking."

"You could take a wheelchair."

"I'm very tired, Leonid."

"What if I hired a nurse to come take care of you at home?" I offered. "You know, like we did for Gordo."

"You're a sweet man," my wife of too many years said, "but you don't want me."

"I want you to come home."

"As your wife or an invalid?"

"Katrina, we have lived in that apartment, raised three beautiful kids, and eaten ten thousand gourmet dinners on that dining room table. There's not one in ten can lay claim to that."

"I'll think about it," she said.

While waiting for her to say more I tried to think of some compelling argument for her to return to our flawed life.

Finally I said, "I'll come by tomorrow."

"Good-bye, Leonid."

It wasn't till after we hung up that I remembered to ask if Twill had dropped by like he'd promised. I wanted to call back but decided that Katrina would have been suspicious and worried at the insistence and so I let that opportunity drop. Twill was in trouble, I was sure of that, but he was a capable young man so would do what it took to survive—I hoped.

———

"Excuse me, mister," a voice laced with Spanish song said.

It was the brown young man that Westley called Quintez. He was my height and so I liked him. Though soft-spoken he still looked me in the eye.

"Yes?"

"A lady at the door to see you, mister."

"A lady?"

He nodded.

"A young lady?" I asked.

He hunched his shoulders. Young for him and for me might have been apples and pork chops.

"Send her on down."

Quintez went away and I took a deep breath. It felt like I'd been on a twenty-mile forced march with eighty pounds strapped to my back.

And the real battle hadn't even begun.

"Hello?" She was young even by Quintez's standards, I was sure. He probably didn't understand what I was asking.

Tall, maybe five-eight, and thin, she had brunette hair and skin that took to the sun; a white girl no more than twenty, her face was plain and pretty by turns with eyes promising intelligence, patience, and empathy.

"Can I help you?" I said.

"Is Twill in?"

"He's out of the office right now. I'm Leonid McGill, Twill's father and the chief investigator."

"Oh. Maybe I should come back."

"No," I said. "Come on in and sit down. Maybe I can help."

While she hesitated I studied her couture. The silk blouse was blue with an underlying patina of gray. Her black pants looked to be cashmere as did the emerald sweater she had draped on her shoulders. No purse. Not much makeup either.

"What's your name?" I asked.

"Liza Downburton," she said with a sigh. This release was enough to get her into a chair.

"Um," she said. "What happened to your front room?"

"Nothing. I'm just making a few improvements to the security system. How can I help you, Ms. Downburton?"

"I just," she said. "Well, I wanted to know what progress Twill has made."

"Which case?" I asked as if there were a dozen projects I had to choose from.

"Getting Fortune away from Jones."

"Yes," I said even though the sentence didn't quite make sense to me. Fortune and Jones. The one thing that I did know now was that Twill definitely took on a job when I was down in Philly on the Martinez case, and that job had nothing to do with some old high school friend. "Why don't you fill me in on the background and I'll try and get you an answer before you leave."

"Oh," she said, wondering what my role in her business might be. "I guess it's okay. Twill told me that you were in charge."

"Start from the beginning," I said.

She turned her body in the chair until she was almost at profile to me and said, "I hired Twill, your agency, because of Fortune."

"A friend of yours?"

"Well, um, not at first. Maybe eight weeks ago I was sleeping in my apartment in Park Slope when I heard something from the living room. I thought it was the dog caught behind the stuffed chair again but when I went out there and turned on the light I saw this young man—Fortune."

"You didn't know him?" I asked. That's always a good question.

"No. He was there to steal."

"A burglar?"

Liza nodded and said, "We were both surprised. For a long time, I mean a minute or so, we just stared. Finally he said, 'I'm sorry about this.' I asked him what he was doing and he told me that he was trying to steal my emerald necklace, the one that my grandmother from East Hampton had left me."

"You didn't know him but he knew about your necklace?"

"He is, was a part of a kind of gang. It's these young people who work for a guy named Jones. Jones has organized dozens of young people, most of them under eighteen. They perform crimes for him. Fortune was one of the older members."

"He told you all this?" I asked.

"After he apologized I offered to make him some tea. He said that he'd never had tea before and I said then he should probably try it with honey. We sat at the little table in the kitchenette for hours.

"He told me about Jones and how he lived in the subway tunnels and ran the gang of young people. He said that when Jones told any of them to do anything they had to do it or they'd be punished or even killed. He said that there were graves all over the subway tunnels that nobody would ever find except in the future.

"I asked him if this Jones man would kill him if he didn't bring back the necklace and he said no. He thought he might get hit but that was all. He said that he'd just say that the necklace wasn't there and maybe he wouldn't even get in trouble at all."

"How did he know about the necklace in the first place?" I asked.

"I go to NYU. My parents wanted me to leave it at home in my dad's safe but it reminds me of my gran and so I brought it here. I told everybody about it. Fortune said that Jones has ears everywhere, especially in places like the Village."

"What's Fortune's real name?"

"He's an orphan so he doesn't know. All he's ever been called was Fortune."

"Why?"

"I don't know."

"And so did this Fortune leave without taking your jewelry?"

Liza Downburton looked like a deer hypnotized by fear. She gazed at me, shook her head slightly, made to rise from the chair, and then fell back.

"I, we," she said, "kind of fell in love."

"I take it he's a good-looking kid."

"Yes but that's not why, I mean, we really connected. Fortune was raised by a woman who worked for Jones. They lived in a tin shack in Queens not far from the Triborough Bridge. When people get too old to work for Jones in the street he pays them to take care of kids that will work for him when they're old enough. Fortune lived in the tunnels after he was eight and now he has a room on Avenue D in the East Village and works at doing burglaries for Jones. He doesn't like it. He wants to leave but Jones has killed people who left him and Fortune didn't know where he could go."

"So you gave him the necklace?"

She nodded.

"How much is it worth?"

"It's insured for one hundred eighteen thousand dollars."

"Oh. And you hired Twill to get the necklace back?"

"No. Since then Fortune and I have been seeing each other, when he can get away."

I sat there looking at the lovelorn Liza Downburton thinking about one woman, Marella Herzog, who takes a man's heirlooms, and another that gives hers away.

"He can't let Jones know that he's seeing you," I surmised.

"No. He's afraid that Jones's people might try to get at me. Fortune wants to run away but he's too scared so I came here to hire your office to help him. I talked to Twill and he said that he'd do it. He seemed so sure that I believed him. But he hasn't called since then and I, and I wanted to find out what's happened."

"Did he ask you for a deposit?"

"No."

Good.

"I talked to him yesterday," I said. "He seemed to be deeply ensconced in the job."

"Did he say anything about Fortune?"

"Not directly. He just said that he was on the job."

"That's something, I guess," Ms. Downburton said.

"Let me ask you a question," I said.

"Yes?"

"How often do you and Fortune see each other?"

"After every burglary Jones gives him three days off. That's when we have the time."

"So Fortune is still burgling?"

"Yes. I told Twill that."

"Has he, I mean Fortune, asked you for more money or jewels?"

"No."

"Well," I said. "That's some story. Like I said, I've been out of town but still Twill works for me. And I don't like the idea of you out there with no protection while my son stirs up the hornets."

I looked at my watch. It was 7:15.

"Come on downstairs with me, Ms. Downburton. I have an appointment but maybe we can talk to Twill before I have to be there."

"You know how to reach him?"

"Come on. We'll give it a try."

20

A t the curb, in a no-parking zone in front of the Tesla Building, sat a black sedan; coincidentally a Tesla. An almost nondescript white man somewhere in his forties stood by the passenger-side door. This man wore a cheap medium-green suit with a white dress shirt buttoned to the throat but sporting no tie. His hair was dark brown and just this side of unruly. He was neither tall nor short, and slight of build.

"Leonid," the man said in a voice that was more an insinuation of resonance than an actual tone.

Hush owned the limo company. He bought the business not long after he gave up his lifelong calling: murder for pay.

"What's the boss doing on the job?" I asked.

"I got my regulars," he said. Liza Downburton came up beside me just then. Hush eyed her with an expression that maybe only I and his wife could read. "I also wanted to ask you a question. Maybe get some advice."

"No problem," I said. "I was going to call you anyway. This is Miss Liza Downburton, one of Twill's private clients."

Hush nodded at the young woman.

"Can you drive us down toward the Village?" I asked the driver.

"Not the restaurant?"

"All in good time."

He opened the back door to the fancy electric car and I gestured for Liza to scoot in. I followed her and Hush went to his driver's post.

As we tooled down Fifth Avenue I brought out a phone and entered a code for a very special number.

Within the last year Bug had made new and improved multichip phones for my use. I could turn off any of the numbers but there was one that my son, Mardi, Zephyra, and I kept on for emergencies. Twill's emergency number was the one I called.

Three rings in he answered, "What's the problem, Pop?"

The last word reminded me that I had found my father and lost him again.

"I'm in a limo with Hush driving and Liza Downburton sitting next to me."

"That's funny," Twill said. "I'm in a green borough cab headed for Liza's apartment."

"You have anything to share with her, or me?"

"Did she tell you everything?" my favorite son asked.

"I have the basics."

"I was gonna tell ya, Pop. It's just I had to figure out what was goin' on first."

"And what, may I ask, is that?"

"I thought that the guy, the burglar Fortune, was settin' Liza up for somethin' but the deeper I got the more I came to understand that this Jones is the real thing. He got him a goddamned army and nobody seems to know about it. And once you get in you can't ever get out—not ever."

"And are you in?"

"All the way up to my nuts."

I smiled then. There was something undeniably lovable about my sociopath boy.

"Are you compromised in any way?" I asked.

"I can't be sure. I only met the dude once. He wears this fake beard and contacts that make his eyes a different color. The way he looks at you is spooky. Anyway—I heard him askin' about Fortune so even if I'm in good with him, Liza and her boy might not be. That's why I was goin' to her place. I was gonna offer to put her at Mardi's for a few days."

"What if you asked Uncle Hush to do that?"

"That'd be like keepin' a Christmas Club account at Fort Knox."

Twill listened to his elders and therefore had many of our outdated references.

"You tell your client," I said. "I'll ask Mr. Hush."

I handed the phone to Liza and leaned forward over the seat.

"Twill needs you to put up his client for a few days," I said to the killer who was something like a friend.

"Twill?" Hush uttered. "No problem. She knows the rules?"

"I'm willing to bet she's a fast learner."

By the time I leaned back Liza was handing me the phone.

"Twill says that he wants me to stay with Mr. Hush," she said with trust in her voice that very few innocents ever had for me.

"Is that all right with you?"

"Can I call my parents?"

"Only if you don't tell 'em the truth. You really don't want anyone comin' around Mr. Hush when he's feelin' protective."

"Are we in trouble?" she asked me.

"You already know the answer to that."

I waited in the car while Hush walked Liza up the stairs to his twelve-million-dollar mansion on Fifth Avenue not a block from Washington Square Park. Hush had more security surrounding his home than most senators or CIA spooks. Tamara, his wife, and Thackery, his young son, would take care of Liza while I worried about my own son's chances at survival.

While I waited I called the Chambre du Roi, telling them to inform my date that I might be a few minutes late if she got there before me.

When Hush returned I moved to the passenger's seat beside him.

"You sure it's okay?" I asked.

"Everybody loves Twill," he replied. "The restaurant now?"

On the way up Sixth Avenue, just around Forty-second Street, I asked, "Have you ever heard of a guy named Jones runs an army of underage thieves?"

"No. New York?"

"Down in the tunnels."

"Wow. You need to find out more?"

"Twill's already down there. What I have to do is figure how to pull him out."

"Need help?"

"Maybe later."

Around Fifty-fifth Hush said, "Dude from the federal government asked me if I could kill a foreign head of state and make it look like natural causes."

"Oh?"

"If I couldn't do that, maybe I could make it look like some other unfriendly leader or group did the deed. Seven figures, legal, no tax."

"Damn."

"What do you think I should do?"

"You need the money?"

"No."

"I thought you wanted to try and go the other way," I said. "I mean whether it's official or not, blood on your hands is still blood."

"Yeah. Yeah. But you know, LT, I've been gettin' this itch."

I didn't need to ask what needed scratching.

"Ever since I quit killing for pay I want to hurt people," he continued. "I never felt like that before. Everything was cut-and-dry in the old days, you know? I killed for my supper and the dinner was always good."

Sometimes there's nothing to say; no rule book to quote, no homily that has weight. There are things about being a human that cannot be excused or even understood. Hush wanted to go out and murder someone just to get his passion under control. That was crazy—but so were thousands of truly senseless deaths from Palestine to Kandahar to Congo.

The car came to a halt and I saw that we were at the restaurant.

"So?" Hush asked.

"How long ago this guy come to you?"

"A week."

"Give it another week," I said. "Think it over. Maybe go to the Zen monastery upstate and meditate a day or two. Then, when seven days are up, call me and we'll talk again."

Hush gave me one of his rare smiles and held out a hand.

When we shook I couldn't suppress the little shiver of fear that ran down my spine.

21

The Chambre du Roi was a big round room with tables set out in an off-center spiral. I got there at 8:12. Monique, the hostess, installed me at a booth that was in the outermost circle. I needn't have worried about Marella waiting for me. She didn't get there for another twenty-two minutes.

She stopped at my side of the stall before I had the chance to stand, and leaned over gracefully giving me a wet kiss on the lips. She was wearing a red dress that was close-fitting on the torso but flouncy below the waist.

"You look delicious," she said.

"You took the words right out of my head."

Depositing herself in the seat across from me, she smiled prettily and cocked her head to the side.

"I asked them to bring a Beaujolais when you got here," I said.

"Thoughtful and sexy," she replied.

I usually feel a lump in my throat when a woman riles me but with Marella the bulge was in my chest. I think she could see the impact she was having because she pursed her lips and let her lovely dark head loll a little farther, bringing her right shoulder up like the back end of an oil derrick.

The wine came along with menus.

"You order for me, Lee," she said. I couldn't remember anyone ever calling me Lee; some encounters are just unique.

"I may have to answer my phone from time to time," I apologized. "My son works for me and he's in a little trouble."

"I guess I'll have to punish you for that."

"Okay."

"What kind of trouble is he in?"

"He's in the company of killers and thieves but they haven't recognized him for what he is . . . yet."

"That shouldn't be any problem for a strong man like you."

There had been many times in my life that I'd come across just the right woman at the wrong time, but it was rare that I chanced upon the perfect wrong woman at just the right moment.

We toasted and I almost forgot my problems.

"You sounded tense on the phone last night," Marella said.

"Son's in deep shit, wife tried to kill herself three months ago—"

"You're married?"

"Yeah."

She shrugged, tossing off this knowledge as unimportant, and I fell a little deeper into the dark passion she offered.

"I turned down a client two days ago," I went on, "and he was murdered. The man who killed him, I believe, hired me this afternoon. Somehow I have to take all of that and make it right again."

"My problems are small potatoes compared to yours," she said, somehow managing to be both light and serious at the same time.

Before I could speak the waiter came to tell us the specials; at least he tried to. I cut him off, ordering the chef's specialty Canard la Maison for myself and coq au vin for Marella.

When he left I said, "You probably have a close relationship with your father."

Frowning, she asked, "Why do you say that?"

"Because only old men use the term 'small potatoes.' "

Marella gasped and stood up. I wondered if I had somehow insulted her and now she was about to walk out.

She held out a hand to me. I took it and she pulled me from the booth.

At the front podium she told Monique that we'd be right back—in French.

Across the street from the restaurant there was a recess between a stationery store and bank. It was a dead-end alley blocked off at the mouth by a large locked plastic crate that was there to hold trash bins. This crate was maybe four feet high.

Marella pulled me until we were partially hidden by the receptacle container. She turned her back to me and lifted the flouncy red skirt. She wasn't wearing anything underneath.

"I know you know what to do with that," she said over her shoulder.

I did know and did not hesitate. There's not nearly enough said about the smooth warmth of entering a woman without protection or worry. When she pressed back against me I noticed that she was clutching the same sacklike black satin bag she'd carried on the train. A sound erupted from us both simultaneously and I began to move with force that threw her against the wall more than once.

The sounds we made got louder over the seconds and minutes. At one point I glanced to my left and saw that a young couple had stopped to watch; a white man in a black suit and an Asian woman in a rainbow-glitter dress. I noted the couple but they didn't matter to me.

"Harder, Lee," Marella groaned.

I can't remember any orgasm being stronger or more satisfying.

When it was over we put ourselves together and walked out from behind the big crate. The young couple was still standing there, still watching us. I wondered if they might take our place when we were gone.

On the way across the street back to the restaurant I checked my phone. I didn't want to but there was too much going on. Nothing from Twill but there were eight messages from Zephyra; most of these about Coco Lombardi—most but not all.

Back in Chambre du Roi, Marella made a stop at the ladies' room.

I spent the few minutes reading over the various texts and e-mails.

"That's much better," Marella said when she returned to our booth. "We needed to get that out of the way before being civilized."

I suppressed the desire to tell her I loved her.

The waiter came, placing garlicky salads before us.

"It was my grandfather," she told me.

"What?"

"My grandfather and I were close. That's why I had to fuck you."

"Who was this guy you were engaged to?" I asked.

"You jealous?"

"As if you were the only woman left in the world."

"You don't have to be," she said instead of answering the question.

"What about that diamond?" I said. I wanted to feel businesslike and sophisticated because Marella was bringing out a beast in me.

"What about it?" Her smile was crazy-making.

"How much did you get for it?"

"Why so many questions, Lee? Isn't this enough for you?"

"It's just that I was wondering," I said.

"About what?"

Neither of us had touched our salads.

"About how you could be so sloppy to have a thug like Alexander Lett get so close."

Her smile faded when she said, "The less you know, the better."

"But I know so much already."

"Like what?" There was a hint of danger in her mien.

"You got engaged to the man somehow knowing that sooner or later he'd break it off," I said.

"You're a smart man, Mr. McGill."

"No."

"No?"

"I'm a fool. Otherwise I would have taken your money and ignored the fact of the three-point-six-million-dollar diamond you tricked out of Melbourne Westmount Ericson. There was an article about the engagement and the ring on the society page of the *Washington Post*."

"Oh my God," she said with genuine surprise in her lovely, deadly eyes. "You really are a detective."

"Yes," I admitted as humbly as I could manage. "I know, for instance, that you have a gun in that bag, that Mr. Lett would have died, or at least he would have sustained serious injury, if he tried to take you. I was the less lethal alternate plan."

"You're the kind of man I like to take pictures with. The kind of pictures that drive fiancés mad."

"You're something else, Marella Herzog."

"What are you going to do?" she asked, as if there was a choice I had.

"You got me in this now, Mar, I got to make sure the Ericson family steamroller don't make me Pancake Lee."

"There's a lot of rage in you," she said. It was true but I didn't know where that fact fit in our conversation.

"Maybe."

"I'm the kind of girl who can let a man express that rage any way he wants, anywhere he wants."

"I can see that."

"So what are you going to do?" she asked again.

"Eat my dinner. Drink my wine. Look at you and be happy. Then walk you home and try to get my mind in the place it needs to be."

22

I surprised Marella Herzog—also known as Mona Briannan, Cassan-dra Massman, Thulia Lewes, and some other names by sources that Zephyra had forwarded to me. I surprised her not with the knowl-edge of her aliases but by kissing her on the cheek at the hotel entrance and saying good night.

"You're not coming in?" she asked.

"Not tonight."

"Why not? It's late."

"It's a matter of self-preservation."

"I don't bite that hard."

"As I told you, I have other business that cannot be ignored." My overly formal reply had the desired effect.

She looked me in the eye for a long moment, nodded, and then said, "Okay," like a confederate, or an accomplice.

I walked the thirty or so blocks back toward my empty apartment. I needed to be on the street to organize my thoughts. Like the table lay-out of Chambre du Roi, my mind was spiraling and off-center.

Marella was the event that had thrown me out of kilter though she wasn't what bothered me. Hiram Stent and Josh Farth posed a mortal danger, but that was just business as usual now that I had taken up the dead man's cause. It was Twill's dilemma that concerned me most. He was down in a hole somewhere and I didn't know if my arm was long enough to reach him.

At Broadway and Seventy-second at 11:47 I engaged Twill's emergency line. He didn't answer but twelve minutes and eight blocks later he called back.

"You kinda leanin' on the emergency button, ain't ya, Pops?" were his first words.

"I need you to come home," I told him.

"In a few days."

"Now."

"Can't right now."

"Why not?"

"Tigers up in the garden and tigers down below," he said paraphrasing his and my, and my father's, favorite Nasrudin Sufi tale. It meant that any way he turned would mean his demise.

"That bad?" I asked.

"I'll be home in seventy-two hours," he said, and then he disconnected the call.

I was pressing the key into the downstairs lock of my apartment building door when he said, "Trot."

Tolstoy wore light-colored trousers, a dark green T-shirt, and a tan windbreaker that was creased and stained. He was hatless, wore glasses, and was as unfamiliar to me as a father could be.

"I thought you was in the wind, man," I told him.

"Never again." He punctuated this solemn oath with a soldier's abbreviated nod.

Back in the dining room, once again swilling cognac, my father and I faced each other across the hickory table.

"You should get over it," he said to me.

"What's that?"

"The rage you feel. The rage that drives you. You were an angry child and now you're an angry man. It's no good."

"That's not the first time I've heard something like that tonight."

"I'm sorry, Trot. I was wrong."

When listing my problems on the way back home from the Hotel Brown I had forgotten about my father and the anger he called up in me. I wanted to answer him but the only words that came underscored the fury that he'd already identified. It galled me that I was little more than a child in his presence, that every misstep I had taken in life could be traced back to him.

He was just an old man, an old black man that could have been a train porter or the Martiniquean ambassador to Cuba or Italy. He was a fool and I had been his fodder. The beast that Marella called up in me wanted to rend Tolstoy McGill. This simple truth made me smile.

"What?" my father asked.

"I'll make you a deal, old man."

"And what is that?"

"You agree to be a grandfather to my kids and a father-in-law to my wife and I'll put away the grief."

"Grief?"

The ex-sharecropper might have been a fool but he was sharp. I had meant to say that I would put away the anger and the rage but instead my tongue said "grief." Grief. It was at that moment I realized that my entire life had been spent grieving the loss of my father and the death of my mom. Anger was just a shield; the rage simple background music for a child who had pitied himself for decades.

Was I really that shallow and self-involved?

"So what do you say, Clarence?" I asked, using my father's given name—what he called his sharecropper name.

"Don't call me that."

"Answer my question."

"Your children are my grandkids. Your wife is my daughter-in-law."

I sat back in the spindly and surprisingly strong dining chair. I took in a deep breath and then exhaled, feeling with that outbreath that I was released from the custody of grief.

"Okay," I said, "now tell me about Nicky."

"Don't you ever relax, son?" my father asked. "I mean are you always on some case, some job? Don't you ever just sit back and watch the TV or jerk off or something?"

Free from sorrow, I laughed and shook my head.

"You know, I killed my first man when I was fourteen," I said for the first time ever in my life. "If anybody had found out and brought me to trial they would have probably called it self-defense but it was murder for me. I strangled him with my hands. I watched him die and then I burned his body with gasoline fire.

"You live a life like that and the *Beverly Hillbillies* jokes lose their appeal."

I had never even imagined that my father's face could hold compassion for anything except the worker and the Revolution.

"You don't have to feel sorry for me, Clarence. I had to kill that man or he would have done it to me. You had to go off and fight your wars. I accept that now. Just don't sit judgment on me. That's all I ask."

My father finished his snifter and I poured him another dram. He drank half of that before speaking again.

"Nikita didn't start off as an armored car robber, as I'm sure you know," he said. "He dealt with hijackers and smugglers for years before deciding to rob that one tank and then retire to Tahiti."

"Do ants retire?" I said, quoting a question my father would ask the straw-man capitalist he so often imagined.

He grinned, showing me his white teeth.

"Nicky never learned his lessons as well as you, Trot," he said. "Anyway, like I was saying, your brother had been involved with certain smugglers that from time to time intersected with other smugglers who from time to time intersected with so-called terrorists. For a modicum of information on these people, and the promise to reinvolve himself in their business, the feds erased Nikita from their system and freed him to steal, spy, and smuggle, incriminate, and enjoy freedom."

"Nicky's a snitch?"

"He likes to say that he's a government agent but yes, he's a snitch."

"Damn. Damn."

"We all cross the line on a daily basis, Trot. It only took me forty years to realize that."

"And what about you, old man?" I said as I poured my fourth drink. I was beginning to feel the alcohol in my fingertips and my lips.

"What about me?"

"Why you stayed in the shadows while me and Nicky roved in the street?"

Tolstoy, who I would almost always from that moment on think of as Clarence, looked at me with apologetic eyes.

"In my years in the Revolution," he said, "I, more than once, was implemental in damaging, destroying, and sometimes assassinating American military and corporate interests and their staffs. I'm on a very special top ten most-sought-after list."

"Because of the people you killed," I concluded.

"Because of the knowledge I have. If I was ever brought to trial the prosecution would be forced to reveal things that no American president, military general, or corporate CEO would like to have made public. I'm a threat and so I try to maintain a low profile."

"Then why come back at all?"

"You and Nicky needed a guardian angel. I watched over you."

I didn't say anything to that. If we talked about him playing the role of father-from-the-shadows I might have rediscovered the anger that I had so recently given up. But I really didn't care about what he thought he was doing or who he feared was after him. I had just solved the most important case of my career. I knew what had happened to me. I knew what he had done and why. So what if there was no pot of gold, no happy ending—truth is its own reward.

23

I told Clarence he could sleep in my daughter's bed. She wouldn't mind. Shelly was away at college living with a man thrice her age.

It was early morning when I awoke in the emperor-sized bed that I'd shared with a woman who hadn't needed love when anyone wanted it with her. But that didn't mean we didn't make a durable team. Katrina and I worked together like a machine constructed from indestructible parts and supplied with an infinite power source. We'd never stop functioning but we were terribly out of alignment. We clattered and struggled, twirled and fell down—but we never stopped working and we couldn't turn off.

I missed Katrina, loved Aura, and wanted Marella so badly that I could taste her in my sleep.

So there I was at 5:47 with the father that had abandoned me down the hall, the women I needed jostling around in my mind, and a cognac hangover from my head to my gut and through every nerve of my body. It wasn't until I made it to the bathroom, standing next to the tub where I had found Katrina in bloody suicide-water, that I remembered Hiram Stent.

As bad as I felt, he had got it worse.

When ice-cold water from the shower hit my skin I wanted to scream; three minutes later the shiver had made it to the bone; from that point I counted to a hundred and then came out of the glass box shower stripped of fear, lust, love, self-pity, and most importantly my hangover.

Leaving a key, automatic lock-release, and note for my father, I began the long walk down to Fifty-seventh Street and the first stop of my investigation.

There was a fancy diner across the street from the art school where Fontu Belair taught life drawing at a late morning class from 10:00 to 12:00. My watch read 7:14 and so I ordered an omelet with jalapeños, goat cheese, and merguez sausage. The fancy young waitress wore a pink miniskirt and a white silk T-shirt so short that it revealed her sapphire navel ring. Her nametag read MIDGE and her lips were painted apricot. When Midge went to deliver my order to the kitchen I took out my phone and made a call.

"Good morning, Mr. McGill," Zephyra Ximenez said, answering before I could hear the first ring.

"Back at ya," I said.

That was it for the pleasantries. From there Z went into her spiel.

"It was really hard finding a Briscoe/Thyme anywhere. I finally located papers filed for them in the Denver offices of a large accounting firm named Feggers and Sons, Ltd. F and S, the name they do business under, was originally a London-based firm that was old enough to have done accounting for Charles Dickens. I followed the trail of ownership back to a Boston company named Braverman Enterprises. Braverman is a holding company that's owned by a private investment bank controlled by a woman named Evangeline Sidney-Gray. The only law Briscoe/Thyme practices comes from her desk in downtown Boston.

"Finding Ms. Gray was difficult but Josh Farth took no time at all. He came up through the Boston gangs making a living on heists, robberies, and extortion. He's been mentioned as a person of interest in three murders but no charges have been made. Now Farth works for Evangeline Sidney-Gray, or at least a company her bank owns.

"I only found a little on Coco Lombardi, mainly phone records when she had some kind of relationship with a guy named Alfred Carr. His nickname is Buster. The majority of her calls were either to Carr in New York or various numbers in the Boston area.

"Finally there's the moniker 'Twitcher.' That was by far my biggest headache. I had to piggyback on an NSA program that Bug infected. His subroutine has been crafted so that the feds can't see it and Bug has it running twenty-four hours a day. I had to drop a key word into the transitional chatter-box and watch it until and if anything came up. Once a key word hit had been made by the box I had ninety seconds to remove it or some bureaucrat in DC would be alerted to the name and the hack."

"I don't need the technical explanation right now, Z," I said. The pink and blue-jeweled waitress was delivering my upmarket eggs. "Just the details will do."

"The name popped up seventeen times," she said. "Four of these were about a meeting on the Upper West Side near the river and One-oh-two."

"I know the place," I said. "Thanks for all that."

"You're welcome," she said. "Will you be needing any more help within the next few days? Because if not I called Petipor and we're going on what he calls a surfing expedition in South Africa for a week or so starting tomorrow night. He's got his own private jet."

"Wow," I said. "That beats my dark green Pontiac."

"I'd rather be in the backseat with you than at Mach two with him."

Zephyra had never spoken a flirtatious word to me before. I wondered what was happening inside me.

"If you need help you have Bean's number, right?" Bean was her backup in times of emergency.

"I do. Just a few more things I need," I said.

"What's that?"

"Make me a first-class Acela reservation for Boston tomorrow morning as much before ten as possible and e-mail all the information you have on Dame Evangeline Sidney-Gray and Coco. And don't take any shit from some royal dude."

"See ya, Mr. McGill. And thanks."

The omelet was delicious. And Midge was an art student at the school across the street. Tiny as she was, she was a sculptor who liked to work in the double medium of iron and stone. I asked if she knew a teacher there named Fontu Belair.

"Oh him," she said.

"Not such a good guy?" I asked, trying not to read too far into her tone.

"He taught me how to draw for sculpture," she said. "Probably the best class I ever had. He said that drawing for a sculptor, filmmaker, or physicist was like dreams for somebody on a psychoanalyst's couch. He was completely right."

"That sounds pretty good," I offered.

"I guess."

"So what was wrong with him?"

"It's the way he looked at women," she said, a little color rising in her cheeks. "It's like love. When he talks to you it's almost like you're dancing with him or something. But then there's nothing to add. When he finishes he turns off completely and if you ask him to get together for coffee he's too busy . . . talking to somebody else."

24

Entering the great copper double doors of the Gotham Artists' Society at 8:28, I went to the reception desk, which was in the northmost corner of a chamber with a high ceiling held up by a dozen marble pillars.

"May I help you?" a middle-aged black male receptionist asked. His nameplate read TITO PALMER. Despite his age he was the same size as Midge, and he held himself with a sense of youth that was unconscious in the waitress/sculptor and engineered by Tito.

"My name is McGill," I said. "I'm supposed to meet a Mr. Belair."

"And what is your business with Professor Belair?" Tito asked with equal parts suspicion and flirtation.

"I'm supposed to model for his new class using sportsmen that have been out of practice for a while."

"What sport did you do?"

"Boxer."

Tito's raised eyebrows expressed mild interest. There was something going on with me; all of a sudden I had become a magnet for the usually hidden passions of humankind.

"Third floor, studio F," Tito said as if the words were a loan that he expected a return on.

Studio F was occupied by four souls. Three of these were students who had come in early to work on very technical and equally uninteresting studies of a woman with sagging breasts with well-defined nipples and a small protruding tummy.

The fourth resident of the light and airy space was a burly man just a centimeter or two north of six feet. He was dressed in a brightly stained white artist's smock, bald on top, and filled with the passion of his self-imposed importance. If I wasn't a boxer I'd have been a little intimidated by his strength and the energy that crackled around him.

"Can I help you?" he asked, more as a threat than as a request.

"Leonid McGill," I said, handing him a card that said the same. "I'm a PI looking for a woman named Coco Lombardi."

"Do you see her?" he asked, gesturing at his students, two of which were women.

"I see you," I replied easily.

Something changed in the art professor's eyes just then. He looked at my big scarred mitts and at the powerful slope of my shoulders. I wasn't a minion and he wasn't a lord—not right then, not right there.

"What do I have to do with this, this . . . whatever her name is?"

"She was a model for your class."

"I have dozens of models. Do you expect me to remember them all?"

"I expect, from all my fellow citizens, the same things," I said. "Civility, respect, and honesty. It's rare to receive any of those commodities but I keep hope alive."

"Are you threatening me, Mr. McGill?"

"If I was, your jaw would already be broken," I said.

One of the drawing students was glancing in our direction. She was middle-aged and looked it.

"Let's go to my office," Fantu offered when he saw his student studying us.

Behind a screen of very large canvases there was an institutional-green metal door that opened onto a good-sized office space. Inside, the twenty-foot-high walls supported dozens of drawings and paintings in cheap frames hung very close together. They were all rendered by the same hand. If I were to bet I'd've said that Professor Belair saw this office as a museum dedicated to his work.

The furniture was a green metal desk and chair, a pine visitor's chair, and a daybed with a sponge-sized pillow and a gray army blanket.

The bed was made, military style, and the blue linoleum floor was spotless.

"Have a seat, Mr. McGill."

"Thank you, Professor."

We achieved our seats and Fantu sat back giving me a stare that probably worked on people who hadn't strangled a man to death when they were fourteen and living in the street.

"That's not your real name, is it?" I said.

"Why are you looking for Coco?"

"You admit that you know her."

"I just want to know why you're looking for her."

"Her family fears that she has fallen in with bad company and that her well-being is threatened."

"You don't talk like a detective," he said suspiciously.

I took out my duly licensed .38 caliber pistol and laid it on the green blotter that clashed with rather than matched his desk.

"How many detectives do you know, Professor?"

Some people you just have to take shortcuts with. We could have talked for an hour about how the police and private detectives on his TV and in his library don't talk like I do. But put a pistol on the table and that whole block of thought just disappears.

"She was modeling for my classes six, seven months ago," he said, exhibiting his proclivity for not answering the question he'd just been asked. "I liked her very much, as a model, because even though she worked in the nude there always seemed to be something hidden."

"You ever find out what that something was?"

"No."

"Did you fuck her?"

"Excuse me?"

"I thought you wanted me to talk like Mickey Spillane so I threw in a curse word. I'm not sure if he cursed in his books but you got the feeling he might any second."

"She stopped modeling for my classes at the beginning of last summer," Fantu said. "I haven't heard from her since then."

"Did you fuck her?" I enjoyed disturbing the bully with my words.

"We were"—he stopped and looked up the way people do when they're reaching for a difficult word—"friends."

"What was she like?" I asked.

The question surprised him.

"She," he said and then hesitated again. "She was very intelligent. She knew more about the history of art than most of my colleagues—myself included. She had a friend, a man who was not the same kind as her."

"What does that mean, not the same kind?"

"He was shifty, unpleasant. For a week or so he'd come around after a session and take her away. Finally she left and never came back."

"What was this man's name?"

"She never said and he didn't speak to anyone but her."

"Did they meet here at the institute?"

"No. But I don't think she knew him when she first came here. Soon after they met, our friendship faded and then she was gone . . . Why are you looking for her, Mr. McGill?"

"I already told you. Her family thinks she's in trouble. It's my job to find her and see if they're right."

"You're supposed to drag her home?"

"I would if that's what they asked for but all they said is that they'd like me to ask her to call them. Did she have any other friends here?"

"Not that I know of."

"Have you seen her at all since she stopped modeling?"

"Well . . ."

"Where?"

"There's a gentlemen's club somewhere around the theater district, I don't remember the name. I was there one, one afternoon and Coco was, um, serving drinks. I tried to talk to her but she ignored me and then she was gone."

"That's it?"

"Yeah."

"Well, thank you, Professor Belair, you've been a lot of help."

"Mulligan," he said.

"What?"

"Frank Mulligan. I went to university at Santa Cruz in California. Some of the other art students and I did acid every day for two weeks. Soon after that I changed my name to Fantu Belair. I really don't know why but I think it has helped me."

25

"Excuse me, mister," a woman called out from somewhere behind me. I was almost to the broad marble stairway that led down to the first floor. Turning, I saw the late-middle-aged woman who had been watching me and Mr. Mulligan. She wore a knee-length khaki skirt and a loose red blouse that partially hid her large breasts. She'd let her hair go gray but her face still had the creamy complexion of youth.

"Yes?" I said.

"You're looking for Coco?"

"Yes?" I said, wondering if Mulligan had confided in her. It didn't seem likely.

"Professor Belair is a wonderful teacher," she said. "It's almost like he can inhabit your soul and bring art out of you that would never happen otherwise. He sees inside, you know what I mean?"

She was wearing simple white-plug earphones connected to some music device in a khaki pocket.

"What about Coco?" I said, feeling like a shepherd of conversation.

"They had an affair," the elder art student said. "She spent afternoons and evenings on that cot in his office. After the first few modeling sessions he let her stay there the first three months she worked here. I think he paid her extra, too."

"There's a name for that," I said.

"She was in trouble."

"How do you know that?" I asked. "Did she talk about it?"

"It was the way she was always so jumpy. She'd actually flinch if anyone, I mean anyone, walked into the room. And when she'd walk with Fantu it looked kind of like she was using him as a shield, you know what I mean?"

I nodded and asked, "Was she a friend of yours?"

"No. We never spoke other than to say hello now and then."

"So Fantu told you I was looking for her?"

"He doesn't talk to gray-haired ladies unless it's about their work. Don't get me wrong, he does his job. He's a good teacher and can't help it that he's a man." These last few words had the ring of a deeply held conviction about the entire gender.

"Then how did you know I was asking about Coco?"

Smiling, the lady brought out a small white plastic box that was connected to her earphones. It didn't look like any digital music player I'd ever seen.

The lady smiled, revealing two missing teeth; one upper and one lower.

"It's what they called on the late-night TV informercial an omnidirectional listening device," she said. "All I have to do is switch this knob on top and I can hear anything anybody says, in any direction within fifteen feet or so. I'm always eavesdropping; on the street, in classes, at church. You wouldn't believe some of the things that people say and do. I heard this one guy say that he raped a woman. I called the police from a pay phone and told them, but they didn't do anything. That's why I decided to tell you what I know."

"Why's that exactly?"

"Because I think that girl's in trouble and you're already looking for her. I thought maybe if I told you I might be some help."

"What kind of trouble was Coco in?" I asked.

"Somebody was after her. I heard her tell Fantu that there was somebody she needed to help her get out of trouble. I never learned why they were after her or what the trouble was."

"If you think she's in trouble, why wouldn't you suppose that that trouble was me?"

"Is it?" she asked, innocent as a child.

"No." I smiled, hoping there was somebody to keep *her* out of trouble. "I'm a PI working for her family like I said."

I handed her my card and she glanced at it.

"I didn't think so," she said.

"Did you hear the name of the guy she needed to help her?"

"It could have been a woman," the old-school feminist objected.

"But it wasn't, was it?"

"No. I guess you're a detective and can see things that maybe I don't understand," she allowed.

"You can really listen in on people's conversations with that thing?" I asked.

"They think I'm an old lady listening to rock and roll or something."

"Damn."

"Paulie DeGeorges," she said.

"The guy she was waiting for?"

The gray head bobbed and gave me her best serrated grin. "You could tell when Fantu was flirting with her that she was just mouthing her answers. She just needed a place to sleep and a few bucks in her pocket. Soon as she found something better she was gone."

"How did you hear the name of the guy she was looking for?" I asked more from habit than anything else.

"He came into the class one day," she said, triumphant. "He was short. Not so much as you, and skinny. He wore a silly suit and bow tie and his hair was too long for a man of his age. Fantu asked him what he was doing here and he said his name was Paulie DeGeorges and he was there to talk to Coco. He said something about her brother but somebody sneezed and I couldn't make that part out."

"Paulie DeGeorges," I said aloud.

"That's right."

"And what's your name?" I asked.

For a moment there was suspicion and fear in the matron's round brown eyes. But then she came to some kind of internal resolve. "Irene Carnation. Carnation like the flower."

"You have my card, Irene. If Coco comes back you should call me. And maybe if you get tired of classes and street corners one day, you might want to call a real detective. I might could give you some work from time to time."

"This little jigger only cost forty-nine ninety-five," she said. "You could buy one yourself."

"It's you that's the jewel, Irene. Somebody sees me and they know to worry. You . . . that's money in the bank right there."

A look of wonder came over Irene Carnation's face. A door was open and she was wondering if she had the courage to walk through.

Early afternoon found me uptown at a high park along the Hudson River looking down on a concrete wall. The barrier was a blank slate except for a door-sized hole thirty feet below, almost at the waterline. There's a very official-looking iron ladder that leads down to the hole but neither that opening nor the ladder is supposed to be there.

I made my way down to the water, maybe two hundred yards from the wall. From there I could keep a watch on the portal and use the fishing pole I'd picked up from home to give anybody looking a reason for why I was there.

Clarence had left by the time I got home. He'd taken the keys and so I expected to see him in less than a year.

I threw my line pretty far out. My secret for fishing was learned from an old guy named Cranston. He taught me that you needed a heavy weight, at least eight ounces, on your line and that the best bait was a giant gutter cockroach. I had both bug and pyramid-shaped lead weight and so I sat down on a craggy concrete plank that had been dumped there to maintain the shoreline. After I had my hook in the water and the pole between my knees I took out the Canadian socialist paper *The People's Voice*. Adam Clayton Powell, Jr., was once associated with a paper by the same name, and I think it was out of a soft spot I had for him that I kept up the subscription.

From time to time a young boy or girl climbed down the ladder to the hole and then scrambled inside; a few minutes later they'd clamber back up again. They looked like ants filled with a purpose laid down in their DNA millions of years ago. Watching them come and go, I remembered the man named Tusk who came from Australia and fabricated an underground pied-à-terre deep within the man-made wall.

Tusk was more of an artist than a survivalist. There was running water and electricity in the cave. I'd shown the place to Twill when he was no more than fourteen.

I sat there for hours reading about dreams that my father had taught me and then abandoned. I caught two good-sized flounder and an American eel that was more than a yard long. I cleaned the flounders and put them in a pink plastic bucket I'd brought along. I let the eel go.

At twilight Twill, replete in blue jeans and a stained T-shirt, came scrambling out of the hole. I picked up my bucket and pole and climbed to the street. From there I followed my wayward son until he was headed east from Broadway on Seventy-second.

"Twitcher! Hold up," I called from maybe ten feet back.

Twilliam McGill, as usual, was unflappable. He turned and smiled as if to say, "What took you so long, old man?"

26

"What you got in the bucket, Pops?" my son asked as we walked.

Twill is five-ten, slender, handsome, and dark as our West African ancestors before the slave ships came. There was a small scar just under his lower lip; a reminder of folk heroes like Achilles and Cain. Twill didn't have an evil bone in his body but he knew no laws except for Family, Friends, and Free Will.

I held up the bucket for him to see my catch.

Looking at the fish as if they were a calculus equation on a college blackboard, he said, "You musta heard my other name on that phone call, huh?"

"What were all those kids doing climbing in and out of Tusk's place?" I asked. Tusk had migrated back to Australia after he'd gotten into trouble and I got him out again, but I always thought of the illegal apartment as his domain.

"Jones don't see everybody," Twill said. "A lotta the kids get written orders that he has somebody older pass out. Today was my turn."

"The kids read?"

"He has most of them go to school. That way they get smarter and hear stuff that might be some help."

"Like burglary jobs?" I asked.

"Like that."

"Let's sit on that bench," I said, pointing to a pedestrian stopping point near the Seventy-second Street subway station.

We perched and I put the fish under the concrete seat. And there we sat side by side, father and son with nary a gene in common. Both of us were under threat of mortal danger, but our demeanor was more like two women friends taking a break after an afternoon of window shopping.

"Regale me," I said to my boy.

Twill shook his head slowly and did not smile.

"This dude Jones is the real thing," he said. "He like the black plague and almost no one knows about it. He deals in underage prostitution, got a bigger burglary ring than I ever heard of, uses little kids and young women who pretend they're the mothers for international smuggling, murders anyone who goes against him, and has underground public floggings for even if somebody steal somethin' the wrong way. It's like living in the Middle Ages here today in twenty-first-century New York."

Somehow Mardi had gotten Twill to start reading. He used the knowledge he gained to further his understanding of the flaws of humankind.

"How many people work with him?" I asked.

"I only seen a dozen or so at one time but it's got to be hundreds. He been doin' it more than twenty-one, twenty-two years and the ones that grow up still do things his way. Fortune says that there's at least two dozen dead in a graveyard below the tunnels."

"What about the police?"

"Nobody seems worried about the law. Kids get grabbed sometime but Jones got a law firm called Bedford-Rule that gets them out. There's a lotta talk among the kids, say that if somebody turns on Jones he's not safe even on Rikers Island."

"You believe that?"

"That man got a system, Pops. He got some serious people in his pocket."

"And you couldn't figure all that out before you got yourself this far in?"

"I just didn't believe it, man," Twill, my peer, railed. "I mean how you gonna have some crazy dude with a false beard only come out in the tunnels under the city and run a crime syndicate made mostly of children?

"When Liza come to me I figured that either Fortune was playin' her or they were just believin' some kinda hype. If he was scammin' her I'd cut her loose and if he was for real I'd just move 'em out of harm's way.

"Then, two days after Fortune brought me in, Jones sent us out on this one job where all we had to do was go to this warehouse in Long Island City. There was a young guy made night watchman two years ago. He'd been layin' out plans to steal a truck that had more than a million dollars of electronics in it. We drove that suckah to an abandoned building over in Brooklyn where there was people waitin' there to take it over and break it down."

"What happened to the watchman?"

"Who knows? Vanished in the tunnels till Jones need him for another job."

"Somebody broke into the office," I said. "Used explosives on the front door and then broke down the wall to the back office. That sound like your man?"

"Naw," Twill said through a sneer. "That's too loud for him. Jones want everything to be quiet like."

One shore achieved but there were still many rivers to cross.

"Why would they trust you on a job when you just got there?" I asked.

"The only weakness they have is that they don't think they have no weakness," my brilliant son opined. "Trouble is, they might be right."

"Why didn't you go to Carson?" I asked then.

"The way I see it, Jones got the uppity-ups by the nuts. You know your friend wouldn't back down so I figured tellin' him wouldn't help my client and probably hurt him."

"You think they might suspect that you're a plant?" I asked.

"Why would they? I haven't done nuthin' except what they said. I did that one job okay. Today I gave out his letters. They don't suspect me but Jones got these two lieutenants called Marcia and Deck, little younger'n me but serious as a land mine in a nursery school playground. I saw Jones gesture at Fortune with his eyes when Fortune was leavin' a few days ago and Marcia walked out behind."

"Fortune get you in?"

"Not really. He told me who to go to. It's this newsstand near Grand

Central. All you had to do was say you was lookin' for a sales job and that was the way in."

I stood up and Twill did too. He picked up the pink bucket and we were on our way north.

"Maybe you should get in touch with this Fortune kid and point him over to Hush."

"A'ight," Twill said with a nod. "You know I was thinkin' that maybe we might need Hush on this one anyway."

"Why?" It had only been recently that I'd read Twill in on my friend's old profession.

"Jones don't let anybody share the throne," Twill said. "Cut off the head, you know."

"We're detectives, Twilliam, not contract killers."

"A'ight."

"So you think this Jones keeps his power by blackmail?"

"That's the only thing makes sense, I mean if you got pictures of some council member or mayor's aide havin' sex with a twelve-year-old girl, that's like gold."

"You know where these records might be?"

"No idea whatsoever."

27

long the way to the apartment I picked up some chives and ice for my fish from a greengrocer. Once home I rinsed the two flounder and put them in the refrigerator while Twill changed clothes. Fifteen minutes after we got home we were off again.

Neither of us recognized the Filipino nun at the front desk of Tivoli Rest Home. When we came up on her she was staring off into space. She had a round face and golden skin. I didn't know that woman from Eve, as I said, but I was willing to bet from that look in her eye that whatever it was she was thinking it had nothing to do with her Catholic vows.

"Katrina McGill," I said and she jerked back to awareness. The face of wonder was replaced by one of atonement and loss.

"Sixth floor," she said.

The only thing different about my wife's room was that Katrina was not in it. She hadn't been walking in the hall with Sister Agnes. Her bed was unmade so I thought that she might have gone to the toilet. Without discussing the mundane fact of her absence we decided to wait. I leaned against the windowsill and Twill arranged himself elegantly in the padded visitor's chair. He was now dressed in black trousers made from light wool, a black silk T-shirt, and a pearl-gray jacket with no lapels or buttons.

"At least she's walkin' now," Twill said after a minute or two. "That first six weeks I don't think she got outta bed on her own at all."

"You think she's doing better then?" I asked my son.

"Better than at first but she kinda stalled the last month or so. I try to get her to walk with me but when I give her my hand all she wants to do is hold it."

"I told her we could get a nurse at home but she wasn't interested."

"I think she wants to be the woman she was before all this," Twill surmised.

Looking at my son I thought, not for the first time, that he was something like a creature, a baby puma or panther, that I'd found in the wild and brought home. There he slowly took on the form of a human child but his nature was still feral and unfathomable. He had deep feelings for his mother but these emotions were not nostalgic or self-indulgent. She was his mother and I was his father but the world was vast and we, all of us, were just a small part of that immensity.

"Mr. McGill, Twill," someone said from the doorway.

In her fifties, broad-shouldered, and brown like cured mahogany, Sister Agnes stood there, a questioning look on her face.

"Sister," I said, propelling my bulk from the window. "Where's Katrina?"

"I thought you knew," she said, almost as if the words formed a question.

There are moments in life when the heart makes itself known to the man that lives with his feelings but rarely recognizes them. When Sister Agnes spoke those words I felt the emptiness of the room and a coldness went through me. I could taste the grief that had escaped my lips when talking to my father. At that moment I was beginning to mourn the loss of my wife.

"Didn't Sister Alona tell you?" Agnes asked.

"Tell me what?" I said in a tone usually reserved for lowlifes and gangsters I intended to hurt.

"That, that she was down at the corner at the Trattoria Lucia," the big woman stammered.

"What the hell is she doing down there?" My anger would not heel.

"She went there with your father."

"I thought your father was dead," Twill asked as we headed for the little restaurant.

I had never told the family that Clarence was probably alive. Why would I? I could hardly believe it myself.

"I just found him recently," I said. "He came by the apartment last night. I forgot about it because of the break-in and tryin' to find you."

"Is that what's wrong with you?"

"What do you mean?" I said, stopping there on the sidewalk.

"There's somethin' definitely wrong with you," my son averred.

"Wrong how?"

"Like you went crazy or sumpin' an' haven't made it all the way back yet."

Marella, I thought, or something Marella meant to me; something I had been missing for a long time; but whatever it was, that something didn't fit where it used to be.

"Let's go," I said.

Trattoria Lucia had a smallish dining room with a high ceiling that was deceptive because there were many hanging plants drooping down from overhead. Through the foliage I could see a table for four in the far corner. Seated around various plates of food was Dimitri, my only blood son; Tatyana, his Belarusian girlfriend recently delivered from the East European underworld; Katrina, wearing an alluring blue dress; and Clarence Tolstoy Bill Williams McGill. Katrina, most recently a depressed invalid, and Dimitri, who had always been a sour child, were both laughing.

"Trot!" my father called out. "Twill, come on over."

He spoke to a waiter who pulled up another table.

Twill went to join the family affair while I remained there at the entrance trying to get all the pieces of my life into some kind of semblance of order. I stood there for a full minute and was at work on the next revolution of seconds when Dimitri, whom we all called Bulldog, came over to me and put his hand on my elbow.

"It's okay, Dad," he said. "Everybody's fine."

Looking at my son was very much like peering into my own face.

He was almost a walking facsimile of me except for the fact that he was five inches taller and almost always brooding.

"Come on, Dad," he said. "Come sit with the family."

Twill took to Clarence like his wild feline totem; more by scent than logic.

After we were settled the party went back to the way it had been before we arrived. Clarence was telling jokes and Katrina was laughing at them. She had color in her cheeks and that look in her eye that always told me when she was falling in love.

After a while I got my equilibrium back and asked, "How did you get Katrina out of that bed?"

"He came in and told me who he vas," my wife answered. "That made me sit right up. Then he asked me vhen vas the next bus due in? I said there is no bus and he said ve better hurry then if ve want to get out of there in time for dinner. It vas so silly that I started laughing. I'm still laughing."

A waiter came up then to refill Katrina's wineglass, but my father waved him away. Katrina saw this exchange but said nothing. If I had tried to keep her from a drink we would have fought the rest of the night.

"And where'd you pick up Bulldog and Taty?" I asked, feeling oddly jealous of my father and family.

"Taty finally got me to come by," Dimitri said. "Twill told her that I might help Mom get up or something but when we got to the front desk the sister told us to come down here."

Dimitri was grinning while Katrina beamed, placing her palm on my father's forearm from time to time. Everyone was saying how happy they were that Clarence came out of the shadows and rejoined them. No one questioned his long absence except to ask where he'd been. My wife and sons were all happy just to see him. Only Tatyana and I seemed somewhat somber. She caught my eye at one moment there and we both smiled.

"I'm checking out of the sanatorium tomorrow," Katrina announced after devouring a plum tart. "Will you come get me, Tolstoy?"

"Me an' Trot'll be there with bells on."

What could I say? The only way to get Katrina on her feet again was for her to be enveloped in the euphoria of love. I wondered if any hospital had ever used love therapy to cure their depressives and other psychosomatic sufferers.

At about eight o'clock the party broke up. Tatyana and Dimitri trundled off to their new place.

They went maybe fifteen feet when Tatyana turned and came back, to me. She took my arm and leaned in close so that no one else could hear.

"Are you all right, Mr. McGill?"

"Sure I am, Tatyana. Why?"

"My father left me, my mother, and sister and never said a word. He left and I hated him." She was looking into me.

"What can I say, honey? You're right."

She kissed me and then went back to her boyfriend.

I watched them walking away, wondering at the complexities of the semisocial, partially civilized human heart.

Twill went off to find Fortune and remind the Jones gang that he was still with them. Clarence and I saw Katrina back to her room. She kissed us both good-bye but the caress lingered on my father.

"Tomorrow," she said, looking at him.

"That's a fine woman you got there, Trot," Clarence said on our walk back to the apartment.

"Not hardly," I replied.

"What do you mean by that?"

"She hasn't belonged to me in many a year."

28

After a month of a dedicated housekeeper's hard work the smell of old socks and twenty years of brooding had finally been cleaned away from Dimitri's room. My father, whom I would always and forevermore call Clarence, was asleep therein. He told me that he felt best sleeping in a different bed every night; that he felt safer moving around.

I should have been asleep too. My days had been strenuous and the drinking wasn't light. But there I was in my den/office wondering how it could be that I had discovered hidden feelings for my wife and once again lost her in just a few minutes' time?

I picked up the phone at four minutes shy of midnight and dialed a number. After four rings a recording of Aura Ullman's voice said, "You have reached me, so talk to me." I hung up before the beep.

I'd called Aura hoping that there might be love somewhere for me, too. But if I couldn't have love I had to dig deeper.

"Mr. McGill," she said after the Hotel Brown switchboard operator connected us. "What revelation do you have for me at this hour?"

Just the sound of her voice brought up a vibration like a growl in my chest. The creature making this sound in me was like a wild thing—both hunted and free.

"I want you to know that I'm not asking you for anything, but . . ." I said.

"But what?" There was a lot of satisfaction in those two words.

"I'd like to come over."

"I understand," she said with no underlying gratification. "Come along."

I walked there. The whole time I was thinking about how foolish it was to pursue a woman like that; a woman as dangerous as any killer I'd gone up against.

I was so wrapped up in these thoughts that I bumped into a pedestrian waiting for the light at Seventy-third and Broadway—a very large pedestrian male.

White, short-sleeved, and generously tattooed, the man made a sound like the one in my chest.

He said, "What the fuck's wrong with you, nigga?"

We live in a brave new world. Many white people in their thirties, and younger than that, take the derogatory slang from the music they listen to with no notion of insult based on race. I felt, however, that this particular individual had learned his slurs behind bars and under guard; at close quarters and in situations that were life and death on a daily basis.

I smiled broadly and held my upturned palms near shoulder level.

"Bring it on, my brother," I said. "Bring it on."

The tattooed man moved his left shoulder to put himself in an advantageous position for fighting. My smile deepened. He took me in with well-trained eyes, and the anger he carried around like a weapon suddenly faded. The light turned and he walked away at a pace he hoped I wouldn't try to match.

If there was anything that should have dissuaded me from going to the Hotel Brown it was that ex-con's reaction to me at that moment in time.

Marella and I didn't speak until after 4:00 that morning. With her eyes, teeth, and clawlike nails (both hand and foot) she dared me to do things to her that most women have no stomach for. And no matter how far I went she was ready for more. It wasn't fun and it certainly was not love but more like an operation to amputate a gangrenous limb or to excavate a diseased organ. We were doing each other for survival, not edification.

When it was over I wondered how far I'd have to go to get back to some version of civilization.

"I know a man in New Orleans named Gregor Vincent," she said as she was washing the sex off both of us with a warm hand towel.

"Yeah?"

"He thinks I'm a virgin."

"And?"

"His family owns half of South America and they do business in gold, not currency."

"Sounds like your kinda guy."

"We could make enough off him to take a five-year vacation and not even feel it."

"Why you need me?" I asked, turning the notion of a criminal on holiday around in my mind. "I mean you're the whole business on your own."

"It's good to have a strong man in the wings," she said. "And even people like us need somebody to talk to from time to time."

Despite my better nature, my desire to make up for my transgressions, I was tempted by this woman. She had touched a part of me that I hadn't even known existed.

"We could take a piece of the next score and set up a trust fund for your wife and kids," she offered.

"You don't really care about the money," I said, experiencing a sudden epiphany.

Marella smiled.

"Money's nice," she said. "It's necessary, too, but . . . But I like to feel alive, you know? Love and money are fine but they're only useful if they bring you to life."

"And do you love me?" I don't think I'd asked that question since my single-digit years.

"That's not really a possibility for people like us now is it, Lee?" she said.

She reached out and took my damp penis in her left hand. As it engorged, her smile broadened. Looking in her eyes I realized that I was ready to go with her, to leave my family and office, loved ones and enemies to fend for themselves.

She had me, so to speak, by the balls.

Her stare brought to bear a will that was bending me like she was my dick. I didn't resent her power any more than a bear resents the warmth of the sun waking him from blissful hibernation.

It was 5:00 a.m. and Marella was my escape hatch, my enlistment papers for the Foreign Legion.

It was 5:03 and the tune of the song "Seventh Son" played on my cell phone.

I reached for the phone while Marella clung to my erection.

"Twill?" I said on a hollow breath.

"Hey, Pop."

"What do you need?"

"From the sound of it maybe what you gettin'."

One of the reasons I loved Twill was that I couldn't hide much from him. With this thought I realized that I did have the potential for love. My erection waned and Marella released her hold on me.

"Where are you?" I asked my son.

"At the front of your hotel. That GPS shit work like magic."

"I'll be right down."

"Are you leaving me, Lee?" Marella asked as I was pulling my pants up.

"I got to get downstairs and see about my son."

"You know what I'm asking."

"When I was your age, Mar, I did everything you're doin' now. I stole and cheated and lied and worse. Meeting you makes me realize that I miss those wild days. I miss it. I got friends that miss it. But I know, and you should know, that one day one of us would have to stab the other in the back—have to. That's as much a fact as Gregor Vincent's gold."

There was a feral genius glowing in Marella's eyes. She nodded ever so slightly and then shook her head.

"A few nights like the one we just had might be worth a knife in the back," she speculated.

"Not if you see it comin'."

"Will I see you again?" she asked.

"I'll fix this thing with your DC ex," I said. "And I'll come spend the night again if you still want that."

She kissed me with a fierce passion and then kissed me harder.

29

will was parked in front of the hotel in my 1957 dark green Pontiac. I smiled at the young man and the car; both boy and machine were classic in their own way.

When I was putting on my seat belt Twill handed me a paper cup of black coffee.

"Thanks," I said. I took a big gulp of the bitter liquid, burning my tongue and groaning.

"What's wrong, Pops?"

"Burned my mouth."

"No, man," he said. "You still actin' kinda off."

I had brought Twill on as a trainee detective to keep him honest; but if the truth be told he, more often than not, performed that function for me.

"I feel like a kid when his testicles have just descended. Nothing's the same and somehow I know that it never will be again."

He turned over the engine, pulled away from the curb, and asked, "She that good?"

"You know you should respect your father."

"Cecil's?" he asked instead of taking the bait.

"Sure."

Down in a part of Chinatown that used to be Little Italy is a workman's coffee shop simply called Sicily. It opens every morning at four thirty and serves breakfast until just about twenty past eight. Over time the people that frequented the diner began calling it Cecil's.

The restaurant had a counter that sat nine, and six tables. Tomas and Donna were the owners, cooks, janitors, and dishwashers of the establishment. When they opened the place, sixty years earlier, they had been married but then Donna had an affair with a wannabe gangster named Michael. Tomas divorced Donna, who in turn married Mike, who was then gunned down by a real gangster.

Tomas and Donna still ran the breakfast joint. I only ever heard them talk about the work they were doing. Once, when he was nine, Dimitri asked me if Tomas and Donna were still in love.

"There are things in the world more important than love," I said to him.

Those words came back to me as Twill pulled up to the curb across the street from Cecil's Sicily.

We sat in a corner booth that I liked. I ordered oatmeal because my stomach was a little raw from too much booze and agitation. My son had half a grapefruit and a rasher of bacon. Old Italians, Chinese laborers of various ages, and a few knowledgeable partygoers at the end of their night were there eating and talking in low tones.

"Fortune's gone missing," Twill said after Donna took our order. "I went to his room over on Avenue D. Somebody had broken down the door."

"Any blood?" I asked.

Twill shook his head.

"So maybe the ones busted in missed him, too," I suggested.

"That's like I see it. But you know he ain't gonna make it long if Jones has his people after his ass."

"It's a big city," I offered. "Fortune might be the kind who knows how to hide."

Donna brought our fruit, cereal, and meat on a cork-lined cherry-wood platter.

"Don't see you in a long time, LT," she said.

"Not enough trouble around here anymore," I said in way of explanation.

"Used to be your old man and his brother would come here when they was just kids," Donna said to Twill, one bony fist on her skinny hip. "They'd eat honey cakes and ham and then help Tomas empty the garbage."

"How old was he?" Twill asked, though he'd heard the story a dozen times.

"LT was twelve-thirteen and Nicky was two years less than that. They come and listen to the old gangsters after a night of partying or maybe a job. That's where both boys learned all their bad habits."

"We got customers," Tomas shouted. His back was turned and he was leaning over the grill.

Donna sucked a tooth and moved on.

"Jones got a LoJack on all his people," Twill said.

"What?"

"It's this tube that they put under the skin, usually behind the knee. He got this one nurse cut you open, shove it in, and then sew up the wound with one stitch. I got one the first day. Fortune told me that Jones got this computer that locates people good as your GPS."

"Damn."

"You better believe it."

"So he could look and see that you're here right now?"

"Naw."

"Why not?"

"Bug."

Tiny "Bug" Bateman had lived and worked for a decade in a cellar under the apartment building he still owns in the West Village. But after he started dating Zephyra he abandoned that property and bought a brownstone on East Twenty-ninth. His computers and other electronics occupied the upper floors and the basement of his new place, but at least now he spent most of his time aboveground.

His paranoia is still in evidence however: the windows are bulletproof and there are high-yield explosives knitted into every wall. After many years of therapy Bug had figured out that living under a perceived state of siege was why he had ballooned up to three hundred eighty-five pounds.

"But I'd rather exercise four hours a day and eat protein powder than give up my guns and bombs," he told me the day after he stopped going to his analyst.

Twill pulled my Pontiac into Bug's attached parking garage.

Bug opened the front door to admit us at a few minutes past 7:00 a.m. He was wearing a plush burgundy robe and bright yellow slippers. He usually slept late but I figured that he'd want to see us as much as we wanted him.

The caramel-colored young man was a shade under six feet with the physical conditioning of a young heavyweight. He'd lost so much weight that even his face had changed shape.

"I got breakfast in the kitchen," he said.

"We already hit Cecil's," Twill told him.

Bug's living room had been designed by Zephyra. The pine floor had been replaced by bamboo and the furniture was original eighteenth-century French Provincial. I think Z just liked being able to spend two hundred thousand on settees, chairs, and tables.

"We need to find somebody in Jones's system," Twill said when we were seated.

"You told LT about the location devices?" Bug asked.

"The question is," I said, "why didn't *you* tell me?"

"Twill's a man," Bug said gravely.

I wanted to argue about blood, a father's duty, and the chain of command but there were more important things to concentrate on. Anyway Bug left the room.

He came back in a few minutes with an oversized laptop under his arm. He summoned us to an ornate table set in the bay windows. We pulled chairs next to him while he unfolded and switched on the computer. He spent a few minutes answering security questions and setting us up among the dozens of projects, operating systems, and external systems that his machines straddled.

Finally he got to a screen where each of the pages had an electronic watermark—JONESDOWN.

"Explain to me how this system works," I said.

"It's pretty rudimentary," Bug began, leaning forward hungrily. "But really efficient. The units are always on, always transmitting to a satellite system that a trucking transport company uses."

"How did he get wired into that?" I asked.

"From what Twill tells me he probably had something on one of the controllers, maybe even the CEO . . . Anyway, I was able to isolate the pulse and then piggyback into the system. I downloaded the virtual addresses of eight hundred ninety-six units implanted in the people he keeps track of."

"Eight ninety-six?" Twill and I both said.

"Yeah. It's probably more than that but that's the people active today. I just mapped it out last night after you called," Bug said to Twill. "I can track or derail any monitoring of the eight ninety-six. Right now I have Twill sleeping in an apartment building up in Washington Heights."

"What about Fortune?" Twill asked.

"Wait a minute," I interrupted. "These devices identify themselves?"

"No," Bug answered. "They just have four-byte hexadecimal addresses, but the Jones system associates those addresses to files. I'm tied in there so it's easy to put a name to a pulse. The only problem is that the devices can't be monitored underground. The last time I have a reading on your friend is him down around Wall Street."

"Shit," Twill said. "How long ago?"

"Six hours."

"And he hasn't showed up since then?"

Slowly Bug wagged his head from side to side. For a moment I remembered him as a fat man gazing through semiopaque rainbow-colored glasses at a dozen monitors hanging from a ceiling in a hole in the ground.

"I know where he is," Twill said to me. "Problem is he been down there with half the girls on Jones's crew. It's this subbasement room in a construction project that's been stalled. Fortune snipped off all the padlocks and replaced them with his own."

"So he thinks he's safe?" I asked.

"Prob'ly so."

"We should be going," I said. Then to Bug, "Do you mind if we leave our car in your garage for a bit?"

"Sure you can."

"And turn off Fortune's tracker," Twill said.

"You got it."

At the door Twill said that he had to retrieve something from the car. As soon as he was down the front stairs Bug put a hand on my shoulder.

"I wanted to ask you something," he said.

"About Zephyra?"

"How'd you know?"

"Because you only ever want advice on exercise or her."

"I hear she went away with some guy, some prince, to South Africa." There was a vein standing out in the middle of Bug's forehead. It throbbed, resembling an earthworm undulating just under the surface of wet sand.

"How many women you been with in the last three months?" I asked the math genius.

"She said she wanted an open relationship," he protested.

"That don't mean she wants you to rub her nose in it."

"What does she expect me to do? I asked her to marry me. She said no."

"In my line of work, David," I said, uttering his rarely used given name, "I find that what people say and what they mean are often quite different entities."

"What's that supposed to mean?"

Twill waved at me from the curb.

"You're a smart guy," I said. "Work it out."

30

The construction site was on Rector Street not far from Trinity Place. It was a half-block lot surrounded by a high pine-board wall. On one side there was a slender corridor that separated the site from the brown brick wall of its neighbor. Twill led me down there about thirty feet or so until we came to a jury-rigged door that had been secured by a padlock threaded through the raised eyes of two metal slats. I say "had been" because the slats had been ripped free and the door hung open.

"I thought you said he had a key," I said.

"He does."

I took out my .38 and Twill pushed the door open.

We entered a long pine passageway that ended at another door with the lock ripped off. The inner sanctum of the building was a broad concrete floor with the seventeen-story metal frame of the would-be office building hovering above us like the reconstructed bones of some long-extinct dinosaur.

There was a chill in the air that I hadn't felt outside.

"This way," Twill whispered.

On the southeast side of the site stood a box tent made of heavy brown canvas. Its door was just a slit that flapped around a bit.

"There a guard in there?" I asked my son.

"No. I mean if there was somebody he would have found out about the locks, right?"

I was about to say that maybe a guard had come and ripped off the locks but just then five men came through the slit in the canvas tent, disproving my unspoken speculation.

Five men, all of them under the age of twenty-five. Four were what must have passed for muscle in Jones's army, and one, bleeding from the mouth and nearly unconscious, was being held up by the arms between the two largest volunteer soldiers.

We were, all seven of us, surprised.

There was no more than a few feet between us.

"Stop right there," I said, expecting my words to become their actions because of the gun in my hand—but I was wrong.

The men holding the prisoner dropped him and lunged at me, completely ignoring the potential for death. There was a split second for me to choose—death or bruises.

My greatest weakness is that I'm not afraid of a fight and I am always confident that I will emerge the victor. The guy on the left was a light brown hue, like some chicken eggs. He reached me first. Flipping on the safety with my thumb, I slammed him in the temple and then moved to the far side of his falling body to block his compatriot while I shoved the pistol in my right-front pants pocket.

My second challenger cut a second off the time it took to reach me by leaping over his fallen comrade; too bad that this opened him up to a straight left to the jaw. He fell also.

I heard a scream of agony and turned to see that Twill had buried a medium-sized hunting knife into one of his opponents' left foot. The young man looked to be a mixture of Asian and Polynesian genes. He fell on his butt grabbing at the haft of the knife. Before I could help Twill with his other challenger I felt a blow to my right cheekbone.

The light brown guy I had felled with my gun was up again like some tireless zombie in a B movie. He threw another punch that I was able to avoid. I hit him six times to the body and he went down. But it was like a tag-team match because his partner, who was white, jumped at me again. I blocked his blows and hit him with my best.

He went down as his partner staggered to his feet.

"Stay down," I told him.

He threw himself at me but I sidestepped, allowing him to crash into a steel girder.

Twill was on the move. The guy left standing was black and wiry but he wasn't trained. Twill had been working out in Gordo's Gym beside me from the age of eight. He knew how to bob and weave. He knew how to hit, too.

Looking back at my enemies I saw that the light brown guy was unconscious. He was beefy and had thrown his full weight at me. When flesh and bone hits tempered steel there's no instant recovery.

The white member of the Rainbow Coalition of Street Fighters was still coming though. I sidestepped once and he failed to grab me. I sidestepped again and the frustration began to show in his face. Now I was looking at my opponent and at Twill and his man beyond. The Far Eastern soldier was still trying to staunch the bleeding from his foot. He'd taken off his shoe and sock and was holding the injured appendage with both hands like a yogi attempting some advanced blood-asana.

I took a deep breath and for the first time the white attacker stopped, looking for a way past my fists. That was okay by me, I could use the breather. But then Twill's guy got in a lucky punch, hitting Twill in the gut, which lowered him to one knee. The black attacker was closing in and my common sense diminished with each inch. But then the man who was being dragged from the tent leapt on the attacker's back and Twill picked up a chunk of brick and hit the guy multiple times to the rib cage.

I smiled broadly at the outcome, and this confused my enemy. He turned to see if something was coming up behind him and I took the opportunity to land a haymaker on the side of his jaw. The jaw was definitely broken and the man was surely out.

I was breathing hard and so was my son. Two of the four we fought were unconscious and the other two couldn't get to their feet. Twill was supporting the prisoner and smiling at me.

"You okay?" I asked my son.

"Just fine, Pop."

I took a handkerchief from my inside jacket pocket and handed it to the kid we'd saved. He pressed the cloth to his mouth, pulled it away to see his blood, and then pressed his mouth again.

"Fortune?" I asked.

He nodded.

"We better get out of here," Twill said.

The three of us walked and staggered through rush-hour foot traffic across to the E train station. Fortune had cleaned up his face pretty much and the bleeding had stopped. Like his four assailants he wore blue jeans, knockoff cross-trainers, and a black T-shirt. He was what people descended from the colonized world called white, and quite beautiful: full lips, blue eyes, and tawny hair that formed into ringlets. He might have been a minor god from a Mediterranean pantheon come to Earth to see what the big deal was about love and death.

"Why didn't they kill you, man?" Twill asked as we waited by the southmost stairwell for a train to come.

"I don't know," the slightly woozy godling replied.

"Why would they?" I asked.

"When Jones sends bodies after you he expects bodies in return," Fortune said, mouthing a homily probably repeated a dozen times a day by the Jones acolytes. "When they busted in on me I expected 'em to cut my throat."

The train came and we got into a car that had only a few straphangers headed uptown at that time of morning.

I appreciated the sharp pain in my cheekbone. It was like a Zen bell ringing in the darkness of deep meditation. This clarion note obliterated the passion unleashed by Marella, leaving my mind open and free.

"Those boys are gonna report to Jones," I said.

"Yeah," Twill agreed.

"Maybe we can leave Fortune off here at Hush's place."

"What about me?" Twill asked.

"No," I said. "I want you somewhere else."

"Why?"

"For easy access." I didn't want Twill around Hush too much or for very long. Both my friend and son were psychopaths and sociopaths. Together they might create something that I couldn't protect Twill from.

"Who's Hush?" Fortune asked.

31

We called Hush while walking from the West Fourth Street station. He was waiting for us at the door when we got there.

"Come on in," the killer said, ushering us into the posh entrance hall of his old-time Greenwich Village mansion.

Waiting for us in the octagonal room was Tamara, Hush's wife. She was a black woman with a plain face but with spirit so powerful that it seemed to add a dimension to her visage; next to her stood Liza Downburton wearing a pale blue kimono that she must have borrowed from the lady of the house.

"Fortune," Liza cried, and she ran to the pretty young man, caressing him, kissing his face. "What happened to you?"

I had never seen the young burglar except with the bulges and bruises on his face, so he looked normal to me.

"He sent the four after me."

"And you fought them?"

"More like they took turns fightin' my head. Twill and his father come to save me."

"The two-man cavalry," Hush said softly.

"Come on in the living room," Tamara said. She'd put a hand on my forearm because she had a soft spot for me since I'd saved her life and her son's.

"Where's Thackery?" I asked as we moved from the red tiling of entrance hall to the oak floor of the living room.

"At the French school," Hush and Tamara said together.

There were eight bright yellow padded chairs set in an oval around a pink marble table of the same shape. Everyone but Tamara took a seat. Liza pushed her chair closer to Fortune so that they could hold hands.

"I'll go get us some ice tea and biscuits," Tamara said.

"Don't put ice in Fortune's," Liza said. "He's got sensitive teeth."

The two women glanced at each other and I saw a connection.

Hush saw it too. He didn't look bothered, but anyone knowing Hush didn't want his attention on them for any reason.

"What happened?" Liza asked again.

Twill gave the explanations with a word or two interjected here and there by Fortune.

For his part Fortune had gone to ground under the construction site. The entrance was hidden by the brown canvas tent.

"I didn't wanna dig out the transmitter till I knew for sure that they were serious," the young burglar said. "You know it's a death sentence to do that."

"Didn't you realize that people in Jones's army knew where you were?" I asked.

"Yeah," he said, "but nobody ever told about it before. You know Jones didn't want us gettin' high or hookin' up away from the places he controlled. We liked to keep places like that a secret."

"But didn't you know he was after you?" Liza asked.

"Yeah but I just thought it might'a just been for a beat-down like. I didn't know he wanted to kill me."

"But he didn't kill you," Twill observed. "Why not?"

This question raised Hush's attention.

Tamara returned with a silver tray holding our tea and cookies.

"I don't know," the orphan named Fortune said. "I mean that's what the four usually do."

"What do you mean—the four?" Hush asked.

Fortune's first response was a worried expression. He avoided Hush's stare and did not speak.

"It's okay, Fortune," Twill said. "He already sent 'em after you. As far as Jones is concerned you're already dead."

"I'm not supposed to say," Fortune said to Hush. "Jones got these rough dudes, four of 'em, and their job is to handle problems. If they don't get the job done then he sends Marcia and Deck, and sometimes this dude named Thune. They got guns."

"And they kill children?" Hush asked.

"If they do sumpin' bad enough."

"You're bleeding," Liza said.

There was a trickle of blood coming from Fortune's mouth. He must have bit the cut worrying about telling strangers Jones's secrets.

"Come on," Tamara said, "let's go clean you up."

She and Liza helped Fortune up from his yellow chair and guided him out. I looked at the fabric but didn't see any specks of blood.

"He's got a concussion all right," Hush said. "I'll get a doctor I know to come look at him."

"Thanks," Twill said.

"You sure know how to get in trouble, young man," Hush told my son.

"I get it from my pops."

"You mind if we leave the lovebirds here a few days?" I asked.

"T loves Liza," Hush allowed. "So I'm sure she'll be happy. The kid looks street but he'll be okay too. This Jones sounds like a mother-fucker."

Twill nodded and I said, "Yeah."

"Where to now?" Twill asked when we were on the street again.

"Let's walk a ways," I suggested.

We headed north on Fifth Avenue, each of us a little stiff from the construction site rumble.

"Thanks a lot, Pops," Twill said as we were crossing Sixteenth Street. "You know I should'a been more careful before jumpin' into this shit."

"The one thing you learn in the ring," I said. "If you climb through them ropes trouble will find you."

"Yeah. Ole Jones will have two hundred people on the street lookin' for me."

"And you will be at Uncle Gordo's helping him and Sophie get ready for their wedding."

"Who's Sophie? I thought he was marrying Elsa?"

"Another of his ring lessons," I said. "Sometimes you got to change it up."

"What about Mardi and her sister?" my son asked, accepting change faster than I was ever able to.

"I gave her a few days off. You think Fortune told anybody where Liza found you?"

"Never think," Twill said, repeating my words to him. *A detective never thinks, he knows.*

"Give her a call," I said. "Gordo got eight bedrooms in that rabbit warren on the top floor."

An hour later my son and I were sitting at the cramped dinette table off of Gordo's kitchen, on the fifteenth floor of the building he owned. With us was Sophie—a short and slight woman with big eyes, a patient demeanor, and skin the color of some dark pears. Iran Shelfly was there. He'd lost his shot at contention in Philly and had the black eye to prove it. Gordo was leaning back in his chair. He was a veteran of the Human Wars, having survived everything from Jim Crow to Willie Pep to cancer.

"Damn, LT," he was saying, "you look worse than Eye-ran here and he went up against a top-twenty middleweight."

There was a bump on top of my head and a swelling where I got sucker punched on the cheek. My eyes were probably bloodshot from too much liquor, too much sex, and very little rest.

"It's been a good week," I said.

Gordo chuckled.

"It's good to see you again, Sophie," I said. "Must be thirty years."

"I'm surprised you're still alive, Leonid."

Remembering that Sophie was an incurable truth teller, I said to Gordo, "If you guys take Twill, Mardi, and her sister for the next few days it will be good for all concerned."

"And how do you see that?" Gordo argued. He liked sparring in and out of the ring.

"Mardi is the most organized woman I've ever met," Twill said. "If you need a sharp eye planning this wedding then you should probably pay her to come."

"Twill has spoken," Gordo intoned.

"Iran, I need you to keep watch on them," I interjected. "They shouldn't be down in the gym at all until after it's closed, and the doors need to stay locked."

"You got it, LT."

Iran loved me because I'm the one that got him straight after he got out of prison—of course he didn't know that I had framed him to get the conviction in the first place.

"As long as we're all here," Sophie said to Gordo, "you should tell them."

"What?" I asked.

"I had a will drawn up leaving everything to Sophie. But she said she didn't like that, that she wasn't marryin' me to become my heir. So we compromised that everything can be hers but that you are the executor. You dole out the cash and cover the bills for the first seven years."

"And what if somebody shoots me in the back?" I thought this was a valid question.

Gordo did too because he said, "If you aren't able then the job goes to Twill."

"Me?" Twill said.

"Yeah, man," Gordo said. "You the best of all of us."

Twill stared at the unsung master trainer a moment and then nodded.

"Okay, man," he said. "We all know you gonna live to two hundred anyways."

I hung around for an hour or so until a limo from Hush's fleet delivered Mardi and her sister Marlene to Gordo's. After that, Gordo walked me down the fourteen flights to the first floor.

"Must be some serious trouble you got everybody hidin'," the man I considered my true father said.

"Yeah, yeah. But now everybody's in place and I can take care of other business."

"What other business?"

"I got to see a woman in Boston about a killing or two in New York."

32

I got home in the early evening. I was looking forward to the solitude of an empty apartment for the first time in many weeks. It had been a rough few days even if I had made some progress. I still had the business of my dead client, Hiram Stent, to settle up. And there was Hector Laritas to avenge.

"Leonid?" she said as I was making my way toward the dining room.

The voice came from behind, from the door of the little front TV room that we rarely used.

"Katrina."

She was wearing an off-white silk blouse and a black woolen skirt that came down to her knees—no shoes.

"We're in here," she said.

We.

"Come join us," she said, sober and happy.

My father was sitting in the blue stuffed chair and Katrina returned to her perch on the maroon sofa. It was a tiny room that the kids used to watch TV when they were small. The last time Katrina and I were in there we had passionate sex for the first time in years. That was a few days before she tried to take her life.

"Trot," my father said.

"Clarence."

"Your father has been telling me all about the Revolution," Katrina murmured. She looked much younger than she had in the sanatorium, ten years younger than her actual age. She wore no makeup. Rather the youthfulness came from an inner light.

On the small, child-scarred maple coffee table was a hardback book with no jacket and a bottle of our good port with only one glass.

"What you readin'?" I asked no one in particular.

"First volume of the *Prison Notebooks* by Antonio Gramsci," my father said.

"Bill said that he was the greatest thinker in the socialist movement," Katrina told me. "He was arrested by Italian fascists and died in prison."

I knew Gramsci's story. My father had drilled the whole socialist pantheon into my brain by the age of eleven. But what interested me was that he wanted my wife to call him Bill; the third name he'd taken on looking for the man he wanted to be.

I sat on the opposite end of the sofa from my wife. She pulled her legs up under her, shifting her body so that half her back was toward me, giving her full attention to my father.

"How's that boy of yours?" Clarence asked.

"Safe and sound."

"Twill seemed tense at our dinner," Katrina said.

"You came home today," I replied.

"Bill got me just as he promised."

I had spent so many years hating my father that his charisma was lost on me. I really didn't see his power except through Katrina's eyes. But there I saw what brought her home. If Katrina survived it was bound to be because she fell in love again. That was her nature.

I looked from one to the other of the people who were supposed to define the love of my life and saw only distraction and reckless folly.

"I got to get to bed," I said.

I stood up expecting to spend the rest of the night alone.

"I'll come with you," my wife said.

She also stood.

"Good night, Bill," she bade to my father.

"'Night, Clarence," I added.

I was naked under the blankets with Katrina pushed up against my side wearing a gown that was more like an extra-long red silk T-shirt.

"What's wrong, darling?" she asked. I could feel her warm breath on my ear.

"Lots."

"Is it a job?"

"Twill got himself in a mess I can't even begin to work out and then there's these two dead men, a missing girl, and a marital job I got to work with. But that's just a week's work."

"So it's something else?" She traced the swelling on my cheek with a single finger.

"It was like magic you gettin' up out the bed and coming home."

"Your father made me laugh," she explained.

"Are you better then?" I asked. "Because you laughed?"

She laid a hand on my chest and after a minute or so said, "You have a strong heart."

There was no answer to her declaration and so I gave none.

"I have never been so strong as you," she continued. "I have always looked for someone or something to, to save me. I wanted money and love and something magical and you were always holding everything up. I could have other men's children and you loved them. I could go away and you always took me back. Somewhere in all of that I got old and lost myself and couldn't think of any way out but to die . . ."

She talked and talked about the ways she failed and my place in her world. At some point the language stopped having specific meaning. I just listened to her tones of love and loss, grief and understanding. There was something wonderful in the sound of her words and I might have wanted to make love to her if I wasn't dead tired.

In the morning neither of us had budged. Katrina's hand was still on my chest. She was asleep with a smile on her face. I could feel the heavy beat of my heart under the light touch of her fingers and palm. I wondered if she and my father would become lovers; if I would care at all or kill them both.

But that crossing was many miles ahead; beyond Boston and Washington, DC.

I removed Katrina's hand gently and got out of the bed silently like a fat serpent uncoiling from a warm den.

I slept again in the quiet car of the Acela train going from Penn Station in New York to South Station, Boston.

Just south of Beacon Hill on Tremont Street across from the public garden was a four-story brick home that I knew from the phone book was the nerve center of the Evangeline Sidney-Gray Foundation and corporation.

I was wearing one of my four identical blue suits and black shoes that shone dully; standing in front of a doorway that had a door with no knob. At seventeen minutes shy of eleven in the morning, with at least a dozen hours of sleep behind me, I looked for a button but there was none. I glanced from side to side for another entrance; all I saw was wall. I chuckled to myself speculating that I'd taken a train to the future where the citizens were hermetically sealed into homes that were self-sufficient and unassailable.

"May I help you?" a man's voice asked through some kind of ampli-fied medium.

"Ms. Evangeline Sidney-Gray," I said to the knobless door.

"And you are?"

"Leonid Trotter McGill of New York City."

"And your business is?"

". . . with Ms. Evangeline Sidney-Gray," I said.

"Do you have an appointment?"

"With destiny and your mistress."

"I'm sorry but I have no record of that meeting." A bodiless voice with a reciprocal sense of humor.

"I'm here representing Hiram Stent," I said boldly.

"Hold on."

The voice went away or at least stopped communicating and I turned my back on the door. It was a lovely, chilly morning in Bos-ton. There were joggers in the park along with nannies pushing baby-buggies, businessmen and -women striding purposefully among the hoi polloi, and various vagrants looking for anything that might afford them some relief.

A police cruiser slowed down as it drove past. Both cops were looking at me with curious, unfriendly eyes.

"We have no record of any Hiram Stent having business here," a new voice said.

I turned away from the cops and answered, "But Mr. Stent was employed by a law firm representing Dame Gray's holding company."

"What firm is that?"

"Briscoe/Thyme."

"I've never heard of that firm."

"It is a subsidiary of a London holding company that she in turn holds."

I quite liked talking to a neutered door. It was a unique experience.

Looking to my right I saw that the police cruiser had parked up the block and that its uniforms were walking my way.

"You might tell your boss that Briscoe/Thyme engaged Hiram Stent to locate Celia Landis and Coco Lombardi, two women, one soul, and a whole lotta grief for us all."

"Hold on."

The policemen reached the foot of the stairs I was standing on. They were both white men but, even in Boston, this didn't necessarily have to be the case. They were tall but I was standing on the topmost stair in front of the impossible door, so I didn't feel like retaliating.

"Excuse me, sir," the policeman on the right said. He was hatless and fair.

"Yes, Officer?"

"What's your business here?"

His partner, who was of equal height but had darker *white* skin, frowned and put his hand on the butt of his service revolver.

"With Ms. Evangeline Sidney-Gray," I said jauntily.

"Do you have an appointment?"

"Do I need one?"

"She is a very important woman."

"This is America, Officer, all citizens are of equal importance here."

"Come down here."

"Please?"

"What did you say?"

"I was wondering if you were making a request or giving me an order," I said. That strong heart that Katrina liked so much was about to get me in trouble—again.

"I told you to come down here."

"Mr. McGill?" a voice said.

Looking around I saw that the door opened like a regular door. I was sure that it was a slider but it had swung inward just like any door with a knob.

The man standing there wore a blue suit of a different species from my own. It was darker and had some kind of highlights, was cut from a cloth that made mine seem like peasant's wear.

"Yes?" I said to the superior being.

"Ms. Gray will see you."

"These young men have asked me to go with them," I countered.

"That'll be all right, Officers," the well-dressed, cocoa-colored man said.

I gave an inquiring look to the constabulary. They frowned at me and then shoved off.

33

The home behind the brick facade must have been an impressive Victorian at one time. The entrance hall was large, twenty-four feet deep and twenty-four yards wide, with a desk and secretary in each corner. Maybe eight yards from the wall on the left was a larger desk that was untenanted.

"Have a seat, Mr. McGill," the black man in the better blue suit offered. He gestured at a box-shaped oak chair that had arms and a maroon pillow in the seat. This furniture was set before the larger, empty desk.

I did sit. From there I could appreciate the various office workers typing, talking on headset phones, and tracking unknown scenarios across broad computer screens.

"How may I help you?" my host asked. He lowered into a chair behind the formidable oak desk that was obviously the seat of his domain in the foyer of the Great Woman.

"Not at all," I said, looking anywhere but at him.

"But you said you were here on the behalf of Hiram Stink."

"Stent," I corrected.

"So what can I do?"

"Either bring me to Ms. Evangeline Sidney-Gray or bring her here to me."

The master of the reception area had a round head and long fingers. My head was more angular and my fingers could have been roughly rolled Cuban cigars.

"One does not just meet Ms. Gray or bring her anywhere," the man said.

I noticed that the hubbub of the office area had slowed.

"What's your name?" I asked.

"Mr. Richards."

"Like in the Fantastic Four?"

"Excuse me?"

"You know, Reed Richards of the Fantastic Four," I said as if I were talking Shakespeare to a cretin. "He married the Invisible Girl. She had a dalliance with the Sub-Mariner but finally came to her senses and married Mr. Fantastic."

"My name is Henry Lawrence Richards."

"Well, I tell you what, Reed. You call Ms. Gray and ask her if she's willing to break protocol and meet some man off the street."

Two big men walked up to the edge of a double-wide doorway opposite the knobless entry. Their dark suits were not as fine as Mr. Fantastic's but still much better cuts than my poor ensemble. They were watched by the three women and one man stationed at the corner desks. The big men were looking at me but they refrained from actually entering the room.

"You will be talking to me," the comic book hero said, "or you will be leaving."

I luxuriated in the roomful of threats. My whole life had been spent in the company of enemies. If I listened to my father the whole world was my enemy; at least that's what he used to say.

"A man named Hiram Stent," I began, "approached me to locate a woman named Celia Landis. Ms. Landis it seems was the heir to a great fortune and she was Hiram's distant cousin, though, before speaking to the representative of the lawyers from Briscoe/Thyme, he had not been aware of the relationship. He offered to pay me out of his finder's fee but he wouldn't obtain said fee unless he found Celia. I turned Hiram down and then someone broke into my office . . . Oh, yes, I'm a private detective. Anyway, someone broke into my office, knocked a hole in my wall, and murdered a young man who, though not legally married, had a significant other and three children. Hiram Stent was then slaughtered by persons unknown and a fellow named Josh Farth came to me and asked if I would find a woman named Coco Lombardi who fit the description of Celia to a tee."

Staring at me with great concentration, Mr. Fantastic then raised both his palms and his eyebrows, asking, *So what?*

The big men took this as a sign to take three steps into the room.

"Briscoe/Thyme works solely for Ms. Gray. That means that she is the one who started the ball rolling; a big scary ball that has killed two men and which is headed for a young woman. I considered taking what information I have to the police but, as the policemen outside your door told me: Ms. Evangeline Sidney-Gray is an important woman. So I figured I should ask her what it is I should be doing. Now if Mr. Fantastic and two Things wish for me to depart, I'm willing to call the cops. Cops like to hear names associated with murders. They like to find missing persons and to press charges."

The muscle had flanked the back of my box chair by then. They were ready to pluck me up and chuck me out the door.

"Send him up," a dignified, if a bit wavering, woman's voice commanded.

The black man in the blue suit swallowed hard and then nodded at the two men standing behind my chair.

"Stand up," the one on my left ordered.

I pondered the command for twenty seconds and then rose. I turned to face the men and realized how much like an oversized boxing ring that entrance-hall-turned-office was. The suited muscle on my left wore dark gray. The one on the right was clad in burnt umber. The men were white, burly, and not unacquainted with violence and its uses. This combined knowledge brought a smile to my lips.

The brown-suited man put a hand around my right biceps. It was a big hand but when I tightened that muscle he realized that his fingers couldn't even encircle half of the circumference.

"Let me go or we gonna rumble," I said. "Right here, right now, win or lose, the three of us will fight."

It was, most probably, me talking about dead Hector and the family he left behind that brought out the desire to hurt someone.

The man released me but now I posed another problem. If I was this violent what would their mistress say if they brought me in front of her? Maybe I'd start throwing punches in her den.

"Bring him up here now," the woman's voice ordered, punctuating each word.

"Right this way," Gray Man said.

Beyond the entrance hall there was a room that could only be called the Staircase Room. On both sides and in front of me were stairways that seemed to be leading to completely different areas. I wondered if this structure was once three different buildings that had been cobbled together by an idle rich mind that had nothing better to do.

We headed up the curving, carpeted stairs on the left. I took the steps two at a time to keep my guards on their toes. On the fourth landing I was faced with a humongous library that had no doors or even a doorway. The entire floor was a room, thirty feet high and as wide and deep as the building it capped. The far wall was a window that looked down on the park and beyond. In front of that window was a big desk that was blond and not wood.

Behind the desk rose a tall and elegant woman wearing a cranberry-colored blouse and khaki riding pants. As I approached the woman I began to see subtler details. She was lean, gray-eyed, with the mostly erect posture of an arthritic ballet dancer. At one time she could probably have crossed that room in four or five leaps.

There was a spiteful sneer on her lips. Maybe she loathed anything that rose from the lower level to her aerie.

"Mr. McGill," the brown suit said to the woman.

"Leave us," was Evangeline Sidney-Gray's reply.

"But, ma'am . . ." Gray Man protested.

"Leave us."

And they did.

"Bones?" I asked when the help was gone.

"What?" she asked, insulted that I spoke without being spoken to.

"This desk," I said. "It's made out of bones. Done well, too. Tooled so that they fit together almost like real wood."

I had never seen a sneer morph so seamlessly into a smile before. Her moods could switch from superior to vile to magnanimous in moments. I couldn't think of a more dangerous personality.

I sat in the chair before her desk. It was cobbled from bone also.

The mistress of the mansions lowered into the chair behind her saying, "When I was a child my father told me that they were the bones of his enemies. Later I found out that it was even worse, that he slaughtered three bull elephants to get the right ivory and bone matter for his desk and your chair."

"That's worse than people's bones?"

"Elephants are innocent."

I was speechless mainly because I believed that she believed what she was saying.

"Why are you here, Mr. McGill?"

"I assume that you heard what I was saying to your man Richards," I said.

"I did."

"Good. I hate repeating myself. The man murdered in my office might not have been innocent but I liked him. He was just doin' his job and people, probably working for you, cut his life short."

"I have never been the cause of a murder, Mr. McGill. I mean, I pay my taxes and the president uses it to kill people but that's as far as it goes. If, as you say, people working for me committed such a crime I should want them to be prosecuted."

"Is that all you have to say to me?" I asked. I could be haughty too.

"What else can I say?"

"What about the murder of Hiram Stent?"

"I've never heard of that individual."

"And Josh Farth?"

Ms. Sidney-Gray didn't respond immediately. Her gaze honed down on me and there was something almost human in her eyes.

"You're threatening to go to the police?" she asked.

"It's not a threat but a duty, ma'am."

"If it is your duty then why haven't you already gone to them?"

"There are multiple responsibilities in most men's lives," I said.

"Women's lives too. Hiram Stent came to me, I turned him away, and he died. I feel responsible for that. Hector Laritas was trying to protect my property and he died. The police don't care about the women and children that either man left to fend for themselves, but I do. I was abandoned as a child and so I'm here to give you a chance to do what's right."

What might pass for a knowing smile crossed the lady's lips.

"What do you want?"

"Tell me why you're after Celia Landis and give up the man who killed the people I represent."

"You represent the dead?"

"I could just leave and let the NYPD take charge. I know a cop in Manhattan who's not afraid of any sum of money or persons that bleed blue."

"Is that a threat?"

"The cop is the threat," I said. "I am merely the conduit."

Evangeline Sidney-Gray took in a deep breath through her long, distinguished nose. She moved her head in birdlike fashion, taking me in from a series of slightly different points, like snapshots.

Finally she said, "There's a library in Cambridge, Mass., called the Enclave. It's a private institution that gathers collections of old books, documents, and letters. It is a very old organization funded by some of the wealthiest people in the world. Mostly people bequeath their libraries to the Enclave, but now and then they purchase a collection. A few years ago I donated a selection of my great-grandfather's cache of forty-two-line Gutenberg Bibles. It turns out that, quite by mistake, mixed in with that lot was a thirteenth-century handwritten version of Herodotus's *Histories*. It was never my intention to donate that book. It was my father's favorite manuscript. It was turned over by mistake. I can prove this by my copy of the bequeathing letter to the Enclave.

"This Celia Landis worked for the Enclave and then left. When she departed, my great-grandfather's manuscript disappeared. I want it back."

"And are you sure this Celia Landis was the one who stole the book?" I asked. "It might have just been misplaced."

"She sent me an electronic communication demanding money for the return of the book. She knew its value and that it was not consciously included in the gift."

"May I see the e-mail?"

"I deleted it."

"Oh. Okay. Well . . . let's say I could do something for you," I said. "What would that something be?"

"Bring this Landis woman to me."

"And the manuscript?"

"Of course the manuscript."

"Why not just the book? You don't really need the thief if your property is returned."

"I like to look my enemies in the eye," Evangeline uttered.

"I could turn her over to the police for the theft," I said, thinking about her father's enemies and the material of her desk and chair.

"No. I will pay you one hundred thousand dollars for the woman and the book."

"That's a hefty late fee."

"I'm paying for your discretion, Mr. McGill."

"Most people already know the general content of the nine books of the father of history," I said, feeling the need to sound knowledgeable in that room of rarefied access and wealth.

"Do we have a deal?"

"One hundred thousand dollars, you say?"

"Yes."

"Sounds good. One hundred for me and also equal amounts for Hiram Stent's and Hector Laritas's families."

"All right," she said as if the amounts were nothing.

"What about Josh Farth?" I asked.

"What about him?"

"What if Mr. Farth resents my intrusion on his business?"

"Mr. Farth works for me," she said. "He will do as I say."

"Some of us down below the top floor don't see the world the same way you do, Ms. Gray. And anyway, I might have a problem with Mr. Farth's way of doing business."

"If Josh is guilty of some felony having to do with my requests then he will find himself on his own," she said, rapping her knuckles once and with finality on the tabletop of bone.

Henry Lawrence Richards, not of the Fantastic Four, was tasked by the woman on the top floor to give me a cash down payment of ten thousand dollars. He handed me a brown envelope with the money sealed inside, the two bodyguards flanking me.

I tore the envelope open and counted the cash, twice, because when I was a child my father taught me that you could never trust the rich.

34

I flew back to New York's LaGuardia Airport and took a taxi, arriving at the Tesla Building at 3:56.

I was looking at my watch, just inside the big brass doors of that perfect Art Deco feat of architecture: a huge room replete with blue walls lined with brass plating; pink, black, and green tiled floors done in a curving abstract design, and a broad fresco of workers, naked women, and saints that had no pantheon, just the faith of their people. I liked the classical and yet revolutionary decor despite my dislike of my father and his beliefs. I think I might have smiled a moment before something hard pressed into the right side of my upper back. I looked up at the high reception desk and twisted my lips even before the man behind me spoke.

"Let's take a walk, Mr. McGill," an unfamiliar voice said.

I turned my head sixty degrees or so and saw the man I'd first beheld on Monday looking at Marella Herzog and ignoring me. The probable gun he held against my shoulder blade was hidden under the fabric of his dark yellow trench coat. This supposed weapon was held in his left hand, as I could see his right encased in a plaster cast, its swollen fingers poking through.

Beyond the paid stalker's angry visage I could see that Warren Oh, the Jamaican black-and-Chinese senior guard for the Tesla, was talking on the phone.

"What can I do for you, Mr. Lett?" I asked pleasantly.

"We can go upstairs to your office and you can tell me where Marella Herzog is and how I can get to her."

"You plan to shoot my receptionist, too?" I asked as if requesting extra butter on my vat of movie theater popcorn.

"Don't fuck with me, brother," Alexander Lett said. "I got a cushion on this piece. I'll be a block away before they even know you're dead."

I was beginning to detect a pattern in my life. This model of behavior was a hybrid of capitalist necessity and proletarian existentialist angst; or, more accurately, modern-day potentates and their anger-driven gunsels.

"But surely no one has asked you to kill me, Mr. Lett," I said. "I mean you didn't even know me when you took on this job."

"Move it, McGill."

"I'd like to, Mr. Lett, but my assistant is a delicate thing and I'd feel terrible if I brought fear or worse into her life."

"Have it your way."

These last few words he might have meant for my epitaph. I didn't think that this was the case but human nature is not always predictable. Lucky for me—prediction had no place in the equation of our interchange.

"Hold it right there," a third, very authoritative voice demanded.

Alex and I both looked in the direction of the command. There we beheld four policemen; three in uniform and one plainclothes Captain Carson Kitteridge.

Once again I could feel the heartbeat of my wife calling me strong, realizing that strong could also be scared.

Alexander Lett's olive profile was the epitome of desperation. I could see in that visage the questions that beset men when they've taken one step too many down a bad path. *Why did I do it? How can I get out of it?* These are the unanswerable and useless questions that go through our minds when someone shoves a gun in our side or calls for us to halt.

"Let me see your hands," Kit said clearly.

The civilians crowding the foyer of the Tesla Building were now pressing toward the edges and exits.

"I got a gun in my left," Alexander Lett admitted loudly.

The fleeing crowd became a bit more frantic.

To his credit Warren Oh stayed at his post.

"Bring it out holding it by the butt," Kit said, and I wondered if I'd be shot.

There was a tense moment in which many thoughts and sensations transpired.

As the pressure of the muzzle eased from my side and Alexander Lett's sour breath assailed me, I was thinking that the most important moments of my life had nothing to do with intelligence or insight. I was a brute among brutes and would die according to my nature and its affiliations. This thought comforted me; it allowed that Fate was my master and not free will.

It was then that I saw the long-barreled pistol emerge from under the yellow fabric. Alex held the butt with his forefinger and thumb. The three uniforms moved quickly then, grabbing the gun and throwing the already injured Lett to the hard, multicolored tile floor.

"Go easy on him, Kit," I said loudly enough for the prisoner to hear. "Alex here an' me is old friends. He was just jokin'."

"With a loaded gun?" the captain asked.

"You know, man, you work with dynamite long enough and you start to forget how dangerous the shit is. Right, Alex?"

"Uh-huh," the confused thug agreed.

"I'm still takin' him down. If he doesn't have a license he's gonna do time. He might anyway. Reckless endangerment."

After Lett was searched, chained, and trundled off in a police car, Warren Oh and I were informally deposed by a sergeant named Reese. After all that, Kit and I took the elevator upstairs to my office.

The door had been replaced and the wall inside rebuilt. My keys still worked and everything was right with the world.

"How'd you get here so quickly?" I asked Kit when we passed into the empty reception area.

"You know we always have a few men on the Tesla. That many tourists always attract your people."

My people. Captain Carson Kitteridge would always see me as a criminal and my race as like-minded felons.

"But why were *you* here?"

"I came by to ask a question."

"Serendipity then?" I said as I entered the key-code to the back offices.

"Why'd you give Warren the high sign if Lett was a friend of yours?" Kit asked when we were seated in my personal office.

"We don't have to worry about that, Kit. Lett is representing some angry ex-boyfriend and he got mad that I sucker punched him, that's all. We got bigger things to talk about."

"Like what?"

"You know anything about a guy named Jones got a whole bunch'a kids doin' crimes for him?"

It was a rare moment to catch Kit off guard; he blinked—twice. He was small and delicate as far as the physical goes, but his will had a steel jacket. Any breach in that armor was a major achievement.

"What do you know about him?"

"Twill got himself mixed up with the dude tryin' to help a girl lost her heart to one'a Jones's men."

"Put Twill on a plane and send him to Pakistan," Kit said. "I doubt if even Jones got clout there."

"Who is he?"

"The question is what is he? Child molesting, kidnapping, forced prostitution, blackmail, murder, extortion, smuggling, and sadism. I got a file with forty-six persons either missing or dead, and we think Jones killed 'em all."

"Then why not arrest him?"

"I don't even know what he looks like. No one does. He wears disguises and only makes himself known to the orphans and runaways he controls. Every time we arrest somebody that might know something, either a power from on high lets them go or they die. I'm surprised that Twill even got in without having his throat cut. Jones is bad business. He's never been arrested. There's no photo or fingerprint, not a signature or single strand of hair on him."

"What's he got on people?"

"What did Lucky Luciano have on J. Edgar Hoover?"

With that sentence Kit was telling me that he would do anything to bring down Jones.

"What would you give to get at him?" I asked.

"I'd lay off your ass for a month of Sundays."

"Is that a February month or August?"

Kit's smile was anything but friendly. "If you bring this man down I'll even lay off the Hiram Stent business."

I think I must've blinked then. Kit smiled as I wondered how he could have possibly linked me with the homeless dead man.

"Who?" I finally managed to utter.

"Hiram Stent. Homeless guy. He was murdered a couple of days ago in Brooklyn."

"What's that got to do with me?"

"I don't know," Kit admitted. "When he was being murdered I was at your office trying to keep you from coming to blows with my sergeant."

"And?"

"Stent was killed in a mugging, at least that's the way it looks. But he had your address and phone number written on a piece of paper that he'd hidden in his shoe."

"That doesn't mean I know him."

"I don't care, LT. You bring me Jones and I'll send Stent to potter's field."

"Why you hate this guy so much?"

"I got my reasons."

"Like what?"

"Like a dozen children murdered and tossed off in alleys and abandoned buildings," he said. "Like judges, city hall officials, and senior cops getting in the way of every case related to him. I'm a cop, LT. I put people like you behind bars. Either I succeed or I don't but the people on my side should never block my investigations."

I gave that minor soliloquy a moment to settle. There was real passion in the angry cop. Whenever a man as dangerous as Kit expressed rage, you needed to give it a moment to breathe.

That moment gone, I asked, "You got a private cell?"

"Why?"

35

our years ago that block on the Grand Concourse in the Bronx wasn't even a "neighborhood in transition." Most of the houses and small apartment buildings were abandoned or lived in by squatters. Back then the four-story house I was going to had two residents: Luke Nye, who passed for a black man but who actually looked to be a direct descendant of the moray eel, and Johnny Nightly, a midnight-colored enforcer who might have at one time been mistaken for Nat King Cole's younger, more handsome brother.

That was then.

Today Luke's building houses eight apartments, six of which are inhabited by Hispanic ladies and their children, and maybe a temporary man or two; one unit for Luke and another for Johnny.

The basement of Luke's place was his main source of income: a huge room that housed three regulation-sized pool tables. It was here that the best players in the world came to compete. Johnny rented the room for anything from ten thousand to one hundred thousand dollars a night, and also ran book for people around the world who both watched and bet on the contests.

But now Luke's neighborhood was becoming gentrified. The billionaires' and multimillionaires' colonization of the island of Manhattan had driven the middle classes out to Brooklyn, Queens, and even to the Grand Concourse. Luke bought buildings up and down the block, selling to would-be homeowners who wouldn't cause him trouble.

Other than real estate, Luke's side business was information. He would, for a thousand-dollar fee, answer solitary questions for people he trusted. Luke knew a great deal about the underworld from New York to New Mexico and all the way to New Delhi.

I was one of those special customers to whom Luke deigned to sell.

The building had a front door but I rarely approached it. My usual route was a concrete path that led around the back, arriving at a weatherworn door that was four steps down from ground level. I could have knocked but, as at Evangeline Sidney-Gray's door in Boston, there was no need. I waited for maybe a minute and the door opened inward.

Asha Graham stood there. Slender and brown, disdainful and quite lovely, Asha wore an emerald dress that came down around her calves. She had run with half a dozen gangsters, gamblers, and gunmen over the past ten or twelve years; she'd outlived them one at a time. After a while bad men would avoid Asha whenever she came around. They could face a beating or bullet because there was some chance they might survive those encounters, but Asha was a death sentence and no sex in the world was worth that.

The thirty-something beauty might have become an old maid if not for Luke. He had seen everyone around him perish before their time. He believed in curses of course, all gamblers did, but he felt that his juju was at least as strong as Ms. Graham's.

"Mr. McGill," she said. It wasn't quite a friendly greeting. Asha wasn't the kind of woman to smile and fawn; she came from the guffaw and fuck, drink yourself senseless and die finishing school for young women.

"Asha."

"You here for Luke or Johnny?"

"Can I have both?"

Asha let go of the slightest of smiles and stood to the side. I went past her, going down twelve more steps into one of the most important pool rooms in the world. Past the three tables was a sitting area with three red sofas set in a triangle about a circular table with a top made from a single piece of lapis lazuli. The room was bright because there was no game. There was a bottle of gin and a teapot on the blue table.

"LT," Luke said, rising up from a sofa. He spent most of his time in the pool room. That was his life now that he had given up pimping, stealing, dealing, and murder-for-hire.

"Luke," I said, shaking the hand he offered.

"Leonid," Johnny Nightly said. He also rose and shook my hand.

When we were all seated Luke asked, "Who can do what for you today, LT?"

"The who is you," I said, "and the what is two names. An underground Fagin wannabe named Jones and a guy who's probably in the life named Paulie DeGeorges."

That was one of the few times I saw a moment of hesitation in Luke's face.

"DeGeorges," he said, pondering. "What's his thing?"

"I'm not sure. There's a girl way out of her depth that has stolen something that's very valuable and maybe important for other reasons. She's probably hoping to use this guy to help her work it through. But I really don't know anything about him except for the name and that the one time anybody saw him he was wearing a bow tie."

Luke thought for a moment more and then went to an oak wall at the back of the room. There he slid a panel aside and pulled out an unusual contraption. The greater part of the machine looked like an old-fashioned complex shortwave radio. This was attached to a very ordinary, if outdated, black rotary phone. He set a few dials on the radio portion of the machine, the phone gave a short burp of its ring, and then Luke raised the receiver, dialed six numbers, and, after a forty-five-second wait, said, very clearly, "Paulie DeGeorges."

He then hung up the phone and returned to a red sofa next to Asha. I had a couch to myself and Johnny occupied the other.

"Tea or gin, Mr. McGill?" Asha asked.

"Better give him tea," Luke suggested. "With the kinda questions he's askin' he's gonna need all his wits."

While Asha poured my English Breakfast, Luke continued, "If you can forget Jones, that would be your best option; maybe your only one. He the baddest motherfucker in three states. Slick as oil and deadly as a volcanic eruption. Only man I ever heard of could make somebody commit suicide rather than go up against him."

"What's his thing?" I asked, to see if there was more than what Twill and his clients knew.

"Children," Luke said simply. "The greatest weakness of any species is its young. If they don't survive, the story is over. If they do, they will bury us."

"In English, Luke."

"He got children doin' his work. They steal for him, prostitute for him, and they will kill, too. He brings 'em in and makes them his creatures. If they cross him they die. If they talk it don't matter because they don't really know nuthin'. Nobody knows his name and he's got dirt on at least a few people in every court, precinct, and government office. Nobody knows what he looks like, or where he calls home. If I was to make book on it I'd say that he was once a part of the juvenile protection department. From there he found out how to use children. But no one knows."

"No way to beat him?" I asked the man who many believed had all the answers.

"Get somebody in close," Luke speculated. "Close enough to kill him and brave enough to die. I don't think he's the kind of guy trusts anybody with his secrets, so a suicide run would end whatever problem it was that somebody had."

I was hoping that Twill hadn't come up with the same conclusion.

The rotary phone rang once, then the sounds of a dot-matrix printer started up. After maybe eight minutes the sounds stopped and Johnny went to the back wall, pulled out a drawer, and removed half a dozen sheets of paper. He glanced through them and then handed the sheets to Luke. Without reading the contents he passed the pages on to me.

I folded the papers and put them in my inside breast pocket.

"What is that?" I said, gesturing at the apparatus.

"That is to me what I am to you," Luke said.

"What do I owe?"

"The same," he said. "Always the same. One thousand dollars."

"What about for Jones?"

"I hand out death notices for free. Public service, you know."

"LT," he called.

I had almost made it to the sidewalk in front of Luke Nye's house.

I turned and waited for Johnny to reach me.

"You need some help on this, man?" he asked.

I took a moment to consider the offer. Johnny was long and lean, powerful and deadly. He was the kind of guy you wanted on your side when the shit came down. I had three deadly forces to contend with, and only two hands. Luke was right when he said that our children are our greatest weakness. Twill was my son and I felt vulnerable for him.

But Johnny almost died the time before last when I needed his help.

"No, Johnny," I said. "I got this one covered."

36

From time to time there's a Rembrandt on display at the Metropolitan Museum of Art, twenty inches wide and maybe two feet high. It's an oil rendering of a peasant girl who is looking beyond you into a history of pain and loss. She's beautiful and you could tell that the artist and many others had fooled themselves that they could love her and that that love would be a good thing. But the longer you sit watching those haunted and haunting eyes, the more concepts like love and beauty drain away; all that's left, if you look at that painting long enough, is the awareness of the hopelessness that eats at the human soul.

The curators bring that piece out only once every dozen years or so; something to do with anomalies in the medium and their exposure to light. It's on display for six weeks and then brought back to its dark closet in the lower levels. I have a friend, an old guard named Franz Jester, who tells me whenever that painting is on display.

I sat there in front of the dead but still dangerous peasant girl, looking at her between bouts of reading and rereading the information I'd received on Paulie DeGeorges.

Whoever sent the pages on Paulie was probably a highly placed bureaucrat in some government office. There were six hazy black-and-white photographs of DeGeorges from his teen years up until near his current age, which was forty-three. Four of the pictures were taken by police photographers after an arrest. One picture was taken by a surveillance lens when Paulie was coming out of a restaurant on the Lower East Side. He was standing next to a platinum blonde who would have been beautiful if she could have just gotten the hatred out of her smile.

Paulie was naturally slender, even skinny, with randomly placed prominent bones about his face. He always wore a sports jacket and bow tie, even as a teenager, and he was pale and freckled. He was the kind of thief that stole your car and then offered to sell it back. Sometimes, oftentimes, he worked in collusion with the victim. He'd been arrested a dozen times and convicted four. Six and a half years in prison were behind him and he would definitely be sent up again; his last stint ended five weeks ago.

There were no violent offenses in his jacket. His stats told me that his hair was light brown and his eyes blue. His wife was named Violet Henrys. His mother, Bea Trammel, lived in a retirement home on the West Side about twelve blocks north of the Financial District.

No Violet Henrys in the phone book or on the smartphone Internet. No Bea Trammel either but there was a listing for the Oak Village Retirement Home on Hudson Street. There was a phone number but I didn't see any reason to call.

It was a very modern, very nice place to die. The ground floor was surrounded by walls made of glass that allowed sun in at any time of day. To the right was a broad platform, a few feet lower than the entrance, where three or four dozen retirement home denizens sat and spoke, wandered and babbled, or simply stood staring out through the wall, or not. To my left was a wide counter behind which stood two women and one man. These attendants wore clothes that could have been civilian wear except for the fact that they were all cut from the same cloth and dyed the same unlikely color green. The women wore skirts and jackets of that color. The man was allowed to wear pants.

"May I help you?" he asked when I approached the desk.

"Ms. Bea Trammel."

He tapped around on an electronic tablet until coming to a page of data.

"Yes," he said, "are you a relative?"

"Bradford Littles," I said. "I was her son's fourth-grade math teacher.

I ran into Paul quite by accident the other day and he told me that his mother was here. He was always in trouble and so his mother and I met pretty often. He said that she might like a visitor. I have a meeting not far from here this afternoon and thought I might see her."

"Did you make an appointment?" The man was the color of aged ivory, in his thirties, and officious in a reserved way. He was also a little suspicious.

"Is she really that much in demand?" I said.

"So you taught Mr. Paul Trammel at a New York public school?" said the man, keeping our string of interrogatives alive. He wore a badge that read SHAW.

"Paul DeGeorges went to school in Columbus, Ohio, where I lived until I retired."

Shaw pursed his lips while pretending that he could read into my intentions. Finally he shrugged, thinking to himself that he'd done his due diligence. He reached under the gray plastic counter and came out with a plastic badge that held a card with a big red V on it. He handed the general identification to me.

"You understand, Mr. Littles, we have to make sure our residents are protected."

"From what?" I asked as I clipped the yellow-and-red badge to my blue lapel.

"Last month a man came in here saying that he was a resident's nephew and managed to get her to sign over the rights to three very expensive properties. Thank God we were able to nullify the transaction. Otherwise Mrs. Dunn would have been forced to move out."

"I see," I said, wondering if Shaw heard his own acceptance of the venal code of his job while talking about protecting his elderly, dying charges.

Bea Trammel was on the seventeenth floor in room 21. The teal door was open. There was a clipboard in a little pouch hanging from the door. ALL VISITORS MUST SIGN IN was written on the paper pouch. I took up the clipboard and a ballpoint pen dangling by a string from the pouch and signed the name Bradford Littles while perusing the other signatories. I had enough information right then but I knocked on the open door anyway.

"Come in," she said sweetly.

The room was very small with pink walls and a yellow desk, a single bed against the wall, and a love seat made for very small lovers or maybe one fat-bottomed solipsist. There was a well-used chrome walker in the far corner.

The window looked out over New Jersey. Bea Trammel stood there, her back to Hoboken, facing me.

"Yes?" she asked.

"I don't expect you to remember me," I said, approaching her and gently holding out a hand. "But my name is Bradford Littles and I was Paul's fourth-grade math teacher."

She took my hand, squinting at me.

"Of course," she said. "Have a seat, Mr. Bradford."

She gestured at the purple love seat and moved to sit on the bed.

Maybe five feet in height and weighing no more than ninety pounds, she wore turquoise-colored pants, a brown blouse, and a blood-orange sweater because of the air-conditioning.

"What brings you here?" she asked with the insincere smile that many old people adopt to protect themselves from the rampant and often unchecked powers of youth.

"I ran into Paul at a club on Fifty-fourth Street," I said. "He told me that you were here and that he, that he had just gotten out of jail over some mistake about insurance and a stolen car."

"He did? That must be some kind of mistake. Paulie was working for an Internet company in San Francisco for the past three years. He worked so much that he didn't have time to come back east until the job was over—but he certainly wasn't in any prison."

"Oh?" I said. "Maybe I misunderstood. Maybe he was talking about some other student in our class."

"That's probably it," Bea said. "There were a few of Paulie's friends that were bad eggs. Maybe he was talking about Robert Hrotha, that kid from Panama."

"Maybe so," I replied, thinking that I had made a misstep.

Bea looked to be in her seventies. She'd moved slowly from the window to the bed. Her body was weak but her gaze was not.

"Is your name really Mr. Bradford?" she asked.

"Littles. I said my name was Bradford Littles."

"Is that true?"

"No."

"Are you after my son?"

"Looking for him," I admitted, "but not after him. He knows a woman who has stolen a valuable book. It's my job to find her."

"You're a cop?"

"No more than you are, Ms. Trammel."

"Paulie's a fool," she said in a level, almost threatening tone. "But he's my son first. And so whatever you want, you won't get it from me."

I considered leaving her my name but then thought better of it. Bea Trammel had been something in her early days; and I doubted if that something was a suburban housewife.

37

At an art store on Grand I spent two hundred sixty-four dollars and forty-seven cents for a beginner's set of oil paints and brushes, an eighteen-by-twenty-four-inch canvas stretched on and stapled to a sturdy wooden frame, and a spindly easel made from uncured pine.

I set myself up on Ninth Street just past Avenue C at a spot down the block and across the street from a row of low-income housing bungalows, each of which had doors that opened onto the sidewalk. Instead of having screens, each of these doors was protected by a gate of heavy bars—each of these gates was equipped with a heavy-duty lock. The entrance of unit 4A was visible from where I stood in front of my future masterpiece. I had also purchased a folding blue-canvas stool that I could sit on to appreciate my work and keep an eye on the barred door.

Once I had read the only other name on Bea's visitors' list, I knew my next step. I couldn't find a listing for Violet Henrys but Violet Trammel lived in 4A on that block of Ninth. I knew the units because Alphabet City is full of the lowlifes and grifters that are my stock-in-trade.

I didn't want to knock on the door because Bea had probably warned Violet that I was looking for Paulie. So I decided to wait until either she came home or went out before settling on how to make contact. If I was lucky Paulie might be with her. If I was very lucky Celia would be there too.

My disguise consisted of a Red Sox baseball cap that I'd found in a trash can on St. Mark's Place and the fact that I had doffed my jacket, folded it, and placed it under the stool. I had it in mind to try to re-create the haunting stare of the Rembrandt Girl I so loved. After maybe two hours I had a graded gray-blue background and one eye. A few people stopped to watch me but nobody said anything except for a homeless woman that looked familiar. She was older than she should have been, clad in a dress that was a step down from being rags.

"Got a cigarette, mister?"

"Sorry, honey, I quit." I gave her a dollar. But now that cigarettes cost a baker's dozen times that, I didn't know what she'd do with it. Maybe she could buy a loosie from someone. The police had laid off killing men for selling loosies for the time being—bad publicity.

Watching her shamble off, I was reminded of Twill and the way he dressed down to join Jones's crew.

"Hello?" he said, answering his private line.

"Where are you?"

"At Uncle Gordo's."

"Mardi?"

"Her and Marlene are here. I called Liza and she said that she and Fortune were okay but then Hush got on the line. He said that he saw some people walk past his place three times." Hush had surveillance cameras all around the outside of his house—professional necessity.

"Did he want help?"

"He didn't say so."

"I want you to keep it close, Twilliam."

"I know, Pops. I know."

"I know you know," I said. "What I want is for you to do."

"Yes sir."

I raised my head at that moment, relieved because Twill usually stuck to his word. There at the door of 4A stood a woman twenty years older, and quite a bit blonder, than the woman in the photograph with Paulie. There was still hatred woven into her expression but this time she wasn't smiling.

Violet Henrys a.k.a. Violet Trammel.

"I got to go, son. They just called my number."

"Talk to you later, Pops."

In those few seconds Violet had unlocked, opened, passed through, and closed her barred gate and door.

She was Paulie's wife pretending to be Paulie's mother's daughter so that she could take over Bea's low-income home. It was part of a scam that a local contractor, who built that housing for the city and state, used to sell to qualified grifters. Crooks need a place to live too.

At any other time I would have played a waiting game. Sooner or later either Paulie would come to see Violet or she would lead me to him. I could spend a few days working on my painting, waiting for the fly to come to me. But on that particular day I had people from DC to Beantown wanting to kill either me or mine.

I needed to speed up the process, so, abandoning my art materials, I went to a local bodega and bought a small box of envelopes. I wrote a simple note on the front of one, sealed in a hundred-dollar bill, compliments of Josh Farth, and slipped the packet through the bars and under Violet's front door; then I fast-walked down to the corner of D and waited.

Usually I would have charged that hundred dollars, plus the cost of my artist's disguise, to my client; but my client was dead and so I spotted him.

It took seventeen minutes for her to call.

"Hello?" I said to what my phone told me was an unknown caller.

"Did you put this note under my door?" Violet Henrys-DeGeorges-Trammel asked.

"Yes, ma'am."

"You'd really pay a thousand dollars just to talk to Paulie?"

"That's what I wrote."

"But you'd really do it?"

"I will."

"Were you the man who went to Bea's place today?" she asked.

"I sure was."

"And did she tell you how to get to me?"

"No. You signed the visitors' clipboard and I knew that Paulie is married to a woman whose first name is Violet."

"*Were* married," she corrected. "We cut the knot just before the last time he was sent up."

"Sorry to hear that."

"No need," she said; I could almost hear the sneer. "People get divorced because they want to."

"And why do they marry?" I asked.

"Because they're fools."

"Nine hundred dollars for me and your ex to talk." I had already started walking back toward her door.

"I thought you said a thousand."

"You got a hundred of that in your hands."

"That's just for the call," she said.

"How do we work this?" I asked. I was only a few steps from her address.

"You pay me and I get Paulie to call you."

I was about to say that that was a bad deal for me when I noticed the man walking toward me.

I disconnected the call and said, "Hey, Paulie."

38

He wore a brown jacket, skinny black jeans, a gray-and-blue-plaid shirt, and a bright orange bow tie. His shoes were blunt-toed and brown, and the generous thatch of brown hair was shot through with strands of gray. He still had those freckles and if I was forced to report on the color of his eyes I would have said blue-gray.

Those pale eyes opened wide when I greeted him.

"You Violet's new man?"

"Leonid McGill," I said, extending a hand.

We shook, him squeezing to test the strength of my grip.

"What do you want, Mr. McGill?"

"I need to have a talk with you. I was going to offer Violet nine hundred dollars to put us together. I'll be happy to give it to you instead."

"Talk about what?"

"Let's go grab a coffee and make the exchange," I said. "Cash for information."

The skinny scam artist considered his options. He didn't want his business messed with but I posed a threat whether we talked or not. He needed to know what I knew and also there was a shot at nine hundred dollars.

"Okay," he said after a full minute standing in front of Violet's cell-like door. "All right. There's a place I like over on Lafayette. We could hoof it over there."

———

Half a block from Violet's apartment my phone sounded. I looked at the screen, saw it was another unknown caller. I figured that it was Violet, disconnected the request, and turned the ringer off.

On the way Paulie probed me.

"How you know Violet?" he asked.

"Never met her."

"Then what were you doing waiting for me at her door?"

I told nearly the whole story, leaving out Luke's name. By the time I got to the visit with his mother we had reached the Excellent Bean on Lafayette, just a few blocks south of Astor Place.

At the counter I ordered a triple latte for me and a large hot chocolate for Paulie. He'd taken a small table in a corner.

"What is it that I know worth all that money to you, McGill?" he asked when we were finally settled.

"I'm looking for a young woman named Celia Landis but you might know her as Coco Lombardi."

With eyes as expressive as his, Paulie could never be a cardplayer. Those bright orbs darted from my big hands to the door. They calculated his chance of getting away but came up with odds too long for his comfort.

"I, I don't know those names."

"That's too bad," I said. "Because if I can't get to her I'm going to have to tell the people I work for that I came to a dead end named Paulie DeGeorges. I don't know for a fact but I've heard that they already killed two men who didn't know anything."

Paulie's shoulders juddered and he looked down at his hands.

"This is not your regular scam, Paulie. These people have power and money. They don't give a fuck about an ex-con like you."

"You don't have to give them my name," he suggested.

"I do if I expect to get paid."

"So if I tell you where she is you're gonna tell them?"

"Actually no," I said. "I think that book she stole might get me a whole lot more than they're offering."

"I thought you said that they were dangerous, killers."

I sat back in my coffeehouse chair and smiled. All around the café young men and women were sitting and talking. I noted that the women smiled more than did the men. I was smiling too, challenging the odds. It was an easy grin because I was confident in my footing.

"Who do you know, Paulie?"

"What do you mean?"

"In the Life," I said, "somebody that knows the names of the players who could tell you about Leonid McGill."

"I got my people," he said defensively. "Prison ain't on the moon."

"Call him up," I said. "Tell him my name and see what he says."

Paulie peered at me like a sparrow that thinks he might have seen a shadow moving through the bushes. He even turned his head to the side.

Finally he brought an old cell phone out of a green pocket and flipped it open.

While he entered the number I took up my phone and typed in the letters HU.

Hush answered on the third ring.

"LT."

"Twill said you had some worries."

"No worries, brother." He had never called me brother before. I wondered what that meant. "Might be something, might not. Either way I know what to do."

"You need me to come by?"

"Mr. McGill," Paulie said.

I held up a finger for him to wait.

"No, LT, I'm okay. Matter'a fact I'm kinda havin' fun."

I didn't like the notion of a smiling killer but there was no time to deal with that right then. I said my good-byes and turned to Paulie.

"Yeah?"

"My friend asked if I could send him a picture of you."

"That piece'a shit phone has a camera?"

"One of the first."

"Snap away," I said.

He held up the phone for a moment and then turned it around to hit a few buttons. He sat there watching it as the outmoded technology organized and sent the picture, one pixel at a time.

After maybe three minutes he brought the phone to his ear and asked, "You get it? . . . Uh-huh . . . Uh-huh . . . Yeah, yeah, all right. Thanks, T."

He put the phone away and looked at me like a man who had just been convicted and now waited for the sentence.

"You know," he said after a moment or so, "I always felt like I was born in the wrong place and time. I mean the people here and every-where don't know shit about style or sophistication. My own wife went out and had an affair with some dude and then tells me that he made her feel like she never knew she could. He broke it off with her but she left me anyway. That don't stop her from askin' me for help whenever she needs it. There ain't nuthin' right about that. And my mother . . . My mother had this check-kiting scheme she used to use at banks in different cities. She'd hit town for a week and get fifteen, twenty thousand and then move on. Never saw two Mondays in the same town and never even got questioned, much less arrested. She refused to visit me in prison because she was humiliated that I got caught. Here I stole the money to pay for her goddamned nursing home and she wouldn't even answer a letter. Shit. There I am in prison for her and she cut me off.

"You know my old man was no better. Strong motherfucker like you, only taller. Rob banks and armored cars. He said that he was ashamed to have a scrawny son like me. He run off from my mother because he said I was the issue of an affair . . ."

What surprised me was his proper use of the word "issue." There was an education under that bony, sad-sack brow.

"Here I could'a made somethin' of myself but everybody live in the modern world where nobody gives a shit about what's right. And the worst place is prison. Motherfuckers up in there brag on all the crimes they did that no one ever tumbled to. Serial killers in jail for assault; arsonists put away for trespass. I don't have no choice but to do what I do and to be what I am. Nobody does."

"How did you meet Coco?" I asked to get the derailed scam artist back on my track.

"Her brother."

"How you know him?"

"They busted him for smuggling drugs. He was my cellmate time before last. When his sister got in trouble he got in touch with me 'cause he knew I was just about to get out."

"Why didn't he help her?"

"Prison again," Paulie said. "North Carolina. Here every motherfucker and his kid is hooked on pharmaceuticals and they put Timothy in for moving seventeen ounces of hashish. Seventeen! Shit. The best of us are the worst of us. We have lost our right to God."

If I had only heard that one diatribe I would have known that Paulie was a jailbird. The odd mixture of philosophy, religion, and despair marked him as sure as a black man's skin.

"One thing remains the same," I said.

"What's that?"

"You either eat or die."

Paulie looked up at me then and a smile came unbidden to his lips. He was a scam artist who thrived on truth; no wonder he was so sad. He probably thought that his wife's lover was better endowed than he; I was willing to wager that the one-night stand just knew how to laugh.

"What you want, McGill?"

"I want to talk to Coco. I want you to tell her that I know about the book and about the woman that wants it back. Tell her that I say that I can make it right for her and even get her a little scratch, you too."

"How much?"

"More than twenty-five thousand for her and at least five for you if we get this business done. I'll pay you nine hundred right now on good faith."

"And you won't, you won't tell about me?"

"If you help me there's no reason to."

I reached in my jacket pocket and came out with a wad of hundreds.

Paulie jerked his head around and said, "Put it away, man. You can pay me outside."

"Okay."

"Look," he said. "I don't want no trouble with you. My friend T says that you're serious business, that people have to be careful around you. So I'ma say that I'll call Coco an' ask her but if she says no there's nuthin' I could do."

"What more can I ask for?" I asked.

39

It was nighttime in Greenwich Village. I went to a bar on Second Avenue, had three cognacs to toast my lost and long-dead lover Gert Longman, and then trundled down into the subway to make it back home.

My wife and father were sitting in the little front room again, drinking wine punch and telling each other things. She was laughing. There was color in her face. My father might have been blushing too but his skin was as dark as mine so the blood stayed hidden.

"Trot," he said.

"Clarence," I replied.

"Are you hungry, Leonid?" Katrina asked.

"Why?"

"I made chicken and dumplings the way you like them."

Chicken and dumplings brought to mind a pop song from the '60s about a cuckold who came home early.

My father and wife joined me in the dining room. They asked a few perfunctory questions about my day and then went back to talking to each other.

The food was great. To accompany the protein and starch, Katrina had made fried okra in a roux—a dish she liked to call half-gumbo. There also was an apple-cabbage slaw and peach cobbler for dessert.

I found out a lot about my father as he regaled my wife. He'd learned how to be a potter in a small village in Bolivia. There, working on a kick-wheel in a shack the size of an outhouse, he started thinking about the few novels he'd read. When he was a young man he eschewed fiction, thinking that reality was all that mattered. But working at that wheel he had the time to remember the stories he'd read and somehow came to the realization that the novel was the only way a human being could truly express the lives he experienced.

"Lives, not life?" Katrina asked.

"If you live long enough," Clarence explained, "you take on many personas. I've gone from sharecropper to revolutionary to scribbler in my seventy-nine years."

"You seem so much younger," my flirtatious wife chimed.

"I notice you didn't mention 'father' in your list of personas," I anteed.

I almost felt bad about the pain that wrenched Clarence's face.

After the meal I looked at my phone and saw that there were fifteen texts and six calls. I wondered at that and then remembered that I'd turned off the sound to concentrate on Paulie.

In my office I listened to the voice mails first. That was easy because four of them were from Violet Henrys-DeGeorges-Trammel. She wanted that nine hundred dollars—badly. I thought that she'd probably get the money before the night was over; maybe even Paulie would get lucky.

Of the two other messages one was a hang-up and the other from Aura. Just hearing her voice set off a chill in my chest. It was a physical manifestation of love, just as the erections I'd experienced recently were from the lust Marella Herzog brought out in me.

"Leonid," she said, "I need to talk to you right away."

"Hello," she answered, wide awake at 11:49.

"What's up, A?"

There were no preliminaries, no "how are you doing." Aura went right into the problem saying, "A man calling himself Abe Hollyman came to my office today and said that he was working for a lawyer who needed to serve a summons on you."

"He show some ID?"

"Yes, but it was just a business card. He offered me five hundred dollars and promised fifteen hundred more if I would call to orchestrate a meeting with you in the meeting room on the fifteenth floor. He said all I had to do was make the meeting time and he'd be there to serve the papers."

"What did you do?"

"Took the money," she said. "You know I have college expenses for my daughter. Then I told him that I'd call as soon as I got in touch with you."

"Thanks for the warning."

"This is serious, honey," the woman I loved said. "He wore gloves *and* a hat."

Sitting there in my dark den, I got a little light-headed. That, as the old folks used to say, was the last straw. It was getting to be time for me to push back.

"Call Mr. Hollyman and tell him that you set up a ten-in-the-morning meeting with me. Tell him that he can pick up the key from Warren at the front desk anytime past nine. Tell Warren that I'll get the key to the observation room at seven. And don't you go to work at all. Stay home till I call and tell you that it's okay."

"LT?" Carson Kitteridge said at a few minutes after midnight.

"Did I wake you?"

"What do you need?"

"It's not about Jones," I said. "Not yet. But I got this other problem you might be interested in."

There was a lull in the conversation, such as it was, for ten seconds or so. Carson was wondering if he should hang up on me. But we'd known each other too long for that. If I was calling then there was something happening that he should be aware of.

"What is it?" he asked.

I told him Aura's story and we made half of a plan.

———

As a youth, sitting in the dark was always a relief to me. An adolescent roaming the streets of New York, I was often in trouble with the older boys and some men, too. I was a killer before my fifteenth birthday and for some years I'd have night terrors over the man I strangled. If I was very quiet under the cover of darkness this panic subsided, somewhat.

As a man I put away my guilty fears; I was, I told myself, prepared for anything, always prepared. I saw myself like my favorite mammal, the honey badger—a squat brute with exceptionally thick skin, powerful long claws, and always looking for trouble. The honey badger spends his days trampling through the world killing, digging up corpses, and defying even lions if he has to. He's always in danger, and danger is always in him.

With these thoughts I got it in mind to turn on the lights and then, just as if God heard me, there was light.

"You goin' to bed, Trot?" my father said from the door.

"Come on in, Clarence."

Shrugging, he walked across the slender glove of a room to the stuffed chair set to the side of my desk.

"You got trouble, son?" he asked.

"Don't you have a home?" I replied.

"Sure I do. I just thought you needed a little help around the house with Katrina just back and that thing with your office."

"What is it with you and my wife, old man?"

"Is that what's bothering you? You actually think I'd go after my own son's wife?"

"She wants you like a tick craves blood."

I realized then that my father's face used to be rounder. This was why he looked like a stranger to me. He'd been a portly revolutionary but old age and a long list of failures had reduced him. His face was now long and oddly empathetic.

"Women are drawn to me, Trot. It's because I'm always thinking about something else, something that seems like it might be more important than them to me. They want the love I feel for the Revolution or great literature. It's hard for a man to understand a woman because a man just desires her; but women, most of them anyway, desire desire."

"They want you to want them," I said. It felt as if I were a child again at my father's feet.

"That's it. A man feeling deeply about anything makes a woman want him to pay attention to her like that. When his passion is for something else she feels safe enough to look at it. And if you look long enough you want to try it out."

"You know I hate you, right?" I said.

"I told you I'm not after your woman."

"It's not that, Clarence. You killed my mother. You promised me the world and then took it away. You save my wife and then tell me she yours if you want her but you don't want her. I spent nearly half a century tryin' to build back the engine of my life and here you come throwin' a monkey wrench in the gears and ask, what did I do?"

To give him his due, my father didn't try to argue or explain. He looked right at me, taking his medicine. I imagined that there were scars all over his body from South American torturers that didn't hurt as much as the truth he was hearing.

"You want me to leave, son?"

"Not till this week is over," I said. "Twill has to get out from under the mess he got into and it's still a question whether or not I'll survive till Monday. You stay a few days more and then you can get out of my life again."

40

My father asleep in Dimitri's room, Katrina next to me in the bed snoring so softly it sounded more like purring, and I never felt more alone in that home. I didn't sleep at all. Even the darkness could not assuage my conflicted heart. There were three groups of killers after me or mine and three women I had feelings for. None of these people stayed in the right place or were likely to wait their turn.

I wanted to run away with Marella but that would end in tragedy, no doubt. I wanted to live happily ever after with Aura but my life was a Grimm not a grade-school fairy tale. Katrina and my father deserved each other but something in me wanted to tear them apart.

Those were the good things in my life.

Jones, Sidney-Gray, and Marella's ex-fiancé were the slaughter-house three; puppet masters vying for my demise with their marionettes lurching forward, wielding papier-mâché knives even as I lay in darkness.

Tomorrow, I thought, I'd turn the tables on my lovers, enemies, and blood. Tomorrow I'd begin my campaign to take back a life that other people, friend and foe alike, had gambled away.

Somewhere around 4:00 a.m. I realized that tomorrow had come.

I got out of bed, took my ice-cold shower, and shambled down the many flights to the street.

"Hey you, motherfucker . . . yeah you . . . come here!"

It wasn't yet 5:00 and I was just passing Seventy-second and Broadway.

He was a big man, dusk-colored in the darkness of morning. Lumbering toward me he bellowed, "Stop right there!"

I had a neat .38 caliber revolver in my blue pocket but I didn't think it would be called into service.

"Can I help you?" I asked when he came within nonshouting earshot. It occurred to me again that I had become a magnet for both love and trouble since boarding the train from Philly.

"Gimme twenty dollars," he demanded.

"No problem," I said. "It's in my wallet. All you got to do is take it."

"What?" It was both a question and a threat.

"You heard, man," I said, getting as much derision in my voice as I could. "Even a dumb motherfucker like you understand plain English."

His clothes, as well as his heritage, were various shades of brown. He was eight inches taller and a hundred pounds heavier than I, but my hands were bigger. I held up those mitts as I had done on a block not far from there just a few nights before. The last guy was a little smarter however.

Big Brown actually threw a punch at me. I swiveled at the hip, watched the slow blow go by, and then came back with a straight right to his jaw; that set him up straight and back a full step. He was stunned but didn't seem to know it. He looked at me as if he wanted to ask, "What just happened?"

I waited three beats and when he didn't resume hostilities I turned to walk on.

Three steps gone I heard a rustling behind me and turned quickly in the event that the man had decided to come after me again. But this was not the case. Big Brown had slumped down on his haunches and was leaning up against a red, white, and blue mailbox at the corner.

I stopped at a twenty-four-hour diner on Thirty-fourth and ordered eggs and bacon, coffee, and rye toast. For forty-five minutes I munched and read the paper. My temple still hurt from where the Jones thug had hit me. Now there was a tingle in the big knuckle of my right hand. I wondered if my beloved honey badger felt aches and pains like I did.

At 7:00 I was in the observation room on the eighth floor of the Tesla Building. Aura had been forced to put cameras in all of the day-rate meeting rooms because various prostitutes, drug dealers, and other not-legal entrepreneurs had started to take advantage of the opportunity.

"I don't have anything against free enterprise," Aura said when she showed me the dozen monitors that watched as many rooms. "It's just I don't want to get arrested for racketeering."

Aura had agreed to let Abe Hollyman use Suite 9 to serve me my summons. She told him that she didn't care about me because I had illegally obtained a twenty-year lease on my suite of rooms; a lease that her bosses couldn't break. I did have a sweet deal (pun intended) but it wasn't illegal; I had just done a favor for the last building manager that kept him out of prison. The least he could do was give me preferential treatment.

At 8:37, manicured and still ugly, Josh Farth and two other men in hats, gloves, and sunglasses came into the room. They took out dangerous-looking pistols that had extra-long barrels and sleek designs.

It was unlikely that they'd see the camouflaged lens that watched, so I sat back and appreciated the assassins as they waited for me.

Killing is a profession like any job. Some practitioners are amateurs while others are more professional. Slaughtering cows, pigs, and sheep is a legal arm of the killing vocation; soldiers annihilating warlords' encampments in Afghanistan are also allowed to massacre without legal consequences. Paratroopers, police officers, property protectors, private security forces, and presidents all have licenses to kill in a broad range of circumstances. Pest exterminators, pet owners, and prison guards are told that there are times when killing is acceptable, even humane. When it came to killing people within the parameters of the law, there was even a moderating term used—"deadly force."

The men waiting for my appearance weren't legal and had little concern about the law. None of them were from New York, I'd've bet. They'd leave no DNA or fingerprints, images of their naked faces, or signatures. Maybe they planned to kill Aura, maybe even Warren Oh, after the job with me was finished.

My death would be quick and brutal unless they felt I had information . . . but no; Farth was simply eliminating a rival because I had made some kind of deal with Sidney-Gray.

Competition for entrepreneurs like us in the open market is a bitch.

My heart was beating fast. Even though I was safe, forewarned, and armed on another floor, my primitive brain was fully aware that there were men close at hand that wanted to kill me. I had to exert a good deal of self-control not to go up to their floor and engage them in that battle.

When my phone sounded I jumped. I felt so intimate with my executioners that I believed they could hear me. But they just sat around the door waiting for my arrival.

"My pussy itches," Marella said when I answered the phone. "What are you doing right now?"

"If it wasn't life or death I'd be there rubbing ointment on that tickle."

"You should come away with me, Lee. You know I'm the kinda woman for you."

Maybe she was.

"Your boy from the train pulled a gun on me looking for you," I said.

"Really?" she asked in a pedestrian, matter-of-fact tone.

"Bullets and everything."

"Melbourne wouldn't have had him do that. He must be acting on his own. I mean you humiliated him when you dunked his ass in the elevator."

"I don't know why everybody has to take everything so personal," I said. "I mean boxers get beat up in the ring every day and they don't go pullin' guns on people."

"If I had the power to love I would love you, Lee."

That might have been the most romantic thing any woman had ever said to me.

"Look, Mar, I'm into somethin' right now. Let me call you back."

"All right. Don't forget my itch."

As soon as I disconnected the call, the phone sang out again. This time it was Aura.

"Hey, babe," I said, hosting a completely different spectrum of emotions.

"Are you all right?"

"Lookin' at your boy and two of his friends holding guns and waiting patiently."

"Did you call Kit?"

"Sure did."

Watching Josh Farth sitting there so patiently awaiting my death was unsettling. I felt that I had to do something but there was nothing to do. At almost any other time I would have controlled my anxiety by practicing Zazen breathing, counting my breaths until my thoughts released.

Instead I took a card from my pocket and entered a phone number.

The phone rang once, twice . . . Josh turned his head quickly . . . three times and he reached for his jacket pocket.

"Hello," he said into the phone and my ear.

"Mr. Farth?" I said.

"Mr. McGill? How can I help you?"

His confederates were now looking at him.

"I've been considering your case and . . ."

"And what?"

"I don't know if I can take it."

"Why not?"

"It feels wrong."

"Can I come to you and discuss it further?" he asked. "I mean I *have* already paid you."

"Well . . . yes of course. I'll have to return the deposit, I guess. I have a meeting set for ten. Why don't you come up to my place about noon?"

"I'll be there."

At that moment there came loud knocking and a muffled voice from outside the meeting room that said something I couldn't make out. Josh disconnected the call and all three killers got up on their feet. There was no sound for the surveillance equipment but their attention was on the door.

Josh Farth said something loudly at the door. He waited a few seconds and then said something else. One of his partners, a heavyset man wearing a bulky gray suit, moved back toward the corner farthest from the door. Josh and his other friend put their weapons on the conference table. He then said something to his fat friend in the back. After a few words back and forth the big man put his pistol down. The other friend reached for the door and opened it.

With surprising speed the fat man took up his gun again and started shooting. He shot the other man, not Farth, in the back and kept on firing. Then it was like a strong wind, a hurricane, blew into the meeting room. Josh and his big friend were hurled from the door by the hail of bullets.

All three men were dead in less than nine seconds.

41

There were a dozen cops on the fifteenth floor when I got there, maybe four minutes after the shootout. Ten minutes later there were closer to fifty official representatives of the city in and around Suite 9. Two dozen police in plainclothes and uniforms, at least ten paramedics, even a dozen or so traffic cops were placed around the exits to keep gawkers, building employees, and regular customers away. Warren Oh and his number two, Lena Brass, were there.

One of the traffic cops held up a hand to repulse me but a regular cop intervened.

I made it to the side of the doorway to Suite 9 and peered in.

I had seen dead bodies before. There was no attraction for me. I just knew that Kit was going to be angry and I needed him to feel that he was working for the law and not for me.

Two cops had been shot; one through his left hand and another in her bulletproof Kevlar vest. She was winded and he looked chagrined, like a lumberjack more ashamed of having lost control of his saw than unhappy about the fact that he was bleeding.

Kit had come out of the suite and was approaching the woman cop when he noticed me.

"What the fuck you get me into here, LT?" he asked. "Three calls on you this week and every time it gets worse."

"You got somebody could oversee the aftermath?" I asked.

Kit understood and turned.

"Sanchez!"

"Yeah, Captain!" a man said from the other end of the hall.

"Take over till I get back."

———

We didn't speak in the elevator or on the walk down the hall to my suite. We didn't utter a word until we were both seated in my office.

"Don't get mad, Kit," I said. "I came to you in good faith. Aura called about a man wanting to meet with me without me knowing it. I told you that. That's why you brought so many cops with you."

"Dead bodies are never appreciated downtown," he said. "And this new mayor really comes down hard."

"They shot first."

"How do you know that?"

"Aura has a camera on all her day-suites."

"It's recorded?"

"No," I lied. "I turned off the recorder when I got in."

"The NYPD is not here to eliminate your enemies."

"Not my enemies, Kit, your suspects."

"Suspects in what?"

"If you look close enough I'm sure you'll find that it was these three that killed the security guard in here and also that Hiram Stent you said had my name in his pocket."

"So you did know Stent?"

"Yes I did but I didn't know it at the time you asked. A few days ago a man calling himself Bernard Shonefeld made an early morning appointment. He said that he was looking for a missing woman and would I help?"

"What woman?"

"Honey Larue," I said. "It was a stripper's stage name. He said he didn't know if it was real. He offered me seventy-five dollars to find her but I demurred. I didn't care if he was a stalker but seventy-five dollars does not nearly cover my nut."

"What does this have to do with Hiram Stent?"

"When you asked about him I looked him up on the Net. When I saw his picture I realized who he was."

"And you didn't call me why?"

"I would have, Kit. I was busy and when we talked last night I just didn't think about it."

"And so why do you think these three after you have anything to do with Stent?"

"Because one of them came to me the day after Shonefeld and offered me ten thousand dollars to find a Honey Larue."

"Which one?"

"The guy wearing the coal-gray suit."

"But you didn't know that when you called me," he said warily.

"No. I had no idea who was going to show up."

"And Alexander Lett doesn't have anything to do with it?"

"I thought you had him in jail for that gun."

Carson bit his lower lip. I knew that this meant great consternation for the excellent policeman.

"It wouldn't be Lett anyway," I said. "He's working solo looking for a woman he thinks I know."

"Do you know her?"

"I met her once and that's it," I said. "But listen, Kit, it turns out that Twill has a guy on the inside of Jones's organization." I knew that this bit of news would stop any other conversation.

"You put some kid in jeopardy with a madman like that? How'd you let that happen?"

"He was already in. A kid they call Nathan came to Twill, told him about Jones, and asked could my son help him dig out. Twill came to me. I asked you about him but Twill hadn't told me about this Nathan."

"I wanna meet this kid."

"Sure. But he's in the wind right now."

"What's that mean?"

"He's scared. Me and Twill met with him down at South Street Seaport and told him that we need information to give to you so you could catch the motherfucker. He had Twill's number and said he'd call when he knew the next time Jones was meeting his people."

"You don't have an address, a phone number, nothing?"

I stuck out my lower lip and shook my head.

"Where's Mardi?" the canny cop asked.

"After the break-in I gave her the week off. She's down in the Bahamas with her little sister."

"I want to look through her desk," he said.

"Not without a warrant."

"You got something to hide, LT?"

"Always. You know Mardi got information on a dozen clients at her desk. I can't have you stickin' your nose into all that."

From inside my pocket the phone played its little melody.

Kit was staring at me.

The phone finally gave up.

"I could arrest you, LT."

"Don't I know it, brother," I said, reminding myself of Hush. "But I'm telling you the truth. The men shot at you killed Hector Laritas and the man you call Hiram Stent. And I have a mole in the Jones Gang. Give me three days, a week tops, and I will give you the where-withal to bring down that whole mob."

Kit stared at me. It wasn't a friendly gaze. Though almost every-thing I had just said was the truth, it was selective and he knew it. But Jones for him was like a naked pinup model asking directions: wher-ever she wants to go, you do too.

"Three days," the captain said at last. "And the DA will be in touch to depose you about the shootout."

"Always happy to do my civic duty, Captain."

42

I walked the captain all the way to my newly rebuilt front door, saw him out, and watched him until he disappeared around the corner. Only then did I close that door and throw its seven locks.

I was halfway back to my private office when the phone sounded again.

"Hello."

"Paulie DeGeorges, Mr. McGill," the scammer fop said.

"Mr. DeGeorges," I hailed. "And how are you on this glorious fall morning?"

"Fine," he said, a little breathless at receiving true etiquette. "I was just telling Violet that it's warm enough that we could picnic in Central Park."

I heard his ex-wife utter something in the background.

"What did she say?"

"Nothing. She was expecting you to give her that money, I guess," he said to me, and then to her, "Quiet, honey, we're doin' some business."

Violet was not about to be shushed and she said so. I heard her yelling and then a few other noises. Finally there came the sounds of open air and traffic.

"Sorry, Mr. McGill," Paulie said. "Violet gets angry and the only thing that cures it is either time or martinis."

"What you got for me, Mr. DeGeorges?"

"I talked to Coco and she said that she'd agree to meet you but she wanted me there too."

"When?"

"As soon as you can."

My knuckle and cheekbone were both throbbing to the beat of my heart. *That's life*, said the Buddha and Sinatra.

"That Excellent Bean joint only had a front door, right?" I asked.

"Yeah?"

"I'll get that seat in the back," I said. "She and I can sit there and talk. You take a place near the front to make sure I don't do anything hinky."

"I don't know if she'll like that," Paulie cautioned.

"That's the only way I'll do it. Tell her. Bring a gun if you need to. I don't care. All I want is some private conversation with her."

"I'll ask."

"See you there in forty-five minutes."

Fifteen minutes later I was ensconced at the same table Paulie had claimed the day before. I could have made it in ten but first I took some money from the wall safe where Mardi was storing the deposits I'd given her. I put a certain amount in a brown envelope.

At the Excellent Bean I perused a monograph by an uneven writer I read sometimes. The title of the book was *The Graphomaniac's Primer: A Semi-Surrealist Memoir.* The book was less than a hundred pages, printed but from a handwritten manuscript; mostly composed of entire pages of letters written in rows wedged so closely together that they morphed into various textures. The page of lowercase *a*'s enchanted me. It was reading without reading. There was a scattering of prose pages and a few drawings in between. The essays were about neuroses and how humans could not survive without them, and also brief analyses of memoir, art, and even a few possibly autobiographical sketches.

"Mr. McGill?"

I looked up to see Coco/Celia dressed in dark blue jeans and a light blue T-shirt. She wore no makeup or jewelry. Her eyelashes were her own and the blue and white tennis shoes on her feet could have been bought at any time over the last sixty years.

"Coco?" I said. "Celia?"

She glanced back toward the entrance. Paulie was sitting at the table closest to the door, trying to look like a bodyguard. His shirt was yellow, his jacket deep green, and his bow tie white with red polka dots.

"Paulie told me to tell you that he has a gun," she said.

"Good for him," I said brightly. "Have a seat, will you?"

She considered my request, looked back at Paulie, and then lowered to sit at the very edge of the walnut chair across from me.

She was thinner than in her photographs and there were dark patches under her eyes.

"What else did he tell you?" I asked.

"That you were a detective who specialized in cases like mine and, and that you could help me, maybe . . . I mean if you thought that it was in your best interest."

"It's like we were brothers," I said.

"Who," she said and then she swallowed. "Who sent you?"

"A man named Hiram Stent."

The question lodged itself in her brow before making it to her lips. "Who is that?"

"I'm told he's a distant cousin of yours on his mother's side."

"But, but I don't know him."

"And neither did he know you," I said. "But a lawyer in San Francisco sent a man of many names to ask Hiram if he knew about you. The lawyer offered a lot of money for knowledge of your whereabouts."

Celia jerked her head around frantically, expecting to see men coming for her from every corner. She looked so frightened that Paulie stood up from his chair.

I held up a hand to assure both the popinjay and the stripper that there was nothing to worry about.

"Hiram never found out anything about you," I said. "And I didn't take his case anyway."

"Then why are you here?" she said, almost shouting.

A few heads at surrounding tables turned our way.

"After I refused him somebody murdered Hiram; probably the man of many names. I'm willing to bet that Hiram told the man that he tried to engage me but that I had warned him, Hiram, that the whole thing was probably a scam. Most likely that's what got him killed and my office door blown off its hinges."

"I don't understand anything you're saying," the petite young white girl said.

"I know," I commiserated. "It's very complex. But I can cut through the fog by saying that it all started when you stole a thirteenth-century edition of Herodotus's *Histories* from a private library called the Enclave."

The surprise on Celia's face was gratifying. I always liked it when I had a fact by the nuts.

"You know about that?"

"Didn't Paulie tell you?"

"He just said that you might be able to help."

"He's right about that. I might be able to help if you can answer some questions."

She was trembling. Twenty feet away Paulie was still on his feet. I began to think that the scam artist was probably what he said—an anachronism of chivalry lost in the modern world; a fifth or maybe sixth Musketeer.

"Why is Evangeline Sidney-Gray after you, really?"

"She wants her book," Celia said, looking down.

"No. Even a crazy billionaire like her would have to have a better reason than an old book to run a search like she has for you."

There was no hair hanging down on Celia's face but she pushed at phantom strands anyway.

"Tell me about it."

"Why should I trust you, Mr. McGill?"

"Because I found you," I said. "Because if I wanted to hurt you all I had to do was bring a little muscle to drag Paulie off and throw you in the back of a van. Because I knew all the players before we sat down." I took out my PI's license and put it on the table and said, "Because I'm a licensed private detective and if anybody ever needed somebody like me on their side it's you."

"I don't have any money to pay your fee," she said.

"I'm not working for you, darling," I said, feeling as if I was in an old black-and-white movie. "That distant cousin you never met, Hiram Stent, asked me for help and I turned him down. He just needed somebody to believe in him and now he's dead. I'm doing this for him."

Celia was concentrating on my every word. In the past eleven months she'd learned to make decisions independent from family, friends, bosses, and even the law. She was on the run and dreamed every night about the life she had probably taken for granted.

She swallowed hard and said, "There was a letter pasted under the endpaper on the inside of the back cover. I noticed how puffy the page was and that made me curious. You know I studied antiquities at Yale. I knew that some of the royal families of old hid their secrets just like that."

"And was it some kind of ancient secret?"

"No. It was a letter ten or eleven years old."

"From whom?"

"Charles Sidney-Gray."

"Her husband?"

"Son. He had gone on a killing spree in his youth. He killed homeless people, men and women, and buried their bodies under the family summer retreat in Cape Cod. Forty-nine bodies if the letter is accurate. He lured them there because he pretended to . . . pretended to work for a charity helping the homeless that his family ran."

"Did you tell Paulie this?"

"No. My brother told me that I should only say that Dame Gray wanted her property back."

"And what did you tell your brother?"

"I said the letter was about a crime but led him to believe it was like a theft. I don't completely trust Donald either," she said. "We love each other but he doesn't have good sense. I only wanted a little money to get him a lawyer that might help get him out of prison. He's dying down there."

"And you somehow got in touch with Dame Gray and asked for the money in return for the letter."

"Yes," she said, looking down.

"What happened then?"

"Two men grabbed me in front of my apartment in Allston. I

screamed and this vet from Afghanistan came out with a gun. He shot in the air and I ran. I ran. I didn't pack or anything. I just went down to where the Chinese bus is and came to New York. I knew those men were working for Mrs. Gray. I was afraid."

"Changed your name," I said. "First you became an artist's model for that fool Fantu Belair and then, after meeting Paulie, you became a stripper."

"You know Fantu?"

"Met him. He wasn't much help."

"I started out modeling because no one wanted an ID and I got paid in cash," she said. "Stripping was the same only it paid better."

"Smart. But somehow they found out you came to New York. They sent the man of many names after you."

"I called my boyfriend to tell him I was all right. I used a throwaway phone but somehow they traced it here."

"Forty-nine dead bodies under her summer home," I said. "Damn. Did you tell Evangeline that?"

"I think she already knew. The minute I said I had a letter from her son she was worried. I didn't tell her about the storage space though."

"What storage space?"

"Charles Gray killed himself soon after he wrote the letter. Before that he took a ninety-nine-year lease on a storage space in Wyoming. He says that there are forty-nine trophies there."

"Forty-nine," I said again. "The rich always go overboard."

I had a storage space too, with my own variety of trophies. I hadn't murdered anyone to get them but they were various pieces of evidence I had to prove that I had set up people for crimes they had not committed.

"I, I don't think he expected anybody to find the letter for a long time. It was a mistake that the book came to the Enclave. The Gray family made a donation of less valuable books but somehow it got included. That's why I studied it so closely. We don't usually get such valuable gifts."

"Do you have the book?"

"No."

"No?"

"It's too hard to bring things out of there. They search you with one of those machines they use at airport security. It can see if there's a dime in your pocket."

"So where is it?"

"There's an old Bible that Indulf the Aggressor, an old Scottish king, used to hide his flask from his wife. It's hollowed out and I put the book in there. I'm the only one who knows about it. It's a part of the permanent collection and I, I don't know. I kind of liked keeping it a secret . . . like I was helping the old king."

"So it's still in the Enclave?"

"Yes."

"The letter, too?"

"Everything," she said with a nod.

For some reason I thought of Marella. This made me smile. If she and I were working together this would be just another job. A few million dollars in the old suitcase and off to Argentina or maybe Monaco. Hell! This is the twenty-first century—we could go to Moscow or Beijing.

"I can get you out of this," I said.

"How?"

"First we have to cut Paulie loose. He's a good guy and he helped you but he's not to be trusted when it comes to power and money like this."

Not answering was her tacit approval.

I handed her the brown envelope with the money I'd taken from my office.

"There's five thousand dollars in here. Go over there and give it to Paulie. Tell him that you're working with me now and that if everything works out you'll be giving him that much again."

"This is too much," she said. "I'll never be able to pay you."

"Don't worry about it," I said. "In for a penny . . ."

She took the envelope and went over to Paulie. They talked for maybe three minutes. He wrote down something and gave it to her, then he looked at me.

I smiled and waved.

When Celia came back to the table she was ready for business. Good. I was born ready.

43

While Celia used dead Josh Farth's money to purchase our good-bye from Paulie DeGeorges, I made a call. It was over before she returned to the table.

"What he say?" I asked when she was seated again.

"That you had a reputation for being rough," she said. "That he only half believed that people were really after me until you found him. He said that his friend had told him to stay away from you if he could."

"Did Paulie give you the same advice?"

"No."

"Why not?"

"He said that if it was you looking for me then I probably needed the help of someone like you."

"He's a puzzle, that Paulie. Usually the only thing you could expect from a guy with a record like his is to pick your pocket and then ask for a loan."

"Donald said that without Paulie he would have never made it in prison. He said that if you respect him Paulie will do anything for you."

"When's the last time you ate?" I said.

"Yesterday."

"What can I get you?"

"I'm not really hungry," she said.

"You have to keep up your strength to be able to outrun the people Dame Gray's gonna put on you."

"I don't want to run anymore. I'm willing to tell her where the book is without any money," Celia said. "All I need is for you to tell her that."

"You could have called at any time and said that," I countered. "But you haven't because you know that it's not the letter but what the letter says. It's what's in your head that puts you in a sling."

Celia actually started to cry.

"You still need to eat," I said.

I called Bug while Celia ate a concoction called granola-oatmeal along with a chocolate croissant and a glass of factory-squeezed orange juice.

"Hello, LT," he said. "You talk to Zephyra yet?"

"I'm calling you, Tiny," I replied, using his lesser-known nickname. "You make any headway on that satellite connection?"

"Yeah."

"I'd like you to meet me at Hush's house in an hour so we can talk about it."

"No."

"No?"

Celia was eating lustily. Sometimes hope gives you an appetite.

"I'm not going to that man's house," Bug said. "Not ever."

"Why?"

"I don't want to know where he lives or what he looks like."

Bug was a genius. Of course he didn't want to be familiar with a hit man that the president of the United States was willing to give license to.

"Okay," I said. "Where then?"

"You know that place on Christopher called Smokers?"

"Two hours from now," I said and disconnected the call.

"This is good," she said, and I found myself hoping that she'd live to eat ten thousand breakfasts more.

"Hey, Pops," Twill said.

He wore coal-gray slacks, a teal T-shirt, and a light jacket that was such a dark red that it almost ran purple.

I could see in Celia's face what everyone saw when first encountering my son. He was beautiful, willing, and there was something about him that reminded you of Bible stories about great and sometimes evil men that stole hearts that never wanted to be returned.

"Son," I said. "Pull up a seat."

Twill kindly asked our nearest neighbors if he could take their extra chair and then pulled it close to Celia.

"Hi," he said to her, holding out a hand. "I'm Twill, this old guy's son."

"Celia," she said, shaking with one hand and wiping her mouth on a paper napkin with the other.

"Some people would like to talk to Celia here," I said, "and I'd like to make sure that doesn't happen until the time is right."

"Uncle Gordo's?"

"He still owes me a favor or two."

"Okay," Twill said, hunching shoulders. "The more the merrier."

"Don't you even want to know why?" Celia asked Twill.

"If he's hiding you then it must be some kinda mayhem," Twill said easily. "That's how LT rolls."

"My son is a detective in training, Ms. Landis," I said.

Then I went into the story of her difficulties without revealing the secrets of the letter. I kept this secret for Celia's sake, not my son's.

"So should we go there now?" Twill asked.

"First I'd like to ask our friend here a question," I said.

She looked at me. Her light brown eyes all attention.

"Why would you ever try to steal from and extort anybody, especially a woman as rich and powerful as Evangeline Sidney-Gray?"

I could see the question furrow in her brow. She had asked herself the same thing many, many times.

"My parents died when I was eleven. Donald took care of me and he helped me with my schoolwork. He kept me fed and safe. I'm not very good with money so I've never really been able to help him. And so when I saw that letter I just thought that that rich kid could pay for what he'd done by helping Donald."

"Sounds like just the right move to me," my son chimed brightly.

Celia smiled and I knew, and so did she, that I had left her in the right hands.

44

The sign read LANNY'S EATS but everyone who went there called it Smokers. It was the last place in Manhattan, that I knew of, that encouraged its customers to smoke while warning away those who somehow felt that there was a loophole in the Death Clause that came with each and every human body. The front door, on far west Christopher Street, opened onto a long corridor that was usually filled with tobacco smoke; this because the vent fans from the dining room blew through there. At the end of the hall was a sign that actually read GIVE UP ALL HOPE YE THAT ENTER HERE.

I had not asked Bug why he liked to go to Smokers. He had never smoked and, before he turned Mr. Universe, he never even went out. I figured it was a reaction to how much his life had changed since he'd met Zephyra. He didn't want to believe that he'd given up a life of pessimism for love.

Given my druthers I wouldn't have ever gone there. I don't smoke but I love smoking. Sucking on a cigarette and letting the smoke waft up from my mouth into my nostrils made me feel invincible. But boxers in training could not put that kind of strain on their breath. I had been on the treadmill my whole life and so smoking would have to wait until I died.

After spending half an hour at Smokers I had fevered dreams filled with coffins and Lucky Strikes for days.

The floors and ceiling were painted white and the walls tar-black. Lanny Marks was the server and his brother (also named Lanny) worked the kitchen; that way no employee could sue them for health issues later on.

"Can you imagine somebody suing you over gettin' sick?" Lanny the cook asked me one off-night when Bug and I were the only customers. "Everybody dies is sick first. You could kill somebody by kissin' 'em or steppin' on a toe and givin' 'em a blood clot. I swear one day they gonna have a fine for BO."

Bug was at a white table in a black corner eating pastrami and drinking a milk shake. He was hunkered down over the meal, looking like the runt of the litter that had grown into a timber wolf.

"Bug."

He gazed up at me, unconsciously raising a hand to protect the meal.

"LT," he said. "You didn't say if you heard from Z."

Young men and their virgin hearts. Bug had only fraternized with escort service girls before Zephyra, so now all he could think about was her and how he was bound to lose.

"She left a voice mail," I lied, "saying she was on vacation."

"Bitch."

"What you got for me, B?" I said.

I pulled out a whitewashed chair and sat.

"What can I get you?" Lanny the waiter asked.

He was a ruddy-white and my height, so I liked him.

"You got that chicken rice soup today?"

"Every day."

I nodded and he went off.

In the meanwhile Bug pushed away his sandwich, pulled a square and flat panel from a large leather bag at his side, and placed it at the center of the table. The white glass tile was maybe three times the size of an iPad. Bug touched a corner that didn't look any different than anyplace else on the glassy rectangle. A bright light rose up from the surface, constructing what I can only call a pyramid of light above it. Rather than blocks of stone, this form was made from multicolored letters, words, images, and lines connecting them in horizontal, slanted, and vertical paths.

The topmost word was "Jones."

There were eight other tables in the smoke-filled restaurant; three of these had two or more nicotine-addicted customers.

I looked around but Bug said, "Don't worry, LT, in order to see this you got to be within three feet and you have to look at it straight on."

To test this claim I stood up. The words and images blurred into pleasant pastel colors before my eyes. I took three steps away and the colors muted even more.

"In ten years every house in the civilized world will have 3-D TVs like this in the living room," Bug said when I was seated again. "I hear there's a sheik in Qatar and an Internet mogul in China got whole ball-rooms made from panels like these. Not only will you be able to watch the movie, you'll be able to get inside it."

"Pretty great scientific tool," I said aloud. "You could actually postulate a molecule and then get inside it to see what you thought wrong."

"Wow," Bug said. To him I had been a brute until that moment.

"Nice lights," Lanny the waiter said as he put the soup down in front of me. "But don't turn up the volume."

"Tell me what we got here," I said to Bug when Lanny was gone again.

Bug smiled and I knew I was in for a frightful treat.

"Fourteen hundred and sixty-two names active," he said. "Those are the names in red. There are other names but they're coded either inactive, blue, or closed, black."

"What about all these shades of green?" I asked, not needing any explanation on "closed" files.

"Those are what the system calls tasks," Bug said. "A task could be a robbery or the end of the line of a smuggling run. The shade of green is judged by the time that the task is expected to happen. The darkest ones are in the next twelve hours; the lighter to lightest are sometime later than that. I don't show anything happening more than a week from the system clock."

"Damn," I said. "There must be three hundred tasks listed."

I wanted a cigarette.

"Two sixty-seven," Bug said. He took a sip from his milk shake straw.

"And these lines connecting green tasks to red names are telling us who is expected to be involved?"

"The solid ones," Bug averred, "and the lines made up from dashes are probable participants."

"Is the when and where in here?" I asked.

"Mostly. It's a beautiful system but it's like he was never afraid of being hacked. There's no firewalls whatsoever."

"Yeah," I said. "Jones figures either he can blackmail or kill anybody try and use this against him."

"He's got the army for it," Bug agreed. "He must have sent one of his kids to MIT or something. This work is beautiful."

"Here's your pie," Lanny said.

I hadn't heard him come up. He was holding a pink cardboard pie carton by its string handle. Bug took the box and said, "Can you put the whole thing on my bill, Lan?"

"Sure, David. No problem."

"What kinda pie?" I asked when we were alone again.

"Um . . . It's nothing, man. Lemon meringue. I put it in the fridge and take a slice now and then. That's all."

His words were an entire history of compensation and loss—the bookkeeping ledger of a young black man's soul.

"How much information you have on the red names?" I asked to cover the epiphany.

"Almost everything. Addresses, cell phone numbers, even birthdays. There's also a history list of the 'tasks' they were involved in."

"Take the data from this pyramid and print it out like a report. Have it delivered to my office."

I put my black hands on the white table, ready to rise and run.

"What about my question, LT?"

I sat back and gazed at the butterball who had exercised himself into the form of a demigod. He was still a child in my eyes. It struck me that Twill had never been that innocent.

"Why you got explosives knitted into every wall in your house, Tiny?"

"For protection."

"That's right. You know that you got a house full'a treasure. There are things you know that nobody else does. That's valuable and dangerous."

"So?"

"Now think about Zephyra. She can go out with sheiks and kings, princes and billionaires, but she took you."

"And she still goes out with them."

"And so you hit the detonator and blow it all to shit. Live with it, brother, or find a new way."

45

ug and I separated at Hudson and Charles, where he turned to visit the old building that he maintained for storage. I suspected that he was going there to gorge on the pie.

I continued up Hudson double-thumbing my phone as I went.

"Is anything wrong, Mr. McGill?" she asked on the sixth ring.

"How's the southern hemisphere?" I asked.

"We're on a deserted beach," Zephyra said, a little breathless. "It's the most beautiful place I've ever seen. Have you ever been here?"

"South Africa, yeah," I said. "But what I saw was not beautiful."

"Is there something wrong?"

"I think it's time for you to come home, Z."

"But I just got here."

"I know. But you leaving hit Bug so hard I don't think he'll make through all those nights. Know what I mean?"

"I can't put my life on hold for some guy who never learned how to take one step at a time," she said coolly. "I like David but I don't owe him anything."

"That's a fact," I agreed. "But there's another one."

"What's that?"

"If David fell back in on himself and I didn't tell you about it first, I might lose the best Telephonic and Computer Personal Assistant I ever had."

She took a beat to digest my words and then asked, "Do you need anything else?"

"If you have the time."

"He'll fly me back on the private jet," she said. "I can do everything over the Internet on the eight-hour flight."

"It's more like eleven, isn't it?"

"Not if you fly in an SST."

I called the Hotel Brown, got connected to Marella's room, and had her order champagne, oysters, and caviar—all on ice.

"Are we celebrating?" she asked.

"It's more like a going-away party."

"Are we going somewhere?"

"Just me," I said. "Just for the day tomorrow."

"That hardly rates a party."

"There's a celebration in my heart every time I see you, girl."

"You're not going to start talking about love, are you?"

"What's love got to do with it?"

Katrina sounded truly sad that I wasn't coming home.

"Sorry, honey," I said, making a rare apology for an absence. "But I have to go down to Philly to tie up some loose ends. You and Clarence can go out to dinner or something."

"Bill went home this morning. He told me that he wanted you to call."

"You got his number?"

"Hold on."

"No, Katrina. Just text it to me. I'll call him when I can."

"I have a lot to talk to you about, Leonid."

"I'll be back in a day or so."

Marella and I nibbled and sipped the icy treats and then we had sex like two lifers allowed their first conjugal visit in years.

I left her asleep in the bedroom of her suite at 5:30 the next morning, but before I was out the door she called to me, "Lee?"

She was standing three steps behind me, naked.

"What?" I asked.

"Where are you going?"

"Down to Philly."

"Eddie and Camille again?"

I was surprised that she remembered my little story on the train. Then I remembered that she was a con artist; that meant she had to remember everything, both truth and lie.

"Yeah, it seems like Eddie had some unfinished business with a guy selling protection in the mall. I'm going down there to take an elevator ride with him."

"Be careful," she said sweetly, standing there naked, knowing that she was gravity—a force that a fool like me could never break.

The Acela first-class waiting room offered mediocre coffee, loud businessmen and -women who felt that they had to shout to be heard on cell phone calls, and a large space with a big TV that was almost always dialed in to the news. Luckily there was a smaller area with two round tables separated from the television and its loyal acolytes.

Johnny Nightly was sitting at the table closest to the entrance, reading a newspaper and looking like a GQ ad.

I checked in with the concierge and went over to Johnny (whom I had called the night before between bouts with the lovely if loveless Marella).

"LT."

"Johnny."

"The ticket Zephyra sent me says DC."

"Mine too."

"What we got on the itinerary?"

I explained as well as I could. When I finished Johnny simply nodded. Not long after that the train was announced and we, Johnny and I, boarded the first-class car for the three-hour ride down south.

We sat in single seats that faced each other over a table that was little more than a tray.

Johnny brought out a magnetic chess set with red and white plastic pieces that he'd owned since he was a boy of six. Back then, maybe forty years ago, Mrs. Nightly would bring the boy once a week to visit his father at Sing Sing. She would sit off to the side as Ring, the boy's father, taught Johnny the nuances of chess.

Time allowing, Johnny still visits on Thursdays to play his old man.

He gave me a choice of hands. I got white and we applied our wills against each other for nearly the full ride. In two and a half hours we made twenty-five moves.

My iPad told me that Zephyra had traced credit card charges attributed to Melbourne Westmount Ericson to the bar at the Crown Hotel almost every weekday going back a year or more. She'd also sent a few photographs of the man in question. He was short for a man but tall for me, flesh-colored like the old-time Crayola crayon, and had a build that workingmen around the world maintain to keep their jobs if not their dignity. Even his tailor-made suit couldn't hide the bulge of his belly.

Outside the hotel I asked Johnny if he had his gun.

"Two," the good son replied.

I was also armed. As a rule I didn't carry firearms across state borders but sometimes you find that you just have to cross that line.

We decided that Johnny should go into the bar first and set himself up at a point advantageous for interference if things went sideways. I introduced myself to the clerk at the front desk of the posh hotel and asked for group rates if my organization, the Benevolent Association of Landscape Artists of Color, decided to have our annual convention there. I had a business card that identified me as the secretary of that organization. There was also a website and an answering service to cover me.

The manager of the hotel, Michelle Tillman, came out and showed me a folder with all the benefits and special rates that the Crown Group offered. We talked for about ten minutes or so.

"Can you show me the bar, Ms. Tillman?" I asked. "You know, I find that our members, and those that often employ their talents, like to meet while, um, lubricated."

Tillman was a café au lait–colored woman who had the pleasing figure that unmarried professional workingwomen had to maintain. She smiled knowingly and led the way.

When we approached the entrance to the bar my heart rate increased. I might have been going into a life-and-death situation and so my body wanted to give me all the help that it could.

Crown Bar was a perfectly round room maybe a hundred feet in diameter. The central floor was a yard lower than the arc bar that occupied the northern quadrant of the circle. There were three bartenders. The barstools were fewer than half filled because most of the customers were sitting at the thirty small round tables three feet below.

Johnny sat at a table near the bar.

I looked up and saw our quarry seated on one of the barstools. In front of him was a newspaper, a deli sandwich of some type, and a frosty glass mug of beer.

"As you can see," Michelle Tillman was saying, "this room can hold more than a hundred people. At night we have live music, usually jazz. But it's never so loud that it interferes with conversation."

I looked around and nodded, noting at least two men who might have been bodyguards. One wore a tan suit that accented his broad shoulders and the other had a burgundy jacket and black slacks. Both men were sitting alone down in the people pit. Even if they were security they didn't have to be working for Ericson. This was Washington, DC. There might have been half a dozen people in that room who needed protection.

"Do you mind if I sit at the bar?" I said. "To go over the information you gave me?"

"Of course," she said forcefully.

She gestured with her left hand and after a moment of looking I took the vacant barstool next to my target. Michelle went to one of the bartenders, pointed at me, and told him to lubricate me—no doubt. She waved good-bye and I waved back.

I had made it to Melbourne Westmount Ericson's side with an invitation from the establishment he frequented. Any security would have noticed and downgraded my presence from potential threat to unlikely danger.

"What can I get you, Mr. Brownley?" the head mixologist asked, using the name on my fake business card.

"Cognac," I said. "XO."

"On the rocks?"

"Straight up."

"Yes sir."

When the rosy-cheeked bartender went off to pour my drink I looked around, appraising a room that I'd probably never be in again.

"Ms. Tillman says that you represent a union of painters," the barkeep asked when he returned with my snifter.

"More like a brotherhood," I said. "Specialists like landscape artists can help each other out in dozens of ways."

"My dad's a painter," the young man said.

"What kind?"

"I don't know what you call it. Big canvases with a lot of circles and triangles. Real colorful."

"Abstract."

"Yeah, I guess, but if you said that to him he'd just get mad. He gets mad a lot."

Just then the bartender noticed something or someone down the way.

"Excuse me," he said. I couldn't have scripted better dialogue or timing.

"You like this place?" I asked Melbourne Westmount Ericson.

"What?" he asked, turning to me.

He had the kind of face that in some ways defied description. The features themselves were young, possibly placing him somewhere in his thirties, a man who hadn't experienced much and knew little, if any, hardship. But his hair was thinning and the puffy flesh around those features sagged like that of a man nearing retirement if not death.

"My brotherhood is thinking of having our next convention here," I said.

"I heard you and Ralph," Melbourne said. "Some kind of artists' union?"

"No."

"Oh," he said, "I thought—"

I held up a finger, arresting my target with a silent command.

"I'm the piece opposite Alexander Lett in the chess game you're playing," I told him. "Lett's got you, so Marella has procured my services with the proceeds from the sale of her engagement ring."

A look of wonder spread across Ericson's confusing face.

It was then I noticed that Johnny had come up to the bar. His signal to Ralph the bartender was actually telling me that there was danger afoot. Looking up into the curved mirror, I saw the man in the tan suit coming up behind me.

I was ready for the tussle, but before Tan Man could put a hand on my shoulder Melbourne gestured and said, "That's okay, Philip."

Tan Man stopped and leaned against the bar behind me. Johnny Nightly took the same position behind the billionaire.

"What's your name?" the young/old man asked.

I told him the truth.

"Aren't you the one who took her from the train?"

I told the story from my point of view.

"But," Melbourne stammered, "but he was there only to deliver a message."

"There was no message."

"He was supposed to get her alone," Melbourne said. "I know how much she treasures her privacy. He told me that she kept avoiding him and then you, you interfered."

"Huh," I grunted, pondering his words. "That may have been right. But it doesn't say why he came up on me with a gun at my offices."

"You broke his wrist and put him in the hospital. Alex is a proud man. Pride sometimes makes a man stupid. I should know."

"You didn't send him to retrieve the ring you gave Ms. Herzog?"

"Certainly not," he said with real conviction. "I understand why she took the ring. She needed money. I had lost my temper and broke it off with her. She had every right, every right . . ."

"You can see where she has a whole different interpretation about your intentions," I said.

"Yes. Yes, of course. She's a woman alone in the world. She must protect herself."

Anybody who tells you that they're a good judge of character is telling you the truth but still they're wrong. The best liars are impossible to read. They not only give misinformation, they become the lie. I thought I knew what I was looking at, but Melbourne could have been better than I was. There's always somebody better. Mardi had deeper perceptions than I ever did. For all I knew, Jones's man Fortune was a genius of misdirection.

I believed Melbourne but, at the same time, I knew I could be wrong.

"Are you in contact with Mar?" Melbourne asked.

"She calls me at certain times to see how I'm proceeding," I admitted.

"She pays you?"

"Yes."

"What if I were to pay you?"

"That would most probably be a conflict of interest."

"But I told you," he said, oh so honestly, "I don't want the ring."

"So? George Bush told me he was the education president."

"I need to speak with her."

"That's up to her," I said. "My job is to make sure that no more men with guns come trying to get to her."

"After getting the firearms charges dropped I called Mr. Lett back home."

"Excuse me if that doesn't mean much."

"Can you ask her if she'll meet with me?"

"I could ask but I'd have to give her a good reason."

"I want to give her another engagement ring," he said. "I want to apologize for losing my temper and saying the things I did."

If he was a liar he was good; if he wasn't he was a fool.

"Mr. McGill?" he said after maybe a minute of silence on my part.

"Yes?"

"Will you give her the message?"

I hesitated.

"I'll pay anything," he added.

"Anything?"

46

Melbourne Westmount Ericson and I talked for eight minutes more. I timed it on a wall clock over Johnny Nightly's shoulder. It was the most productive eight minutes I had ever spent. When it was over, two-thirds of my work problems had been, tentatively, solved.

On the 3:00 p.m. train back to Manhattan, Johnny and I continued the game. We were averaging fifteen minutes a move so when I placed my knight in a position that might lead to check I went down to the exit area near the toilet and made a call.

"Hey, LT," Hush said. He almost sounded happy, human.

"How's it goin' with the houseguests?"

"The boy said that he went out for cigarettes but I think mainly he wanted to buy some weed in the park."

"That doesn't sound good."

"I told him that I'd kick him and the girl out if he does it again, but it was already too late. Somebody saw him and by the next morning they were walking back and forth in front of my place."

"I'm on a train right now but I can get there in two hours."

"No need, brother." There he was calling me brother again. "I took care of it for the time being."

"Are you going to move to a different location?" I asked. "I could get Twill to take the kids."

"No. I got Tam and Thackery out through an underground tunnel I had built. They went to Baltimore but me and the kids gonna stay."

"You sure you don't need me to come by?"

"I'll call you if I do."

Johnny hadn't moved yet. He was staring at the board, circling the end of his nose with the tip of the index finger of his right hand. His handsome head was tilting to the side. There was a modicum of joy in this pose.

"You look like you havin' a good time, Johnny."

"It feels good playin' against somebody can play back."

"I like the game," I said. "It calms me."

"It's not just the game."

"What do you mean?"

"My father told me that you got to know where every piece is and where they all might go if you just wanna stay in the game. That's you, LT."

"Did you ever ask your father what you can do if your opponent was better than you?"

"Yes I did."

"And what did he say?"

"You be better too."

I left Johnny at Penn Station at around 6:00. We had made eight moves on the ride back. There was no talk of money because I knew he expected me to wire five thousand dollars into his checking account for "services rendered." I'd send him a W-9 and alert the government. Even killers had to pay taxes.

Katrina was weeping.

When I had worked all the locks and opened the door she looked up but didn't have the strength to come to me. She was sitting in a hickory chair from our dining room that she'd dragged down the hall to the foyer. So I knelt down beside her chair, embracing her as best I could.

"Leonid, Leonid," she cried, "what have I done with my life?"

"Three beautiful children just for starters, babe."

"You were always there even though I was so angry, even though I had lovers."

"I wasn't no rose all that time."

"But you gave me this apartment and paid all our bills. You didn't have to stay but you did."

I had. There was no denying that I had stayed. But whenever she left I didn't go after her. Our connection was both absolute and static. I wondered how to say that without hurting her.

I didn't have to try because the doorbell rang.

"Oh," Katrina said, and I knew the story that had led to our vestibule encounter.

"Don't worry," I said, and then I kissed her before standing.

I didn't look through the peephole nor did I ask who it was. Katrina had called him and dragged the chair to the door to wait for him.

I opened the door and said, "Hey, Clarence."

"Trot."

An hour later Katrina was asleep in our bed. I had carried her down and tucked her in. Ten minutes after my father got there her mood had lightened.

"You didn't call me," my father said. We were sitting in the little front TV room drinking port and eyeing each other.

"I thought that there was a man in DC who had put out a contract on me. I went down there to face him."

"Was he really trying to kill you?"

"Probably not."

"Why were you worried that he was?"

"The same reason you might be."

"I just came over because she was so sad and you weren't here."

"She didn't call me."

"You were out of town."

I couldn't argue there.

"I don't want to argue with you, son."

"But, Clarence, we skipped the whole Oedipal thing. How can I ever be a man if I don't kill my father? Metaphorically speaking, that is."

"Even when you were a kid," my father said, shaking his head, "I found it hard to understand you. It's not so much the way you think, Trot, but it's how you treat emotions. It's like they were, I don't know, like they were optional. But you're my son. That means something, in the heart."

I put down my glass and stood up.

"Where you goin'?" he asked me.

"I got a few more showdowns before the end of the week," I said. "Why don't you spend the night? Maybe you can keep Katrina from trying to kill herself again."

I showed up at Marella's door a little past 10:00. She was wearing a pink kimono over a short burgundy slip.

She kissed me when I walked in. I wanted that kiss. I wanted to feel it and to stay with it—but something was wrong.

"What is it?" she asked, leaning away.

"Let's sit."

We went to the brown sofa, sitting at opposite ends.

"Tell me," she said.

"I didn't go down to Philly," I said. "I mean . . . I did go *through* Philly on my way to DC."

From the look in her eye I hoped that Marella's holster-purse wasn't within reach.

"What did he offer you?" she asked.

"Anything."

"Anything?"

"That's exactly what I said. He offered me money, access, connections." I counted out these wages on three blunt fingers.

"And what did you say?"

"At first I said that that would probably be a conflict of interest because I work for you."

"At first."

"Yeah. But then when he told me what he wanted I realized that anything I got from him was dependent on you."

"Did you betray me, Lee?"

"No, no, but I remembered something."

"What's that?"

"You said that Melbourne wouldn't have sent Lett after you or me with a gun. Do you still believe that?"

"Yes," she said, "as far as it goes. You know people can surprise you."

"When you say things like that it makes me want to throw you over my shoulder and take you someplace where they'd never find us."

"I'm ready," she said.

"But first you have to know your options."

"Okay. What are they?"

"Melbourne said that he doesn't want the ring back, that he wants to give you another one. He says that he feels heartbroken that he got so angry and now he wants to marry you with no prenup or stipulations."

"No prenup?" I don't think she meant those words to make it to her lips. That might have been the most honest thing she said in my presence.

"He wants to meet with you," I said, "to make his case."

"Do you believe him?"

"Obviously."

"Why obviously?"

"Because if I didn't he'd be a dead man by now."

Marella's nostrils actually flared. Her pupils opened wide.

"You're never going to throw me over that shoulder and carry me off, are you, Lee?"

"Probably not."

"You'll protect me at the meeting?"

"Like a dog with his bone."

"If I say yes will that dog share his bone with me tonight?"

47

The first order of business the next morning was a taxi ride to Hush's house. I called him on the way downtown.

"It's six a.m.," he complained.

"What time you usually wake up?"

"Four thirty," he said, "but this is still early."

"I'm leaving a case and I got a lotta stops to make. Can you make me some coffee?"

"Sure. Come on by."

He opened the front door of his Washington Square Park mansion before I pressed the bell. He handed me a ceramic mug of French roast and shook my hand. Then he did an about-face and led me through a doorway on the left side of his entrance hall. We went maybe fifteen feet and came to a dead end that was also a door. This opened upon a staircase that went up one flight, ending at a second door that looked like it belonged on a bank vault. It was made from burnished black metal and had an old-fashioned combination lock. Hush twisted the dial back and forth seven times, pressed the chrome handle down, and pulled. He ushered me in and followed.

It was a small room; nine by nine by nine. The walls were no doubt reinforced and there was no window.

They were laid out neatly, side by side on the floor—three dark plastic bundles that used to breathe and laugh. Hush slammed the vault door, which plunged us into darkness, then he flipped a light switch summoning at least a thousand watts of radiance from the ceiling.

"Two men and one woman," Hush told me. "All of them young. They were after my houseguests."

"How the hell did they get in?"

"I left the front door open," he said casually. "I got every inch of this house wired for sight and sound. The observation room is just off the kitchen."

I remembered the door. I was in the kitchen with Tamara once and asked her what was in there. She said it was just her husband being overprotective.

"I waited for them to separate and I took 'em out. They all had guns. They could have killed me. They're packed with limestone powder. I'll get rid of the bodies tonight after everyone else is asleep."

The limestone retarded rotting. There was no odor in the room.

"They have homing devices on them," I said.

"Not in this room they don't. These walls stop any wave, pulse, or radiation."

"Like a high-end coffin," I commented.

"Amen," my godless friend said.

"Where did you have Liza and Fortune while all this was going on?"

"I got a panic room in the subbasement," he said.

"Of course you do. What did you tell them?"

"I told them the truth. I said that a couple of people were nosing around and that they might try and break in. I told 'em to go down there until I was sure it was safe. Then, when it was over, I brought 'em out and said that there wasn't anything to worry about anyhow."

"Where are they now?"

"Asleep of course."

"I'm sorry about this, man," I said.

"You don't have to be. I knew it was serious when you asked for my help. Thanks for telling me about the homing devices."

"They insert them under the skin at the back of a thigh."

"I'll dig 'em out."

There were many things that most citizens could say and feel at a moment like that. Those three Jones kids had come to kill my clients and anyone else they encountered but they never had a chance. I could have felt outraged, sick, or maybe guilty. But it was like my father said: in a business like mine, feelings are optional.

Two blocks away from Hush's house I called the police.

"Twenty-sixth Precinct," a woman answered on the eighteenth ring. "How can I help you?"

"Captain Carson Kitteridge."

"What about him?"

"I'd like to speak to him."

"On what business?"

"My name is Leonid McGill—"

"Oh. Here you go."

The phone went mute for some seconds and then, "Kitteridge here."

"Hey, Kit."

"What's up, LT?"

"You say that like we're almost friends, man."

"I like you," the perfect cop admitted. "But I'd like you better in a prison cell, that's all."

"Can you meet me at Gordo's boxing gym in an hour or so?"

"This is about that information you promised me?"

"Oh yeah."

"I'm on my way."

I picked up my pace walking north on Fifth Avenue. I'd been so concentrated on Hush that I didn't pay proper attention to the fact that I had lost every woman I loved or lusted after. Katrina, Aura, and Marella were all off the table for me. I didn't feel crushed or heartbroken. My losses didn't elicit a harsh feeling, no. For a block or two I wondered what was going on inside and then, somewhere around Seventeenth Street, it struck me: it felt, once again, like I was an orphan on the streets of New York.

I had all kinds of family but I did not, and in some cases never did, belong to them. A man of my age losing love, or some adjacent emotion, was somewhere beyond grief. I imagined that my state of mind was like an innocent bystander being killed by a powerful explosion; one moment you're standing there and the next you never were.

Gordo had shut down the gym to make preparations for the wedding. It was a crazy scene, all contradictions and outrageous juxtapositions. There were the heavy bags and speed bags wrapped in ribbons of bright colored silk; young boxers helping with organizing the flowers and placing the rented folding chairs all around the central ring.

In the ring itself Sophie, Mardi, her little sister Marlene, Tatyana, Katrina, and Aura were all futzing around. They were tying roses of all colors with ribbons of silk to the ropes, and wrapping the posts with bright-colored cloth.

Dimitri and a couple of other guys were stapling white silk sheets to the ring and arranging them so they flowed down from the raised platform.

I was amazed by the crazy transformation, but that didn't stop me from having mild trepidation at seeing my sometime girlfriend and sometime wife working side by side. Just the fact that Katrina was there was a surprise. That made me look around the gym a little closer.

My father was there in Gordo's office having what seemed like a very serious conversation with my mentor. I was about to go over to them when I felt the hand on my shoulder.

"Where you been, LT?" Carson Kitteridge asked.

"Stopped by the Tesla Building to pick this up," I said, handing him a thick manila envelope filled with data and detail compiled by Bug. "In here you have all the information about everyone who does or ever did belong to the Jones Gang. There's even information on how he has surveillance devices on every member and how to access the system. With the proper study from your tech guys you could bring down his whole operation in six hours—less. And I'm supposing you're going to want to do just that because there's over two hundred crimes planned over the next week."

I don't remember ever having seen Kit shocked. He held the hefty packet in one hand and stared.

"Are you kidding me?" he said at last.

"That's my August of Sundays right there."

Even though he was stunned, even though this would probably get him another promotion, even though this promised to be the greatest achievement in his career—I still saw a moment of regret for the promise he'd made me. And I have to admit I experienced a little pride that the cop felt that I was almost as dangerous as the phantom Jones.

48

I spent that night at the Hotel Brown. Looking back on it, I might have spent the time at home but whatever there had been between Katrina and me was over in the marriage department; and, anyway, with a woman like Marella there had to be some time to say good-bye.

When I awoke the next morning she was already awake and dressed and packed. Her black-and-pink-polka-dotted bag was at the door. I sat up and found a cup and an aluminum thermos-pitcher on the nightstand next to my side of the bed.

"I'll go downstairs and check out while you get dressed," she said. "Meet you at the front desk."

Her tone was curt and she wasn't smiling at all. The fact that she didn't kiss me was more an expression of love than any sex could have ever been. Marella was facing the unfamiliar task of weaning herself off of emotional dependence upon another human being. I knew this to be true but it hurt me anyway. There aren't many times in life that you meet another person cast in the same kiln, formed by the same dispassionate hand.

I drank my coffee before putting on my pants; browsed the headlines on my smartphone while tasting the bitter dregs that I needed to stay sharp and focused.

Aldo Ferinni, Max White, and Josh Farth—all from Boston—had been shot dead on the fifteenth floor of the Tesla Building by a squad of New York policemen. The three men had been identified by a private detective, me, to the NYPD as persons of interest in two murders. Two officers were wounded in the firefight. No bystanders were harmed.

Twill was sitting at the nearest round table in the first-class waiting room for the Acela to Boston. He wore a very nice dark gray suit with a bright white shirt and a razor-thin blue, green, and yellow tie. His shoes were matte black and tied with perfect bows.

When we approached him the smile that had been missing returned to Marella's lips.

"You must be the Twill that gives him such sleepless nights," she said, holding out a hand.

"And you're Marella," he said, surprising her with a kiss, "that kept him company through that hard time."

The three of us would have been perfect together for as long as the gravy train ran.

"Son," I said, using the word as an anchor as well as a greeting.

"Pops."

We had stopped playing chess after Twill turned thirteen. From then on Go was our game. Twill set out a tablet device between us on the table in the block of four seats, two facing two. He hit an app that brought up a Go grid and we began to play.

After half an hour or so Marella asked, "What's the purpose of this game?"

She had deigned to sit next to me with her hand lightly on my thigh. Having seen me at my best, or worst, she knew that I had a romantic bent and remained close to keep me going in a straight line.

"It's a game of war," Twill said, studying his next move. "The purpose is to defeat the enemy by surrounding him while maintaining your army if you can."

"That's ridiculous," Marella decreed. "In a war it all happens at once, not one move at a time."

"That depends," my old-soul son replied.

"On what?"

"On if you think a mathematician learns how to add before he takes on calculus."

Twill was never very good in math class but that didn't mean that he lacked understanding.

At South Station in Boston my forces were beleaguered but Twill was hurting also. I had a couple of stones on him but that didn't matter; it was the kind of war that the United States liked to make happen between its enemies. That was a lesson too.

Twill went off for a moment to call his clients while Marella and I had a talk.

"I do believe that that son of yours would have been just as effective as you if he was on that train from Philly," she said.

"He's something else," I said with pride.

"You know I'm trying my best to forget you, Lee."

"There's plenty of time for that," I said. "A whole life."

"You're never going to come with me, are you?"

Instead of answering I took her by both hands.

"It's like we were almost real for a few days there," I said. "I don't think that anybody could ask for more than that."

We, all three of us, checked into a suite that Zephyra had booked for us at the Hotel Bombay.

After I'd shown my ID and credit card I asked the desk clerk, "Shouldn't you be calling this the Hotel Mumbai?"

The red-brown Indian woman, PASHA her nametag read, smiled and nodded. She was in her forties and a beauty on any continent.

"*You* have to call it that," Pasha told me. "But my husband, who owns this hotel, is from Bombay, not Mumbai. Maybe our children will change the name."

"Do you have a conference room available tomorrow afternoon?" I asked.

"What time?"

"We don't know for sure but we'll definitely need it. Can I take from noon to six?"

"I'll have to check and get back to you later."

After we'd lugged Marella's hundred-pound suitcase to the rooms I kissed her on the lips.

"We have to go out and do what needs doing," I told her.

She smiled and said, "You'll know I believe you if I'm still here when you get back."

Twill and I walked to Cambridge. It was little more than a mile.

"She somethin' else, Pop," he said as we were crossing the footbridge that led over to Harvard Square. "I mean that's a woman you could write about in the history books."

"You know what we're doing here, right?" I said, avoiding his invitation to the truth.

"Sure do. If what your girl Celia says is right it should be a breeze."

Melbourne Westmount Ericson was waiting for us near the entrance of the Enclave building. He'd come alone, as I'd asked him to, wearing khaki cargo pants and a pink short-sleeve Polo pullover shirt.

We shook hands and I introduced him to my son.

"You look like a good personal assistant," Melbourne said to Twill.

"That's the job."

"Did you call them?" I asked the billionaire.

"Said that I was considering an endowment," he said. "After reading about them online I might really do it. It's really a very interesting enterprise. Combining historical and literary provenance with the weight of ownership, there could be all kinds of interesting study. But there's one thing."

"And what thing is that?"

"I'm uncomfortable stealing from these people."

I might have hated my father. I might have come to the realization that ants and termites were more socialist than Lenin or Marx could ever be when I hadn't yet reached the age of twenty. But no matter how I feel about blood and philosophy—when I hear a truly wealthy man tell me that he's uncomfortable with theft I have the desire to wring his neck.

Suppressing my natural response, I said, "Only the book was bequeathed to this institution, and that was a mistake, it doesn't even show up on the list of gifts. The papers inside are of a personal nature. Imagine if those pictures of Marella got into the hands of some newspaper in DC or New York. Wouldn't you want me to retrieve them by any means necessary?"

"It's that bad?" he asked.

"Worse by a factor of forty-nine."

"Let's get going," he said to my son.

I sat down at a bus stop across the street, unsure of what to do with my strangling hands.

Maybe the rage I felt had some kind of outward expression, making me look like a threat while sitting on a wooden bench on an autumn day.

"Excuse me, sir," a voice said six or seven minutes after I sat.

I looked up and saw a young white cop. He had a pale complexion and a partner that looked nothing like him and yet also would have claimed to be a white man. Something about the disjuncture of their appearance and supposed race reminded me of the rich man who claimed to disdain theft.

"Yes, Officer?"

"What are you doing?"

"Sitting."

"There's only one bus that stops here and it just went by," the second cop said.

"I said I was sitting, not waiting for the bus."

"This is a bus stop," the second cop said.

"Is there some kind of law in Massachusetts saying that a tired man can't sit down at a bus stop without taking a ride?"

"Stand up, sir," the second policeman ordered.

If I wanted to stay on the case I should have popped up like a tulip in the spring. But there was too much weighing on me: Marella and her man, Jones and those kids, Hiram Stent and his inability to make the right decision.

I looked up at a tree in front of the Enclave across the street. There was a red bird of some kind flitting around the branches, enjoying the experience of dexterity and flight, singing his heart out. For a moment, maybe two, I forgot those cops existed.

Then I felt the hand under my right arm. He, the first cop, tried to lift me. I tensed my muscles and his fingers were trapped. He must have looked frightened because his partner pulled out his gun and said, "Down on your knees!"

I might have died then and there. And those policemen were in as much danger as they feared—maybe more.

But I lowered to my knees while putting unclenched hands in plain sight. That didn't assure my survival but it was the best choice I had.

Sometimes you might forget who you are and where, but that's okay because there's always somebody around that's happy to remind you.

49

The policemen actually arrested me; took me to the station, snapped me face-forward and profile, took fingerprints, then interrogated me about various crimes that had happened with a black face maybe somewhere involved.

The whole show didn't take long. When it was done they allowed me a phone call.

"Mr. McGill?" she said.

"Hey, Z. You back from the motherland?"

"Are you in Boston?"

"Cambridge jail."

Sitting on a cot in a cell built for one, behind slatted iron bars, I felt unusually calm. I *was* the honey badger and Marella was the honey; Ericson, Jones, and Dame Gray were the common death threats along the way. And there I was, in the Cambridge jail, imprisoned for nothing I'd done wrong.

It could have been worse and there was still a chance that it might get that way.

These thoughts occurred to me in snatches because I was counting breaths and breathing ever so lightly.

At some point later a man in a black uniform came to pull me out of my meditation cell. He told me that I was being released.

"On bail?" I asked.

"No," the barrel-shaped pink-skinned man said. "Just released."

He led me to a room much like the one I'd been questioned in, but instead of inquisitors Melbourne Westmount Ericson and Twill were waiting for me. Along with them was a short chocolate-colored man in a ridiculous powder-blue suit that fit him like a medium glove on an extra-large hand.

"Harlan Sackman," the new man said, holding out a hand. He had barely an inch on me.

I suppose he had a strong grip.

"I'll be representing Mr. Ericson while he's in Mass.," the lawyer said. "The police have come to understand that their men were overzealous."

"Overzealous? They arrested me for sitting on a street corner bench."

"Actually," Sackman said, "they arrested you for refusing a direct order."

Sackman rankled me. I didn't like his clothes or his profession, but what bothered me most was that he endorsed the behavior of the police. I never liked it when a person so identified with their oppressor that they forgave them.

"Come on, Pops," Twill said, seeing my reaction. "Mr. Ericson and me did what you wanted."

"Everything?" I asked my son while still staring at the powder-blue suit.

"Oh yeah."

There was a stretch limo waiting outside the stationhouse. The four of us climbed inside and I gave the driver the name of our hotel.

We didn't speak on the short ride.

When we got there I separated from the herd and asked the front desk if they had managed to get us the conference room. They had.

That's when I got nervous.

There were all kinds of things that could have gone wrong. Maybe Ericson really wanted revenge and had his driver call ahead to whatever assassins he might have employed. Maybe Marella had run off as she'd said she might.

"To the room?" Twill asked me.

Ericson and the apologist Sackman were standing ten feet off discussing something.

"You got it?" I asked Twill.

"Of course."

"Let me see."

From inside his jacket he pulled out a packet of folded paper, about seven or eight sheets deep. I took the trove from him and pocketed it.

"Any trouble?"

"No," Twill replied. "No airport machine, no body search. You were right when you said they'd never do a security scan on their own kind. When him and the head man sat down I asked if I could walk around the rooms. I went right to the shelf that Celia told us about. The history book was in the Swedish Bible. The letter was in a hole dug out in between the pages."

Twill said no more because Melbourne and his lawyer approached us.

"Ninth floor," I told them before they could ask.

Marella stood up from the conference table when we entered the room. She wore a tight white dress, its hem somewhere above the knee. Her dark skin against the formfitting fabric sent a chill through me.

She hadn't been reading or writing when we arrived; just sitting there patiently like I had in my jail cell. It struck me that we'd not discussed literature. Maybe she was like most Americans, rarely if ever reading a book. That didn't bother me at all. We weren't all going to be readers. I could study Proust while she shopped for tight white dresses—the division of labor.

"Mar," Melbourne Ericson said, all breathless.

"Sit down, Mel," she said. "And who are you?"

"Harlan Sackman. I'm Mr. Ericson's lawyer. I'm here to—"

"Wait outside," she said as if maybe she was completing his sentence. "Mel and I need to talk one-on-one if we're going to work anything out."

I noted that her little black holster-purse was on the table. That might have bothered me if it wasn't for the sexy white dress; that was the statement of intent for the billionaire.

"That's okay, Harlan," Melbourne said. "We'll speak alone and then, if we need your help, we'll bring you in."

"Are you sure?" the lawyer asked his meal ticket.

"Yes."

"Are *you* sure?" I asked Marella.

"You're cute" was her answer.

Outside the conference room stood five stuffed chairs, placed there for less important players in the larger corporate games. Harlan and Twill were on their phones immediately reading texts, listening to messages, and making calls. I was anachronistic, taking out the handwritten letter penned by Charles Gray on both sides of each sheet. The lines in the lettering were so fine I decided that he must have been using a crow-quill nib.

The content was horrifying. There had been rapes and murders, mutilations and long-term starvations, tampering with genitals, eyes, and fingers; death served in a broad variety of ways and recounted in a dispassionate tone that made the content all the worse.

The only time that Charles showed any emotion in his writing was when he wrote about his mother (who he assumed would already be dead). He blamed her for the homicides, for creating a monster.

. . . it was my mother, who, by withholding her love made me into a thing that has no relation to right and wrong . . .

I read the letter through twice, making my plans. I was almost through the third pass when the conference room door opened and Melbourne and Marella came out. The last words of Charles's confession were in my mind. *I go now to my death having completed a life's work in less than two decades.*

"Congratulate me," Melbourne Westmount Ericson said to Harlan Sackman.

While they were shaking hands and smiling, Marella came up to me.

"Say the word and we can leave right now," she said, telling me many things.

I wanted to go. I wanted to leave everything behind me and, like my father, disappear into history.

"If you ever have a problem I'll be there" was my reply.

Sackman approached us then with his felicitations for the bride-to-be . . . once more.

Melbourne reached out a hand to me and I grabbed it, pulling him close.

"If anything happens to her I will kill you," I whispered. "Don't make any mistake about that. So if it's love I wish you well. Otherwise . . ."

"You don't have to worry, Mr. McGill," he said, managing a calm voice despite the pain in his hand. "I love her more than anything."

What could I say? Marella wasn't in jeopardy, Melbourne was.

50

Soon after the announcement Melbourne whisked Marella away in his limousine while Sackman asked the doorman to get him a taxi. When they'd gone I asked the front desk for a few pieces of stationery and sat down in the bar to pen a note to my lawyer, Breland Lewis. I put the last three sheets of the serial killer's confession in an envelope and sealed it; then I wrapped the envelope in my letter. I put this package into another, larger envelope and brought the whole thing to the front desk. The man there put my communication into a FedEx pouch bound for Lewis's office the next morning.

It wasn't until I was in the elevator that it hit me. In just a few moments my connection with Marella had been severed, hacked off. For the past week, I realized, her name and face had been repeating over and over in my mind like a madman's mantra. She was, in many ways, the perfect woman for me. Sure, that passion would kill me one day but we, all of us, die.

I tried to accommodate the loss in my mind, to leave it in the hotel lobby as I rose upward in the elevator car. But when the doors slid open she was still with me and I knew that the best I could hope for was the pain I felt.

"Pop," Twill greeted when I entered our suite.

"Son."

"That Mr. Ericson seemed like an all-right guy but you know he's a fool."

"Why do you say that?"

"Takin' off with a woman like Marella is kinda like seein' a tornado comin' and runnin' out to say hello." Twill was subject to dialect when he waxed philosophical.

"What does a New York City boy know from tornadoes?" I asked.

"I seen my share," he said. "You want a drink? They got four little cognacs in the minibar."

We seated ourselves at the coffee table in the common room of the suite. I was thankful for both the liquor and the company of my son.

"You know I would prefer it if you didn't get killed," I said.

"I know," he muttered shyly. "It just looked so simple."

"That's not the kind of detectives we are. You keep goin' it alone and one day you won't come back."

"What time tomorrow morning?" he asked and I knew that he had accepted my terms.

"Nine forty-four."

"Okay," he said and then stood. "I'll see you there sometime before nine thirty."

"Where you going now?"

"I know these people."

"What people?"

He shrugged. "You know, a girl and some'a her friends. There's this club over in Somerville where they don't even start up till midnight."

"Somerville? How many times have you been up here?"

"A few. You know."

I couldn't stop him. In the end I wouldn't be able to save him. But in the meanwhile I could run interference.

"You're going in that suit?"

Twill gave me a big smile, beautiful.

He struck a pose and said, "I kinda like it."

"Be careful."

"You know it, Pops."

I was sound asleep, my veins running amber with cognac, when the cell phone sang. If I'd been at home and sure of the safety of my kids I might not have answered.

"Hello?" The digital clock next to the bed read 3:54.

"Do you still want me, Lee?"

Drowsiness, hangover, heartache—all gone.

"Are you there?" she asked.

"Yeah, yeah I'm here."

"Are you alone?"

"From the moment you took off."

"I offered to stay."

"Yeah. That's why I thought you were gone forever," I said honestly. "I had it in my mind to let you go."

"I'll call you from time to time, Lee. Maybe one day you'll be ready."

"That would be nice," I said.

"Good-bye."

I have overslept exactly three times in my life. I've gotten up on time through concussion, blood loss, and fever. But that morning I didn't get out of bed until 9:23.

I staggered to the bathroom but even the ice-cold shower didn't completely revive me.

I was in the taxi on the way to South Station when I realized that I had left my phone plugged into its charger back at the hotel.

When I got to the small table at the coffee kiosk in the great rotunda of the train station, Twill was sitting there with Celia Landis.

"Hey, Pops," he greeted as I let my weight fall into the extra chair set there for me. It was a bouncy metal chair dipped in blue latex the same color as Harlan Sackman's suit.

"You didn't answer your phone," my son said. "Five minutes more and I was going to take Celia and go looking for you."

Even though Twill probably hadn't been to bed, or at least been to sleep in a bed, he was bright-eyed and alert.

"Too many jobs all at once," I confessed. "One day I'm gonna have to retire."

"But not today," Twill assured our client.

"No," I agreed. "Not today."

"Remember," I told Celia. "I'm here representing you and I will do all the talking. You and Twilliam are my silent backup."

We were ten steps away from the knobless door of Evangeline Sidney-Gray's city mansion.

Mounting the stairs, I called out loud, "We're here."

It was a three-minute wait.

Black and beautiful, but not necessarily likable, Henry Lawrence Richards answered the door. He didn't speak at all, just led us through the foyer-turned-office and to an elevator that delivered us to Dame Gray's top-floor library.

The kids stayed half a step behind as I led them to the rich woman's bone desk. This time there were three calcified chairs waiting for her visitors. I imagined that there was some butler whose sole job it was to get the right number of chairs set out for whatever guests his mistress entertained.

"Mr. McGill," she said, looking at my wards.

"Ma'am," I replied with courtesy and a slight bow of my head.

"And who have you brought with you?"

"Twilliam my son and Celia Landis."

The shadow that moved across the rich woman's brow was like the image of a planet turning its face away from the sun.

"I wish to speak with you, my dear," she said to Celia.

"But instead," I interposed, "you will be speaking to me."

"I don't know who you think you are, Mr.—"

She stopped because I stood abruptly. I took Charles's letter from my breast pocket and leaned over the desk to put it in her hand.

"This is who I am," I said.

As she paged through the bloody scrawl of her son's mind, many emotions crossed the elder's face. She was in turn horrified, saddened, and disgusted. There were even a few times where she showed a brief smile. I suppose these few happy moments came when she recognized the son she bore when he was still innocent—or at least seemed so.

"This is not the full text," she said, her voice temporarily drained of authority.

"No," I agreed. "In the last few pages he talks about a place where he kept his souvenirs."

"His what?"

"You know," I said, waving my left hand slightly, "fingers, skin, pictures of frightened faces before the subjects were put to death."

Celia gasped and Dame Gray snapped her gaze from me to the young blackmailer.

"Where is the rest of this letter?" she asked, still gazing at Celia.

"Far away but safe as long as I and my client remain—what should I say . . . unmolested."

"Give me those pages now or you will never be safe again."

My laughter surprised me. After all I'd been through a threat from a face I could see and name wasn't bad.

"Listen, lady," I said. "You will do as I say or the *Boston Globe*, *Christian Science Monitor* online, and the *New York Times* will all have a copy of the last three pages of your son's confession."

Dame Gray was stopped by the threat. She'd probably studied me since our last encounter and knew a thing or two about what I could and would do.

"What do you want?" she spat.

"One and a half million dollars. Five hundred thousand in a trust fund for Hiram Stent's children—"

"Who is Hiram Stent?"

"The first man Josh Farth murdered trying to get at Celia. Another half a million for Ramona Vasquez, the life partner of the second man your people killed. Then two fifty each for me and Celia here."

"That's blackmail, Mr. McGill."

"I've done worse . . . and so have you."

"I will not bow down to extortion."

"Have it your way, Ms. Gray. But I got bills to pay and a few of them come from your people wanting to rob and then kill me."

"You are preying on my vulnerabilities, my weakness," she said.

"Lady, your son's been dead eleven years now. And I'm sure you knew or at least suspected that he was a monster. They didn't find a suicide note but I bet that he left one; that it told you what he had done and probably where the bodies were. That's why you believed Celia. That's why you hired Josh Farth to kill her."

Celia started crying.

"Twill."

"Yeah, Pop?"

"Take her out of here. I'll meet you guys back at the room."

After the young people were gone Evangeline and I continued our conversation.

"So?" I began.

"My son was a monster as you say, Mr. McGill. But I am not. I have a large family. One granddaughter and two of my grandsons have political ambitions and this kind of notoriety would be a deep wound in our legacy. Can you see that?"

"I'll send you the names and all pertinent information about the people you have to pay," I said. "I will also send you the name of a lawyer that will handle the transactions."

"And the letter will remain safe?"

"It will be destroyed the day you die."

She scrawled something on a small piece of paper.

"My private e-mail," she said.

I stood up and almost left but then I remembered that there was one more facet to our business.

"And one other thing, ma'am."

"What's that?"

"You will almost certainly get in touch with people like Josh; maybe some of his friends. You will ask them if there's a way to eliminate me and Celia so quietly that the apparatus I set up will not spring into action." She stared at me, trying to hide this truth. "But when you talk to them make sure you say that I have an insurance policy and its name is Hush."

51

I slept on the train ride back from Boston that afternoon. Twill set up the electronic Go board and I may have placed a tile or two but then everything slowed down and I was having a dream about my father when I was ten and Nikita eight.

Along with my mother we were staying at a vacation cottage in western Long Island that the Communist Party maintained. It was a simple house with three bedrooms and a kitchen, living room, and bathroom with a shower. But Nicky and I loved it because we were only six blocks from the beach. Every morning we got on the communal bikes left by Comrade Hastings, the man who owned the house, and tore out for the water. We spent hours there ripping and running, swimming and exploring.

Nicky usually came back before I did because he'd get really ravenous. I was hungry too but one of my father's lessons was that a true revolutionary could overcome any physical feeling that controlled his actions. So I stayed longer gazing at the water while my stomach grumbled and Nicky was eating apple pie.

One day I was coming back from the beach alone, proud of my hunger. My father and Nicky were in the front yard. Nicky was squatting down in a corner of the lawn near the curb watching something with intensity. All he wore was swimming trunks.

Back near the front porch my father was looking down at the green hose. The nozzle was pushed into a hole in the soil.

Looking at them, I remembered that my father had promised Comrade Hastings, an old white man who smelled like vitamins, that he would take care of his gopher problem. The home owner said that he wasn't a Nazi and wouldn't condone the use of gas. My father told him that all he'd have to use was water.

I was rolling to a stop on my too-large three-speed bike. My father and Nikita were maybe a dozen feet apart with their backs turned to each other. My hunger blended with the hatred I'd learned to feel for the Nazis.

"Hello, Mr. Gopher!" my brother yelled happily.

I saw something small, brown, and maybe struggling at the patch of ground my brother watched.

Suddenly my father yelled, grabbed a hoe that was leaning against the porch, and ran to my brother's side, where he slammed the sharp edge of the tool down on the struggling brown head.

Nicky fell back on his butt screaming and crying. He jumped to his feet and ran for the house shouting, "Mama! Mama! Mama!"

My father brought the blade down again and again.

My mother came out onto the porch and knelt down to embrace Nicky.

"He did it!" my brother said, pointing at Dad. "He killed Mr. Gopher!"

I woke up with a start. From the looks of it Twill and Celia had just finished with a kiss. She'd come along with us because there were things at her apartment that she needed.

"How long?" I asked, the panic I felt tamped down under my groggy demeanor.

"Ten, twelve minutes from Penn Station."

I took up my phone and made the call.

"LT?" he answered on the second ring.

"Yeah."

"I've been trying to get to you for hours. Where's Twill?"

"Here with me on the train. Why?"

"We did it. We busted the whole fucking crew. There's not enough jail cells to hold them all. We got almost everyone except for Jones and a couple or three others. Just when the busts were going down one of our techs intercepted a message that referred to Twill and you by name. I sent cops to your place. Your wife and that friend of your father were there. We moved them out. It's not going to be safe until we have Jones."

"Have you identified him?" I asked.

"No."

I disconnected the call.

"Can you put up Twill here at your apartment until I call to say it's okay?" I asked the ex-stripper.

"No problem," she said. "Of course."

I entered A-U into my smartphone and then hit the Call icon.

"Leonid?"

"You home, Aura?"

"Yes."

"I need to drop by and pick up something."

It was 10:00 at night and I was coming home at last. I had dropped by Aura's to retrieve a heavy-duty .45 caliber pistol I had put there some years before. Black men in my position, from gangbangers to hit men to NRA fanatics, learned that it was best to have a woman somewhere holding your piece.

We kissed at the door. Maybe it was the shootout at the Tesla or just the proximity and the metaphor of the gun. But once we started kissing it just wouldn't stop.

"Will you be coming back, Leonid?" she asked when I was leaving for real at 9:30.

"I think so," I said as honestly as I could.

When I opened the door to the vestibule of my building my mind was already up the stairs and in my office trying to figure out if it was finally time to run. As I was reaching for the door of the stairwell they came out of the super's tool closet—fast.

Two men, each grabbing an arm and pushing me toward the back door of the first floor. That led to the back of my building's property.

"Open!" one man shouted as they slammed my face into the door.

A second later the portal opened and I was dragged in.

I struggled but these guys were big and had some training. Together they were stronger than I and they kept me off balance by shaking and pushing me and kicking me in the legs.

The door opened into a hall that was like a connecting room to another door that went outside. In front of that door was a very large man in a big knee-length coat. He had a full and fake auburn beard. His eyes, open wide, were some kind of false blue created by badly made contact lenses. In his right hand, held high above his fedora-covered head, was an angry-looking fifteen-inch butcher's knife.

"No one defies Jones!" the madman ejaculated.

That was the moment that I should have died. The puppet master was all facade except for the blade that was about to find my heart. The men that grabbed me were plenty strong at first but they had not done a proper study of adrenaline and its power of multiplication.

With renewed strength I, my brother's friend the gopher, turned into that honey badger again. I jerked to the left in the narrow passage, slamming the man on the trajectory side into the wall. I didn't have to worry about the man on my right because Jones's knife plunged deeply into his chest. The sound he made was so human, so mortal, that even in my frantic state of mind I noted it.

As the knifing victim grunted and groaned I turned like a dervish throwing the left-arm man into Jones. The cult leader roared out and lunged at me with his blade. I went low and moved so that we exchanged places in that room too small. Before facing Jones I delivered a blow to the forehead of the last standing minion with the heel of my right hand against his forehead. The back of his skull slammed into the wall and he crumpled to the floor.

Jones roared again and I produced my .45.

"The math is not in your favor," I warned.

He lowered the knife and bowed his masked head. If I hadn't spent thousands of hours over dozens of years studying the referee's line *protect yourself at all times*, I might have died then, because Jones suddenly delivered an upthrust of the blade. He pierced my left shoulder but that didn't stop the bellow of my gun.

I knew that I must have been frightened because I shot the madman six times.

———

After it was over I didn't know what to do. I held on to the gun even though it was empty. I didn't want to go out of the door because who knew what might be out there?

I was weak and getting weaker when the door to the vestibule flew open. Two uniformed cops rushed in, their pistols aimed at me.

"Drop the gun!" one of them commanded.

Gun?

I looked at my left hand and saw that there was blood dripping from my fingers. Then I looked at the right. There was a gun in it. I tried to let it go but the hand refused to respond.

"My hand," I said. "It's not working."

One of the cops, a brave young white man, swatted my hand and the revolver fell.

"Come on out here and sit on the stairs, Mr. McGill," a man said.

"Why?"

"That knife in your shoulder."

I saw the haft of the blade. I thought that it was so deep that it might be sticking out of my back. Jones had come close to my heart; like Marella, like Aura, like . . .

52

When I opened my eyes my father, Clarence, was sitting next to the bed. I could see through the hospital room window that it was early morning. I knew that there was some kind of opiate in my system because the pain in my shoulder was there but it wasn't.

"Trot," my father said to my open eyes.

"How'm I doin'?"

"No organs," he said. "You were a pint and half down but they gave you a transfusion."

"I'll need a blood test in a few weeks," my mouth proclaimed.

"Why's that?"

"He stabbed somebody else and then ripped into me," I said lazily. "That's mixing bodily fluids for real."

"Oh."

"How did I rate a single room?" I asked.

"Police protection," Clarence said. "Hmm. Where I come from those two words are mutually exclusive."

I laughed and coughed, reached out, and my father took my hand.

We might have talked some more. I'm pretty sure we did but I can't remember what was said.

When next I opened my eyes Twill had taken Clarence's place in the chair next to my bed.

". . . yeah, Pop," my son was saying, "those guys we fought at the construction site reported in. They asked around until they found my name and then yours. That was all Jones needed. He was so hyped up comin' after me and you that he didn't know what the cops was doin' until it was too late."

"Did they find out who he was?" I asked.

"Julius Sneed. He ran a private organization that contracted with the city to help children and adolescents in jeopardy. Been doin' it twenty-three years."

"I guess he's dead."

"Yeah. He was the last one to die, though. The guy he stabbed and the one you hit died immediately but they had Sneed in this hospital. Even said that he had a good chance to pull through. Hush came down here with Fortune and Liza. He said he would wait and see what's what, but then word came down that Sneed had a heart attack. Six bullets in the torso and he died of a heart attack."

"White guy?"

"Mostly."

And that's how it went for the next day. Aura came and then Katrina with my father. Katrina was very worried. She assured me that she was going to get a job and take care of us like I had done for so many years for her. No one told my daughter because she would be shattered seeing me in a hospital; but Tatyana and Dimitri came. Taty sneaked in a small bottle of cognac.

The doctor, Christopher Omen, dropped by to tell me I was a lucky motherfucker, his actual words.

And then I woke up in the middle of the night. Visiting hours were over. The moon was three-quarters full through the window.

"You're awake," she said. She was wearing the same deep coral dress she had on when we first met.

"How'd you get here?"

"Twill called me."

"How'd he call you?"

"We traded numbers for something just like this. I didn't expect him to use it so soon."

"I thought you'd be in Fiji by now."

"We're leaving for Hong Kong tomorrow."

"He's treating you right?"

"You're the only man I ever met knew how to treat me, Lee."

There was nothing left to say. If I wasn't so drugged up we probably would have had sex. As it was we held hands for a while, then she kissed me.

I closed my eyes and it was morning again.

"Where are you going?" one of the two policemen guarding my door asked.

Two cops! I thought they must be considering putting Kit in the chief's office. That bust must have netted him a whole month on the news.

"My best friend is getting married this afternoon," I said simply.

"The doctor has to release you," said the other cop, a black man with a belly that suited him for a job like this.

I didn't even answer; just walked past them looking for an elevator or, failing that, an exit sign.

53

'd never seen a boxing gym so festive and nonviolent.

Streamers and flowers and pastel silk everywhere. There were boxers in borrowed suits and all kinds of black people from Houston, Texas—relations of Sophie Bernard. She and my kids and my wife and my sometime girlfriend had done a great deal of the last-minute planning. The only contribution Gordo made was the jazz quintet that usually played in an uptown hotel near Lincoln Center.

It was nice hearing live jazz at a wedding.

The ceremony would be in the center ring. The minister, Lucius Crow, was a Bernard family friend. He'd performed the ceremony for Helen and Gordo thirty-some years before.

"Hey, LT," a familiar voice said.

Bug was wearing a pink tuxedo, blush white shirt, and a red bow tie, reminding me a little of Paulie DeGeorges. Zephyra was standing next to him in a jade-and-cream gown. She was breathtaking. Tall and black and smiling like those Valkyries I loved.

"Thanks, man" was all Bug had to say.

Later on Zephyra told me that I was right to call her.

"David gained twelve pounds in the forty-eight hours I was gone," she said.

Twill was wearing the same suit he'd pretended to be Melbourne's assistant in. He was there with Liza and Fortune and a young cocoa-colored woman named Véronique who spoke only French. Her black skin glistened and Twill seemed to bask in that glow.

I traded a few sentences with Véronique but then Liza took me aside and handed me a hefty envelope.

"I tried to give this to Twill," she confided, "but he said the agency is yours and you collect all monies."

"How much you got in here?" I asked her.

"One hundred eighteen thousand dollars."

"That's too much." I laughed at myself and how much I must have changed to be turning down serious money like that.

"No," Liza said, holding up her hands when I tried to return her money. "I decided when Twill took the job that I would pay the cost of the necklace I gave Fortune if he got us out safe."

Clarence and Gordo were in a far corner regaling each other. I didn't really like it that they got along, but I figured that that was my problem and I'd just stay away and keep it to myself.

"LT," Kit said. He didn't say but I'm sure that Twill invited him to the festivities.

"They make you chief yet?" I asked.

"We failed to find his blackmail files," the cop said as if we were on the site of an active investigation. "You got any ideas?"

"Me? You the one took him down."

"And you're the one that killed him."

"I just shot him."

Kit had to smile at that.

"Doesn't look like he groomed a successor. His confederates, the other ones you killed, were Joe Riley and Max Brown. Not their real names. I don't think we'll ever ID most of the people in his syndicate. Most of them came in as kids under ten."

I was listening but I saw something across the room, something that needed attending.

———

"Leonid," Hush said when I walked up to him. He was talking to Johnny Nightly.

"Hey," I said, eschewing using a name for Hush. "Johnny, can I have a minute with my friend here?"

After Johnny was gone I said, "I didn't know you knew Gordo?"

"We met before."

"You here for the wedding?"

"No. I just wanted to congratulate you on surviving and to say thanks."

"Thanks for what?"

"Bringing me those kids. Putting me in that danger took away all the tension. I knew you were going to be here so I just dropped by to tell you that I told the government men no."

My half-Asian daughter, Shelly, hugged me and kissed me and asked a hundred times if I was okay. She saw me as her father and no mirror in the world would dissuade her. We sat side by side through the ceremony. Katrina sat with Clarence. Iran Shelfly was Gordo's best man. A woman named Reesa was Sophie's maid of honor.

As the ceremony unfolded I began to cry. That was the biggest surprise I'd had all week. Something about love and ceremony and big changes at the last minute got to me.

Lucius Crow was asking Gordo if he would love, honor, and respect and I looked up, tears brimming in my eyes. Aura was sitting on the other side of the ring looking at me. Whatever she saw touched her and she blew me a kiss.

blog and newsletter

For literary discussion, author insight,
book news, exclusive content,
recipes and giveaways, visit the
Weidenfeld & Nicolson blog and
sign up for the newsletter at:

www.wnblog.co.uk

For breaking news, reviews and exclusive competitions
Follow us 🐦 @wnbooks
Find us 📘 facebook.com/WNfiction